Crazy About You

Crazy About You

T.J. Blackley

To Rae -
♡♡♡♡
Love you lots
TJB

jms books

CRAZY ABOUT YOU

JMS Books LLC
PO Box 234
Colonial Heights, VA 23834
www.jms-books.com

Printed in the United States of America

ISBN: 9798795479484

To LA, for loving my boys as much as I do,
and to Pickles, for keeping me humble.

Chapter 1

CONTENT-WISE, GREEK mythology is a cornerstone for a lot of modern pop culture, and D'Aulaires is as good an introduction as any for a young child.

Devante rubbed his eyes and sat back in his chair. A glance at the clock on his laptop told him that this essay, the last paper of his Children's Literature course, was due in exactly ten minutes. He took a sip of water from the bottle to the right of his computer, rubbed his eyes again, and scrolled to the top of the document to read it through.

Nine minutes later, he saved and renamed the file, *DMiller_ LIS481_Final*, pulled up his browser, where the submission form was already loaded, and hit *Submit* just as the clock ticked over to five P.M.

He took a moment to relax, his shoulders sagging with relief, before picking up his phone where it had been sitting, face-down and silenced, to the left of his laptop. *Done, just in the nick of,* he texted Preeda. *You?*

She didn't respond right away, so Devante stood, stretched, and slipped the phone into his pocket. He clicked the laptop closed, pushed his chair under his desk, and turned the light off in his bedroom on his way out.

As Devante stumped down the stairs, he heard his father grumble from the living room. Devante sighed and lightened his steps until he hit the landing.

His father, as he always did, had his face hidden behind his newspaper, as he sat in his armchair by the window. Devante could just see the top of his head, tight curls cropped close to his scalp, and his fingers as they held the pages open.

Brain still a little fried from his frantic paper-writing, Devante pulled a face. Without moving the newspaper, Carl said, "You'll get stuck that way."

"How did you see me?"

Carl twitched one side of the paper down to peer at Devante over his green reading glasses. "You'll figure it out when you have kids of your own," he said. "Finished?"

"Yes," Devante said. "Just in time."

"Good." Up went the paper again. "You can choose dinner tonight," Carl said from behind it. "Menu for that new Jamaican place came in the mail yesterday. It's with the rest."

"It's open already?" Devante had been watching the progress of the new restaurant with interest. "I thought it wasn't supposed to open for a week."

"Got a Grand Opening sign in the window, and I saw customers when I went for my walk this morning." Carl turned the page.

"Jamaican it is," Devante said. "Did you circle what you want?"

"Ain't my first rodeo, kid."

Devante dropped onto the couch, a solid leather structure covered in colorful throw pillows. His father had picked the couch, an investment when Devante was twelve; Devante had picked the pillows. Every now and again, when he was bored or gloomy, he went shopping, and ordered a new one to add to the pile.

Carl Miller had strict thoughts about eating dinner before seven P.M., so Devante had a little under ninety minutes to kill before he could place the order. He fished his phone out of his pocket to see if Preeda had responded.

She had. *Five mins late, hope she doesn't dock me. Drinks 2morrow????*

Of course, he wrote back. He was just opened the TFG group chat when his father abruptly said, "If."

Devante looked at him. "Huh?"

"If you have kids of your own," Carl said. The page of his newspaper was curled down again and he was looking at Devante with a serious expression. "Don't mean to assume. We haven't talked about it."

"Oh," Devante said, a little startled. "Uh, it's okay."

"Do you?"

Devante blinked. "Do I what?"

"Want kids," Carl said. "For next time."

Devante flushed. "I don't know, Dad. I haven't really thought about it. I'm only twenty-five."

Carl grunted. "Fair enough." He snapped his paper back up and Devante, a little winded, turned back to his phone.

Preeda had already texted the group chat, creatively titled The Friend Group.

PC: As per tradition, I'm calling an off-schedule drinks night 2morrow to celebrate Dev and me finishing our semester

MC: HELL YEAH

NM: First round's on me

MC: Good of you, Nat

NM: To be clear: first round for the students and people with taste. You can buy your own Pabst, I'm not sullying my credit card with that shit

MC: Damn

CG: Wait, do you think I have taste?

NM: In beer, yes. In women, no

CG: That's fair

DM: Stop murdering Mike when I'm not here to see it, Nat

NM: No promises

Devante muffled his snort in his sleeve.

Carl had carefully circled *Cowfoot soup* and *Plantains* on the Jamaican menu, when Devante pulled it out of the drawer. Devante perused it himself, then dialed the number on the cover and placed an order for cowfoot soup and curry shrimp, with a side of plantains and some steamed vegetables.

"Twenty minutes," he said to Carl, coming back into the living room.

"Great." Carl folded his newspaper and added it to the stack on the floor by his armchair. "We got something to drink?"

"I went to Lee's this morning," Devante said. "Should be cold by now."

Carl nodded and pulled his shoes on. "Back in thirty."

Devante set the table while his father was out fetching their dinner—stained but impeccably clean white plates, forks, knives, and napkins all in their place. When Devante was seven, his father had taught him how to properly set a table. "It's important for a man to know how to keep house, and how to present himself," Carl had rumbled, his big hand on Devante's shoulder. "Fork and knife on the right sides, crisp fold in your napkin, and you're halfway to a good impression."

To be honest, Devante still didn't get it, but every other day he set the table for dinner, everything in its place like his father taught him, and it did feel good when Carl looked over it all and gave him a nod. On Carl's nights to set the table, he took his time with it, nudging each utensil into exact alignment, and Devante always made sure to give him a smile for it. It was the little things.

Devante took two bottles of beer out of the fridge when he heard his father's key in the lock, cracking off the caps into the trash can and settling one down by each place setting. The kitchen filled with the aroma of well-seasoned food when Carl came in and set the bag on the table. "Soup's on," he said. "Been smelling it the whole walk home."

Devante fished out his packages, shrimp and veggies, as Carl decanted his soup into the bowl Devante had set out for him. They settled into their chairs and dug in. The food tasted as good as it smelled, and for a long while there was nothing but the sounds of two men eating.

Finally, Carl set his spoon down with a sigh. "Damn satisfying," he said. Devante nodded, mouth full of the last of his shrimp. "What was your paper on?" Carl asked, balling up his napkin from his lap and setting it to the side.

Devante smiled. "Had to pick a book I remembered from childhood and write about it in light of what we've learned about children's literature," he said. "One of my easier finals."

"What'd you pick? Plenty to choose from, you always were a reader."

"*D'Aulaire's Book of Greek Myths*," Devante said.

Carl picked up his beer bottle. "That the yellow one you read the cover off of?" He tipped the bottle back and drained the last of the beer inside.

"Yeah," Devante said. "It held up, too, which was nice."

"Good." Carl nodded at Devante's plate. "Done?"

"Yes." Devante slid his plate forward and Carl stacked it on top of his own and put his bowl on top. Devante handed him his silverware, which went into the bowl along with Carl's own, and then Carl laboriously stood up and carted the whole lot over to the sink to start the washing-up.

Devante slept deeply that night, the sort of sleep he could only ever get at the end of a semester, when all the stress and labor rushed out of him for a week until the next one started up. *Only one left to go*, a voice in his head chirped when he woke up. *Then it's nothing but adulthood.* Devante groaned and shoved his face deeper into his pillow.

Devante, when he'd moved back home from college, had re-designed his room to be easy to wake up in. The windows were already southeast-facing, and he hung them with thin, translucent curtains to let the light in without too much of a glare; he'd bought a new mattress, to sleep better and be more rested when he woke up; and before all that, he and his father had spent a messy weekend painting over the dark green on his walls with a much lighter blue. For the most part it worked: Devante rarely made use of his alarm clock's snooze button, and he drank less coffee in the mornings than his father. The only downside was that it made sleeping in when he didn't *have* to be up more difficult.

When he finally gave up and made his way downstairs, his father was just sliding his omelet onto a plate. "Bacon in three," Carl said, picking up the tongs and clacking them together. Devante took the plate to the table, where a chipped mug stood waiting, filled with coffee and just the right amount of sugar.

"You working today?" Carl asked over his own eggs once he was finished cooking, a plate of bacon on paper towels in between them on the table.

Devante shook his head. "Tomorrow's my long day," he said. "Today's off. Gonna clean the kitchen and my room."

Carl nodded over his coffee. "God knows the kitchen could use it," he said. "Don't forget to empty the vacuum out when you're done."

"Yes, Dad."

Carl worked at the Reggie Lewis Track and Athletic Center as a trainer. Decent hours, good pay, and he'd been there as long as Devante had been alive, almost from the opening of the place. He clapped Devante on the shoulder after they'd finished their breakfast and he'd changed into his work clothes. "Back at six," he said.

"I'll be gone," Devante told him. "Drinks with my friends. I'll probably be back late." Carl nodded and headed out, the door clicking shut behind him.

Devante washed and dried the breakfast dishes, then used the momentum to scrub down the sink, counter, and table. The fridge they cleaned together once a month, so he left the machine closed and moved onto the floor.

Cleaning his bedroom took him through to lunch, and the combination of exertion and a hearty sandwich dropped him into a deep couch nap. Perhaps prompted by Carl's questions the day before, Devante dreamed of himself as a father, faceless children running around his knees, a wedding ring on his finger.

He woke never having seen his dream spouse, and a little

shamefully glad of it.

Devante dragged himself upstairs to the tiny bathroom on the landing. There was one downstairs by his father's bedroom that was larger, but Devante enjoyed having counter space to himself enough to put up with the squeeze.

There was only just enough room for him and his body wash in the shower, which kept his showers quick and to the point. He carefully washed his cornrows through his hairnet, then scrubbed his body down and rinsed off.

The bathroom was so small that Devante usually did his drying off in the bedroom; he had a bathmat in the corner to stand on and protect his rug. Dry and sparkling, he went back to the bathroom long enough to hang up his towel and oil his scalp between his braids, then went back and perused his closet.

Dark jeans were a given: wearing slacks out with his friends was a surefire way to spend the evening getting teased. Trickier was the shirt; in the end, he picked his bright yellow button-down with pineapples printed in vertical stripes, top few buttons open over a white undershirt.

By the time he was dressed, it was time to leave. He slipped his wallet into his pocket alongside his keys, shook off the phantom Natasha in his head that screamed about gender-based pocket discrimination, and locked the door behind him.

It was a twenty-minute bus ride and a ten-minute walk to The Friend Group's usual watering hole, a bordering-on-hipstery bar named Mood. When he got there, it was to Mike and Charlie already posted up at their usual table, Mike's Pabst and Charlie's Corona open and sweating onto cardboard coasters between them.

"Dev!" Mike crowed when he caught sight of Devante. "Hey, man, how are you?" He scooted down the bench, even though there was plenty of room.

Devante signaled to Katie at the bar, who nodded at him and pulled a bottle of scotch down from behind her. He dropped down next to Charlie just to see Mike's mock-wounded face and laughed at him.

"I'm good," he said. "Thanks, Katie," he added as she set his scotch and soda and a coaster in front of him.

"Glad to be done with classes?" Charlie asked, slinging an arm around Devante's shoulder. He had to reach up quite a way to do it, and Devante slouched a little to make it easier.

"Glad enough," Devante said, taking a sip from his glass. "Only one more semester to go, though."

"And then you'll be all grown up," Mike said, grinning. "Ready to be a real boy?" Devante shot him a glare and he laughed, throwing his head back. "You'll be fine, Dev."

"Don't jinx me," Dev grumbled.

Natasha arrived before Mike could say anything back. Dev always imagined he could see a whirlwind around her whenever she arrived anywhere, dust and makeup and the powdered remains of her enemies. Her dark hair was perfectly set and her eyeliner, as usual, could kill a man. "I need a drink," she announced, dropping her purse on Charlie's other side and marching to the bar.

When Devante blinked the stars from his vision, it turned out Preeda had entered in Natasha's wake, which Devante discovered when she plopped down next to him on the bench and sighed. Her knee knocked against Devante's under the table. He coughed. Across the table, Mike gave him a knowing glance, which Devante avoided meeting.

Natasha returned bearing a glass of dark red wine, which she passed to Preeda, and something bright blue and terrifying-looking, which she kept for herself, settling in next to Mike. "To the graduates," she said, holding her glass up.

"Don't *jinx* us," Devante and Preeda said together, holding their drinks up too. Preeda caught his eye and grinned.

"To the soon-to-be graduates," Natasha amended. They all clinked and drank. "May they continue to kick every ass at Simmons on their way out."

"Hear, hear," Preeda said.

Natasha gave her a proud look, and then threw an expectant one at Devante. "Hear, hear," he said, a little less sure of himself than Preeda had sounded.

"Good enough," Natasha declared. "Now, somebody ask me about my day."

"How was your day?" Charlie asked obediently. He finally took his arm from around Devante's shoulders, and Devante straightened gratefully.

Natasha launched into a story about some blowhard white boy—"No offense, Mike"—in her ethics seminar who, apparently, wouldn't know objectivity if it waved its tits in his face. Perhaps grateful that she'd let him put her drink on his tab, Charlie took on the responsibility of making all the right noises in all the right places, leaving Devante and Preeda to start up a conversation of their own.

"Remind me what you're taking next semester?" Preeda asked, leaning back against the booth wall and regarding him.

"Library services for children, and organizational ethics," he said. "You're taking cultural heritage outreach, right?"

"Mhm." Preeda rolled her eyes. "Another useless course in my useless-but-necessary degree."

Preeda worked full-time as a cataloging assistant at Boston University, and had a *lot* of thoughts on the requirement that cataloging librarians have a Masters in Library Science. Devante could mouth along with her "It should be an apprenticeship" monologue almost perfectly, after two years in the program together. "It sucks," he said now, in an attempt to head it off.

"It's elitism," she said, but subsided. "How's your dad?"

"Good," Devante said. He checked his watch. "He should be home by now. I told him not to wait up."

"Did you try the new Jamaican place?"

Devante nodded. "It was really good, you should check it out."

"I will." She winked at him. "Maybe I'll crash next time you have it for dinner."

"You'd be welcome."

She raised her finger warningly. "Ah, but then I'd have to stay the night so I can have one of Carl's killer omelets."

Devante fidgeted, tugging a finger under his collar. Preeda's expression was light and laughing, a twinkle in her eyes that he knew well.

Natasha spared him having to respond. "You two aren't listening to me," she accused, pointing a finger in Devante's face.

"Sorry, Natasha," they chorused, turning back to her.

She waved her hand dismissively. "From what I gather, this boy's never had an opinion he didn't share, so I imagine you'll have plenty more stories from me to hang off every word of."

"Truly, something to look forward to," Mike drawled. Without looking Natasha smacked him on the arm.

"Hey, before I forget," Charlie said, leaning forward to get everyone's attention. "I wanted to ask how everyone feels about me bringing someone new on Saturday."

Mike gasped, overdramatic and theatrical. "Are you cheating on us with another friend, Charlie?"

Charlie laughed, one of his big laughs that shook his whole body. "You know I'd never cheat on you, Mike," he said. "No, a new guy moved into the apartment next to mine a few weeks ago. We've talked a few times in the elevator, he seems nice, and he mentioned he was new to the area and looking for new friends."

"Well, I don't know any better friends than us," Natasha said expansively.

"Exactly," Charlie said, pointing at her.

"What's his name?" Preeda asked. "We need a little bit more than, 'He seems nice.'"

"His name's Michael—"

"Uh-uh," Mike said, shaking his head. "Instant disqualifier."

"I asked, and he only goes by Michael, never Mike," Charlie said. "I wouldn't bring a duplicate to you, Mike. I know how you value your individuality."

"Why does that sound like an insult?" Mike asked, looking at Charlie suspiciously.

"Anyway," Charlie plowed on. "His name's Michael, he's new to the area, just moved here from Texas."

"Why would anyone make that move?" Devante asked.

"He's a figure skater," Charlie said, "and apparently he switched coaches to one in Boston. So he's here now for at least a year. He seems like a cool guy."

"Figure skater, huh?" Mike said. Devante eyed him warily, but all he said next was, "Cool."

"I've watched some of his programs, he's good," Charlie said. "So? Can I bring him?"

"I like figure skating," Natasha said firmly. "I say yes."

"Sure," Devante said.

Preeda nodded. All eyes turned to Mike. "You're *sure* he's a Michael?" he asked.

"One hundred percent positive," Charlie declared.

"Then fine," Mike said. "We'll give him a trial run."

"Great! I'll let him know," Charlie said.

The conversation moved on, Devante's scotch and soda getting emptier and emptier. When it was finally gone, he nudged Preeda, who slid off the end of the bench to let him out. "I'm done for the night," he said. "See you all Saturday."

"See you tomorrow," Mike countered. Devante smiled at him and nodded. Preeda slid back in to occupy his spot on the bench and gave him a smile of her own.

When Devante cracked the front door of his house open half an hour later, it was with a clearer head and a desperate need to pee. Seeing his father sitting in his armchair, a different newspaper in front of his face and the final minutes of a football game on the television, Devante gave up attempting to be quiet, dropping his keys into the bowl by the door and kicking his shoes off.

"I don't know why you try and sneak back in after you're out with your friends," Carl said mildly. "You never come home past nine, and I'm not old enough to be asleep by then yet."

"I don't *sneak*," Devante said. "And you never know. What

if one night you *have* gone to bed, and I wake you up?"

"Then I wake up, and I know my son is safely home after an evening carousing with young people."

"I don't know what's worse, *carousing* or *young people*," Devante remarked.

Carl threw him a scowl from behind his paper. "You gonna sit down, or stand in the doorway all night?"

Devante loped over to the couch and dropped down. There were only five minutes left in the game. He could stay up that long before dragging himself to bed.

Chapter 2

DEVANTE WOKE WITH a start, the sound of clattering bowls in the kitchen cutting through his sleep. It took a minute of blinking befuddlement before he realized the reason he could hear his father cooking was because he had fallen asleep on the couch. He grimaced, rubbed his neck, and pushed himself to his feet.

"Why didn't you wake me up?" he grumbled, stumping into the kitchen and dropping into his chair at the table.

"I did," Carl retorted. "Chocolate chip or blueberry?"

"Blueberry," Devante said. "Then why was I still on the couch?"

"Because when I woke you up, you told me you *wanted* to sleep there, and to leave you alone." Carl sprinkled a handful of blueberries into the pancake batter in the bowl in front of him, and started pouring it out onto the griddle. "You talk shit in your sleep, kid."

"Sorry." Devante rubbed his neck again, and then carefully patted his hair to test the damage. Not too bad, he ascertained. Luckily half the throw pillows on the couch were satin.

"Enjoy it," Carl grumbled, flipping the pancakes. "Five years, you won't be able to pull a stunt like that and walk the next day. You've got young bones. Get the syrup."

Devante stood and went to the pantry, coming back with both the syrup and the butter bell. There were no plates or silverware on the table yet, so he got those too; not a full proper table-setting, but enough for breakfast.

Then he ran to Carl's bathroom. He never had gotten to pee when he got home the night before.

When he came back, the pancakes were done, piled onto a serving plate in the middle of the table. Carl was tucking into one, napkin tucked into the collar of his shirt to guard against errant syrup. Devante dealt with the risk by hunching entirely over his plate. "Won't be able to pull that either, in a few years," Carl observed. "Bad for your back."

"Better than looking like a toddler," Devante mumbled. Carl kicked his ankle under the table and grumbled.

Like always, Devante did the dishes while his father got ready for work. Carl was painfully economical with his dishes, so there wasn't much, just the batter bowl, the spatula, the griddle, and the plates and silverware they'd eaten with. By the time he'd dried the last fork, he could hear his father pulling his shoes on in the living room.

"Have a good day at work!" he called, opening the cabinet above the sink and putting the clean, dry plates away.

"You too," came Carl's deep rumble, and then the door opened and shut behind him.

Devante didn't have to catch his own bus until 11:15 A.M., 11:30 if he was willing to risk being a few minutes late to work, which he tried not to do very often. He spent the time watching television on his laptop on the couch, refreshing his course software in the background just in case his grades had been posted already.

At 11:10, showered, shaved, and dressed in black slacks and a button-down pattered with colorful fireworks, Devante locked the front door behind him and made for his bus stop at the end of the block.

Twenty minutes on the 66 and twelve on the 65, and then five minutes on foot, put him at the front door of the Brighton Public Library, where he worked eight hours on Thursdays, four on Fridays, and three on Mondays. "Afternoon, Miss Carla," he said, walking up to the circulation desk and then around behind it.

Carla, a prim and proper Black woman in her fifties, shook her head. "You're two minutes early, Devante. Still morning."

"Well then, good morning, Miss Carla," he said, giving her a bright smile.

She laughed and stood up from the rolling chair at the circulation computer. "Give me your bag," she said, holding out her hand. "I'll put it in the back." Devante swung his messenger bag over his head and handed it to her, and she tottered off toward the staff area.

He lowered himself into the chair, reaching under the seat to adjust the height. Carla was much, much shorter than he was. He'd been working at the Brighton Public Library for almost a year, though, and he knew by feel when the chair was at the right height for his long legs.

There were no patrons at the desk; a few kids were clumped around one of the computers in the front, and a middle-aged white woman was perusing the new releases. Carla came out of the staff room, wrapped in her paisley shawl despite the heat of the early summer afternoon. "Busy day?" Devante asked as she made her way past him.

"Naw," she said, shaking her head. "Should be a quiet shift, if this morning was any indication. Good luck, Devante."

"Have a good day, Miss Carla."

"And Devante?"

"Yes, Miss Carla?"

She winked at him. "Give my best to your father, now."

She wobbled out the front door, on wedges she never could seem to get the hang of walking in despite wearing them every time Devante had ever seen her. He turned his attention back to the computer and pulled up the Simmons University Library Science course website.

He spent the first half hour of his shift perusing the required reading lists for his last-ever grad school courses. Some books, some articles; he placed Interlibrary Loan requests for the books through the Boston Public Library website, setting Brighton as his pickup location, and then logged onto Simmons' library website to pull up the first article through their databases.

Eventually New Releases Woman came up with a stack of plastic-coated bestsellers. She smiled at Devante's shirt, and he smiled back at her, scanning her card and checking the books out to her. "Enjoy," he said, pushing the stack back across the counter to her. She thanked him, tipped the pile into her tote bag, and went on her way. Devante went back to his schoolwork, taking notes into a Google Doc.

His supervisor, Ethan, arrived at four, waving at him and settling into their desk behind circulation. "Any problems?" they asked.

"Nope," Devante said, popping the p. "Slow day."

"Good, good."

At five Mr. Smythwick, one of Devante's regulars, came by with a bag of returns. Devante scanned each one back in, then turned to the hold shelf. "Only four today," he remarked, pulling Mr. Smythwick's holds off the shelf. He opened his mouth to say, "Big ones, though," and then remembered that he wasn't allowed to remark on books unprompted and shut it again.

"Don't be fooled," Mr. Smythwick said, shaking one bony, hairy finger at Devante. "I'll be back up to my regular numbers next week. Interlibrary Loan is just being difficult about finding some of the rarer stuff."

"I wouldn't have it any other way," Devante said. "Carrying your books back and forth is my arm workout."

Mr. Smythwick cackled like a banshee, and, when Devante had carefully scanned all four of his check-outs and printed out his receipt, staggered away again, his rickety, elderly frame somehow holding up the weight of the books. Devante shook his head ruefully and sat back down in his chair.

"I saw you remember about the privacy rules," Ethan said, coming up and leaning on the counter next to him. "Well done."

"Thanks."

"Can you put together a cart for the morning? Shelvers are in bright and early."

"Sure thing," Devante said. Ethan nodded and went back

to their desk.

Devante grabbed a cart and started arranging the day's returns onto it in call number order. It was good practice; if he ever got the job of his dreams, he'd be in charge of his own shelving.

By the time he was finished, it was five minutes past six, and Mike was walking in the front door, a bag of food in his hand, his backpack slung over one shoulder. "Evening," he said breezily, walking up to the desk.

"Evening," Devante said. He turned back to Ethan. "Mike's here."

Ethan nodded and made their way up to the circulation desk. "Enjoy your break," they said. "Evening, Mike."

"Hey, Ethan," Mike said. At Devante's beckon he came around the desk and followed Devante to the staff room.

Mike set the food on the table and dropped his backpack into a chair, wrenching it open as Devante pulled paper plates out of the drawer by the sink and ripped two paper towels off the roll on the counter. "One chicken burrito, no lettuce, and a ginger ale," Mike said, setting a foil-wrapped cylinder from the bag and a green bottle from his backpack in front of one chair at the table. "And one quesadilla and a Diet Coke for me," he said, arranging his own food. He moved the backpack to the floor and sat down, accepting one plate from Devante and opening his quesadilla container.

Devante sat down, cracked open the ginger ale, and took a pull. He tapped at his phone, Venmoed Mike ten dollars for the food, and set into his burrito.

"How's your day been?" Mike asked around a mouthful of tortilla, cheese, and beef.

Devante swallowed to set a good example before saying, "Not bad. Pretty slow, but I've got a lot of prep work done for next semester. You?"

"Grand," Mike said, grinning. "Did a solid five miles on the treadmill before my lab." Mike had the sort of exercise regime, and the body to show for it, that ordinarily would have made Devante nervous about eating in front of him. But Mike had always been decent, never commenting on what Devante ate beyond saying it smelled good, and he never seemed to judge Devante for being able to put away a whole burrito from La Catrina in one sitting.

"How's your crabs?" Devante asked solicitously, before going in for another bite.

Mike rolled his eyes. "Are you ever going to get tired of phrasing it like that?" Devante shook his head. Despite himself, a smile tugged at Mike's mouth. He worked in a lab researching the humble horseshoe crab. Nobody in The Friend Group ever missed a chance to make the obvious joke. "They're healthy," Mike said. "And as happy as we're able to tell, anyway. I'll tell them you said hello."

"Please do!"

They descended for a few minutes into eating, nothing but the sounds of chewing and swallowing. When Devante was about halfway through his burrito, Mike said, voice sly, "You and Preeda looked pretty cozy last night."

Devante froze, then deliberately resumed chewing until he could swallow his mouthful. "I don't know what you mean."

"Sure," Mike said, sounding like he didn't mean it. "Seriously, Dev, when are you gonna make your move already? It's getting unbearable."

Devante wiped his mouth with his paper towel, suddenly uncomfortable. "I don't know what you mean," he repeated.

Mike rolled his eyes again. "You're seriously telling me there's *nothing* there? When the two of you can't stop disappearing into your little side convos at every get-together?"

Devante squirmed in his chair. "We've made out a few times," he admitted quietly.

They'd done a good deal more than *make out*, but that wasn't something he was up to admitting right now. Not to Mike.

Mike pumped his fist in the air triumphantly. "I *knew* it!" he crowed. "Deets, immediately."

"No," Devante said firmly, shaking his head. "I didn't tell you to gossip about it, I only said because you asked. It's between her and me."

"Alright, alright," Mike said, holding his hands up peaceably. "I'm just saying, you gotta lock that shit down."

"Why do you care so much?" Devante snapped, covering his irritation in another bite of burrito, which now tasted kind of ashen in his mouth.

Mike shrugged. "It'll affect the dynamic of the whole group, you two getting together properly. I'm invested in the dynamics of the group." He bit off another chunk of quesadilla, chewed, and swallowed. "Also, you're, like, my friend, and I want you to be happy and shit."

"Thanks," Devante murmured. The serious possibility that being with Preeda, properly, would not make him happy, he kept to himself. Mike meant well, but there were some things Devante didn't want to tell him.

Thankfully, Mike changed the subject to sports after that. Devante honestly knew very little about sports, but it was a topic Mike could talk about for hours without requiring more than the occasional noise to indicate Devante was listening. They finished their food that way, Mike chatting between bites about the end of the hockey season, and the uncomfortable knot in Devante's stomach had almost fully eased by the time his break was over.

Devante walked Mike as far as the circulation desk, ushering him out of the staff-only area and relieving Ethan at the desk. "Thanks for dinner, Mike."

"You know it's my pleasure, Dev." Mike saluted him. "See you at drinks tomorrow?"

"See you." Mike left. Devante pulled up the browser window he'd left open and dove back into his grad school articles.

There was only an hour left on his shift, and the latter half of that was filled with check-outs, people packing up after a day spent in the library choosing books, or rushing in to return something due and check out something new. Ethan locked the door at eight and did the closing checks while Devante powered down the computer. "See you tomorrow," Ethan said when Devante slung his messenger bag across his torso.

"See you tomorrow," Devante said. He pushed the chair under the desk and left for the five-minute walk to his bus stop.

He spent the two bus rides leaning his head against the window, trying not to think about Preeda, and Mike, and the dynamics of The Friend Group, and why it felt like it was all coming to a head much sooner than he was prepared for. Trying not to think about it, and failing.

Preeda was nice. She was sarcastic and cutting, sure, but she was always nice to him, and she was pretty, with her shining dark hair always pulled back into a bun and her dark wrap dresses and her mid-brown skin. They had a lot in common, too, grad school and fantasy novels and bad soap operas that neither of them would admit why they started watching years ago and kept up with until now. She'd make any man a perfect girlfriend, Devante included.

Quickly he tore his mind away from how that thought made him feel.

Carl, as always, was installed in his armchair when Devante got home. "You eat?" he grunted when Devante came in and kicked off his shoes.

"Yes, Dad," Devante said patiently. "You know Mike brings me dinner on Thursdays."

"Just checking." Carl turned the page of his paper. "Brought you a doughnut. 'S in the kitchen."

"Thanks!" Devante padded into the kitchen to find a bag from Dunkin on the table. He checked inside—old fashioned, his favorite. He grabbed a paper towel to catch crumbs and brought it out to the living room, sinking onto the couch. "How was your day at work?"

"'Nother day teaching snot-nosed brats how to run," Carl grumbled.

Devante snorted. Carl loved his job, and he loved all his students, especially the ones who didn't come in knowing how to run properly. The more he grumbled about his day, the better it was. "Glad to hear it."

"You?"

"Quiet. Got a lot of work done." Devante gave his father a sidelong smirk. "Miss Carla says hello, by the way."

Carl rumbled something indistinct under his breath and turned the page a little more forcefully than was necessary. Devante laughed and applied himself to his doughnut.

Chapter 3

SATURDAY MORNING SAW Devante in his underwear and white tank top, smacking the side of the washing machine in the tiny room off the kitchen and praying: his usual laundry day routine. The ancient machine, thankfully, decided to be cooperative, and it rumbled to life with an ominous creak.

The dryer, thankfully, although just as old, was much more pleasant, and in an hour Devante had a basket full of his father's workout clothes and his own brightly-colored shirts and dark jeans, washed so many times there was no risk of color bleed in either direction. Devante lugged the basket into the living room and went back to start a load of sheets and pillowcases, both their beds stripped after breakfast that morning. While that load cycled through, he got started folding and sorting the clothes.

His phone lit up with a text from Preeda: *U ready 2 meet the new guy tonight???*

Devante's stomach sank as he remembered: Charlie was bringing his new neighbor, Michael the figure skater, to TFG drinks that night. *Ready as I'll ever be*, he texted back, setting the phone back down and returning to the laundry. It was a good thing wash day was today, he told himself. He'd have his pick of his wardrobe to make a good first impression.

I hope he's cute, Preeda texted back a moment later.

Before he could think about it, Devante had picked up his phone and typed, *Cuter than me?*

No one's cuter than you, she sent back after a minute.

Feeling both hot under the collar and weirdly guilty,

Devante set his phone face-down on the couch next to him and finished folding without distraction.

He left his father's clothes on his stripped-bare bed, slid the laundry basked into the crevice between the washing machine and the wall, and changed over his own bed linens before checking his phone again. No further messages from Preeda, but there was one from Charlie to the group chat.

CM: Remember I'm bringing my neighbor tonight!!! Everyone on their best behavior.

NM: I'm always on my best behavior

CG: I didn't mean you, Natasha dear. I mostly meant Mike

MC: Hey

MC: What's that supposed to mean?

CG: You're the kind of uber-masculine white dude who might make a Mexican bisexual figure skater nervous

NM: Your neighbor's bi?

NM: WAIT

NM: You're not bringing MICHAEL LOPEZ to drinks tonight, are you?

PC: Who's Michael Lopez?

MC: I'm not some damn homophobe just because I work out, Charlie

CG: I know, I know, I'm just saying

CG: And yeah, that's his name! You know him?

NM: He only had the sexiest exhibition skate at Nationals last year, and his quad Salchow is fire. He won bronze!

PC: You're gonna have to explain all those words to me, I don't know figure skating

NM: Just know he's a super hot, super talented professional athlete

NM: Fuck, this changes *everything* about my wardrobe plan for tonight. G2G

MC: I think you're bringing Nat's next hookup to drinks tonight, Charlie. It's not me you should be worried about

CG: I'm realizing that

PC: Also, Charlie my lad, did you just out him to a bunch of strangers?

CG: Oh, he's very out, it's all over his Insta

PC: Still side-eyeing you

CG: Probably fair

PC: Dinner beforehand???

DM: I'll be there

NM: Can't make dinner, but I'll be at Mood

MC: Got lab up until it's Mood time

CG: Got dinner plans already

PC: Looks like it's just you and me, Dev

DM: Oh no

PC: Rude!

A super hot, super talented professional athlete. Devante's stomach was squirming again for different reasons.

He remade his bed and hung his clothes up, stretching out on top of the covers to watch a few episodes of *The Young and the Restless*. As was happening more and more often with that show, he found himself nodding off, and eventually gave in, set a timer on his phone, and closed his laptop, placing it carefully on the floor before curling up and closing his eyes for a nap.

In the end, he went with his pineapple shirt again. It was his favorite, and fresh out of the wash, with crisp creases, it made him look a little slimmer than he was, which he was starting to think he'd need that night.

Super hot, super talented professional athlete.

Preeda was already seated when he got to their usual pre-drinks dinner place, a greasy diner down the block from Mood. There were no menus at the table. "I told Monique you were coming, and I think she put your usual order in," Preeda said by way of explanation and greeting as he sat down across from her. "Sorry if you wanted something else."

"It's fine," Devante said. "How're you?"

"I'm good," she said, smiling at him. She had a good smile; it always made Devante want to smile back. "Caught up on *The Young and the Restless* this afternoon."

"Oh my God, me too," Devante said, leaning forward.

They were still discussing the show when their food came. Monique had indeed put Devante's usual order in, and she set a burger, extra cheese, no lettuce, plate piled high with French fries, in front of him, and a tuna melt with chips in front of Preeda. "Enjoy," she said, stalking away on heels so high they made her taller than Devante when they were both standing.

"Mmm," Preeda hummed, picking up her sandwich. "Oh, did you look up Michael Lopez on Instagram?"

Devante shook his head, dipping a fry into the dish of mayo Monique always wedged onto his plate for him. He hadn't wanted to; just the sound of the man was intimidating enough. He hadn't wanted to psych himself out before he even met the guy. "I take it you did?"

"*Super* cute," Preeda moaned self-pityingly. "And Charlie's right, he's, like, super bi. Nearly every other pic is him draped in a pride flag or with pride eyeliner or something."

"Good for him," Devante said, as off-handedly as he could manage.

"Oh, totally," Preeda agreed. "I think it's great."

"I hope Natasha leaves enough of him for the rest of us to get to know." Devante bit into his burger to hide his expression as Preeda laughed.

They finished up their meal, left Monique an extravagant tip as always, and made their satisfied way down the block to Mood. It was still early enough that the bar wasn't totally packed yet, and they were able to wind their way through the tables to their usual booth, where Devante could see the back of Charlie's Afro bent close to someone's head he didn't recognize.

"Yo," Preeda said, swinging around to the other side of the booth and dragging Devante in her wake.

"Preeda!" Charlie cried, standing as best he could with his legs tucked under the table. The person to his right made a better showing, tucking one knee onto the bench so he could straighten up more fully. "Michael, this is Preeda Chanthara, and *this* is Devante Miller," he said, gesturing to them both.

"Hi," Michael said warmly, holding out his hand first to Preeda and then to Devante. "Great shirt," he added as Devante's hand closed around his, and he smiled, and Devante's mind whited out.

Oh no, he thought, desperate and suddenly panicked. *Oh no, not now, not like this.*

Michael had a big smile, full of shining white teeth and laughter, and his face was angular and sharp, but his hair was soft, falling past his shoulders in perfect waves that Devante distantly thought Natasha would kill for. He was a good four inches shorter than Devante, and his hand was warm and soft, and *Devante was so, so fucked. Not like this*, he thought again, shaking Michael's hand and forcing himself to let go.

The four of them sat down, Devante sliding in next to Preeda as he tried to make his brain work again. Michael's bag was sitting on the bench next to him, and Devante focused on it instead of Michael's face: a messenger bag, in a patchwork of different styles of blue fabric, covered in enamel pins. Devante saw one that said *Birds aren't real*, and another in the shape of the state of Texas, and, perhaps predictably, the bisexual pride flag.

No. Too dangerous. He tore his gaze away from the bag and looked at Charlie, who was saying, "The others aren't here yet."

"Ooh, let me see if I remember," Michael said. His voice was light and airy, a contrast to his sharp features, but it suited him. Devante swallowed. "Natasha and Mike, right?"

"Well done," Charlie said, clapping him on the shoulder. "Now, a fair warning, apparently Natasha's a fan of yours and she *might* try to eat you alive tonight."

Michael laughed, throwing his head back with the force of it. "Thanks for the heads-up, man."

"Can't let a bro walk into that without a warning."

"So," Michael said, setting his forearms on the table and leaning over them toward Devante and Preeda. "I already know Charlie. Tell me about you guys."

Devante's mouth was still too dry to speak, but Preeda swooped in and said, "We're grad students. Library science, at Simmons."

"Oh, cool!" Michael seemed genuinely delighted. "How much longer do you have to go?"

"Only one semester," Preeda said. "Then it's the job-hunt grind for the both of us."

Michael looked between the two of them. "And are you two…"

"No," Devante rasped, his voice coming out ragged and rough. He coughed and tried again. "No," he repeated. "Just friends."

Michael nodded. "Cool," he said, smiling at Devante. Devante's brain whited out again, just a little bit.

"What…What brings you to Boston?" he managed, trying to remember how many times a minute was a normal amount to blink.

Michael leaned back against the booth wall. "I switched coaches," he said. "My old team wasn't on board with my plan to come out, so I signed with a new coach up north who was more willing to work with me."

Devante nodded. "Sucks," he said. "About your old coach."

Michael shrugged. "It happens," he said.

Was Devante looking at him too much? He still hadn't gotten the hang of blinking again, and it was hard to look anywhere but directly at Michael's face, now that he'd started. But Michael was looking back, and he didn't seem weirded out, so Devante was probably doing alright.

"Hello, lord and ladies," came Natasha's voice singing out suddenly. She was dressed in what she privately called her Slut Uniform, a slinky sheath dress with slim straps that made her ass pop, according to her. She dropped onto the bench next to Michael, gesturing at Katie behind the bar. "First round's on Charlie, right?"

"Is it?" Charlie asked, raising an eyebrow. "Oh, alright then. For Michael's first time."

"*Michael.*" Natasha practically purred his name. She put one elbow on the table and turned her whole body to face him. "It is just a *delight* to meet you. I, as you may have gathered, am Natasha Melnikov. Yes, you may shake my hand."

"A pleasure," Michael said, managing to sound appropriately solemn while keeping an edge of laughter in his voice. He shook her hand, and she grinned, sharp as a knife. "I've heard so much about you already."

"All lies, unless it was bad," she declared, making Michael laugh again.

"Here we go," Devante heard Preeda mutter under her breath next to him.

"All good, I'm afraid," Michael told her, laughter still laced through his voice. "I look forward to discovering the truth."

There was a flash of white in the corner of Devante's eye, and then Mike was there, sliding onto the bench next to him. "You must be Mike," Michael said, turning away from Natasha to smile at the newcomer.

Did his eyes, deep brown and warm, flick to Devante, just then, before returning to Mike? Devante shook himself.

"And you must be Michael," Mike said, reaching out a hand

to shake. "Pleasure to meet you, although I warn you, if you ever switch to Mike, I'll have to kick you out of the group."

"I've been Michael for twenty-four years," Michael assured him, "and God willing, I'll be Michael for another eighty."

Mike nodded. "Glad to hear it."

Katie arrived, bearing a tray of drinks. "New guy!" she observed, passing them out. "What can I get you?"

"A gin and tonic, please," Michael told her, turning his smile onto her.

"First round's on me, apparently," Charlie said. Katie laughed and patted him on the shoulder before sweeping back behind the bar.

"So," Preeda said, folding her arms in front of her on the table. "Michael Lopez. All I know about you is that apparently your quad Salchow is amazing."

"Sal-*kow*," Natasha corrected.

Michael grinned. "Thank you," he said. "Still new, but I'm getting the hang of it."

"So what is a quad Sal-kow?" Preeda asked.

"It's a type of jump," Michael said, leaning forward to match her. He kept talking, insides and outsides of edges, rotations, landings…It all sped by Devante's ears in that dancing, sweet voice. He tried to follow, he really did, but the light was hitting the slope of Michael's nose just right to illuminate the whole of his face, and really, what was Devante to do?

This has happened before, Devante told himself. Every now and again he met someone and his whole body just said *yes*, lighting him up like a Christmas tree. He figured it happened to everyone. *Not only with men, though*, said a slinky voice in the back of his head. *Shut up*, Devante told it. So it had happened mostly with men. *Only with men*, said the voice. It didn't mean anything. He'd never *done* anything about it, never looked closely at the attraction to see if there was any substance to it, and so it didn't mean anything that the only people who knocked him sideways like this were men. It was just a *thing*, a quirk of body chemistry. No doubt it happened to everyone.

Now that Mike was on the bench, Devante was pressed even closer to Preeda, their thighs and arms touching. Devante tried to focus on that, on the warmth of her body heat as she listened attentively to Michael, who was now talking about other types of jumps. He took a deep breath, trying to see if he could smell her perfume, but all that hit his nose was an unfamiliar scent of pine and vanilla that made his head spin.

Enough of this. Devante gave himself another firm mental shake and forcibly tuned back in to the conversation.

"The season starts properly in October," Michael was saying. "I won't know when and where I'll be competing until around August, though."

"What do you do until then?" Mike asked. He was pressed against Devante too, all up against his other side, and abruptly Devante started to feel a little hot and claustrophobic. Sweat prickled at the back of his neck and under his arms.

"Conditioning, mostly," Michael said. "Keeping in shape. I'll start to work on new programs in a couple of months."

His forearms, where they rested on the table, were slender and muscular. His whole torso looked slender and muscular, come to think of it. *Stop it*, Devante told himself firmly.

"So are you on, like, a super-strict diet?" Natasha asked. She didn't seem as predatory as she had at the start, but she was still turned fully toward Michael, apparently hanging off every word.

"Not so much over the summer," Michael said. "But during the season, yeah, it's pretty strict."

"Couldn't be me," Preeda said frankly, and the table laughed. Devante laughed too. Too loud? Probably too loud, but no one seemed to take notice of it. He coughed and covered it with a sip of his drink.

"How's your apartment?" Mike asked. "Were you able to find something decent off-cycle?"

"Off-cycle?" Michael asked, looking a little confused.

"Most Boston apartments run with the school year," Charlie explained. "September to August."

"Ah. Yeah, my apartment's pretty nice," Michael said, shrugging.

"Can't be *that* nice, if it's in Charlie's shithole building," Natasha muttered into her drink.

"I resent that remark," Charlie said mildly. "No, but Michael's place genuinely *is* pretty sweet. One-bedroom, even."

"Yeah?" said Preeda, perking up. "Figure skating must pay well." Preeda, Devante knew, liked to lust after Zillow listings for one-bedroom apartments from her studio, a different one every year due to price hikes.

Michael shrugged again. "I had a good season last year," he said. "Sponsors were interested."

"Sick." Charlie toasted him. Michael clinked his gin and tonic against Charlie's bottle and took a drink. His Adam's apple bobbed as he swallowed. *Stop it.*

"You're awfully quiet tonight, Dev," Natasha said, pointing a finger at him. "Nothing to say to our new friend?"

Devante cleared his throat. "Just trying not to overwhelm him," he managed to say. "You all have such big personalities, I don't want him to get scared off too soon."

Natasha threw her head back and cackled. Even Mike cracked a grin, and Michael's smile stretched wide across his face. "I hope you're not this quiet all the time," he said, "if you've got that kind of a sense of humor."

"Dev's just shy," Charlie said, tipping the last of his beer into his mouth. "He'll warm up to you."

"Fair enough." Michael was still looking at him, an assessing but friendly look in his eyes. Without his permission, Devante felt his mouth quirk up in a smile. Michael winked at him.

"You've gotta get back soon, right?" Charlie murmured to Michael.

Michael blinked, as though he had forgotten Charlie was there. Devante certainly had. "Yes," Michael said. "Unfortunately, I've got an early start tomorrow."

"No fear on that front," Preeda told him, draining her glass of wine. "We're all a bunch of old farts who finish early too."

"I'll fit right in, then," Michael said. "Assuming I make the cut," he added, looking over at the rest of them.

"You do," Mike said. Devante, who hadn't realized he'd been tense, relaxed. "We meet here Tuesdays and Saturdays. Charlie can add you to the group chat."

"Can't make Tuesdays, but Saturdays I can do," Michael said. "I look forward to getting to know all of you better."

A chorus of "You too" went around the table; Devante, afterward, was about ninety percent sure he'd joined in. Everyone finished their drinks and shuffled to their feet, and Michael did another round of handshakes.

When he shook Devante's hand, that scent of pine and vanilla filled his nostrils again, and Michael gave Devante another small, private wink.

Devante honestly wasn't sure how he got out of the bar and onto the bus, but he made it home without incident. Carl was in his armchair, the *Boston Globe* open in front of him. "Evening, son," he said when Devante shut the door behind him.

"Did you ever meet someone," Devante said, "and it's like they just knocked you over? In a good way?"

"Your mother," Carl said succinctly. Devante nodded, acknowledging the point. Carl peered at him sideways. "Anyone I should know about?"

"No," Devante said faintly, shaking his head. *Definitely not.* "Nobody in particular. Just thinking."

This was, objectively, nonsensical, but Carl accepted it, going back to his paper with a slow nod and blink.

Chapter 4

FOR THE MOST part, Devante shoved it aside.

Without Michael directly in front of him, smiling so widely and smelling so good, it was easy to downplay the effect the man had had on him. Michael was, after all, a professional athlete; he had to be in great shape for his work, and charming to win over the judges and the audience. No doubt he'd just had it turned up for his first meeting with The Friend Group, and Devante had just gotten caught in the crossfire, so to speak. It had been a fluke.

Devante had a three-hour shift at the Brighton Public Library on Monday, which he spent shelving the books that had come in over the weekend and unjamming the printer for a group of teens who seemed to be printing an entire novel's worth of Naruto fanfiction. If they'd asked, Devante could have pointed them in the direction of much better Naruto fanfiction, but they didn't ask, and the library's privacy rules meant he couldn't comment on what they were doing, so he kept his mouth shut.

Mondays were pizza nights in the Miller household: half Hawaiian, half sausage and onion. It was the one meal Carl allowed them to take in the living room, his newspaper folded on the arm of his chair while he backseat-refereed a wrestling match. Devante live-texted Carl's commentary to Mike, who had lab on Monday nights and needed the pick-me-up.

Devante had chosen to take his final electives online, in large part so that he could keep his same shifts at Brighton. Ordinarily he'd devote his Tuesday to classwork before meeting up with his friends, but his courses didn't start again until the end of the week. He napped instead, or tried to, wrenching his mind away from the phantom scent of vanilla and pine that seemed to fill his nostrils every time he let his mind wander.

The discussion that night at Mood was almost solely centered around their new addition, who was, as promised, absent until Saturday. "God, he's delicious," Natasha moaned, throwing an arm companionably around Charlie's shoulders. "You did good, Grant."

"I feel like I've brought you a human sacrifice," Charlie grumbled. "Just don't fuck him and run him off, alright? I like the guy, I'd like him to stay around."

"Fucking me is not what runs guys off," Natasha proclaimed confidently.

"No, it's your personality," Mike put in, grinning.

"Ugh." Natasha wrinkled her nose. "I hate when I let you get a good one in like that."

"I'll get a good one in—"

"Don't finish that," Devante and Preeda begged at the same time.

"Anyway," Charlie said, laughing at Mike's pout. "He said he really likes you guys, on the way home. Although, Dev, he thinks you don't like him."

"What?" Devante asked, startled. "Why would he think that?"

"You were, like, weirdly quiet all night," Mike supplied, taking a swig of his Pabst.

"I had a headache," Devante mumbled. More clearly, he said, "Tell him I like him fine, Charlie, and I'm sorry." Clearly, he hadn't been as chill as he'd thought. He'd have to practice before Saturday.

Practice being chill around a hot guy, that damn voice in his head said. Good thing you're straight, or this would be a lot more pathetic.

Devante sternly told it to shut up. Straight or not, hot people were intimidating.

And oh, Michael Lopez is definitely hot. Objectively speaking.

"You alright?" Preeda murmured to him, blessedly cutting

through his thoughts. When he looked at her, her brow was furrowed in concern.

"Fine," he said, mustering up a smile for her. She didn't look entirely satisfied, but she patted him on the knee under the table and turned back to the conversation.

She left her hand on his knee. Devante swallowed hard and tried to feel anything at all about it.

Devante spent the rest of his week off from school lazing around the house, exerting effort only to cook dinner on Wednesday and clean the living room and both bathrooms after his shift on Friday. He caught up on all his soaps, live-texting Preeda with each new development until she texted back an all-caps, *SPOILERS, BRO.*

Sorry, he texted back, and then paused the video to make popcorn.

Dressing for drinks on Saturday was a nerve-racking affair, made infinitely worse by his dogged attempts to bully himself out of being nervous. "You're being pathetic," he told himself in the mirror in his bedroom after he caught himself spending five minutes deciding on an *undershirt* of all things. "He's just a guy."

"What was that?" Carl bellowed up the stairs.

"Nothing," Devante shouted back. "Just talking to myself."

That rush of irritation at himself saw him through to getting fully dressed, dark blue jeans and a shirt with kittens on it, and out the door. Everyone else had dinner plans, so he went to the diner alone, intending to drown his sorrows in a plate of French fries.

That plan worked perfectly until the steaming-hot plate of fries was actually placed in front of him, at which exact moment the door to the diner opened and Devante's living nightmare walked in.

Michael was dressed for the heat, salmon shorts and a short-sleeved yellow t-shirt that hugged every inch of his outline, messenger bag slung over his body, wavy light-brown hair pulled back into a sharp ponytail. Devante seriously considered diving under the table, dignity be damned, but then Michael looked around and saw him.

"Devante!" he cried, beaming all over his sharp face and walking toward him. "I guess we had the same idea, huh?"

"Yeah," Devante said, pulling up a smile.

"Mind if I join you?" Michael asked, gesturing to the empty chair across from him. "Totally cool if you'd rather eat alone. I don't want to harsh your vibe."

"No," Devante heard himself say, "no, it's fine."

"Great." Michael beamed at him and sat down. Monique wasn't working tonight, but Randor brought him a menu, for which Michael turned his smile onto *him* and, thankfully, off of Devante. "Any recommendations?" he asked, scanning his eyes down the menu.

Devante shrugged. "It's diner food. It's all tasty; this place has a five-star Yelp rating."

Michael laughed, and then his eyes lit up. "Oooh, chicken tenders," he said. "I can pretend it's on my meal plan."

"Thought you said it wasn't as strict over the summer," Devante said, and then flushed hot, but Michael only laughed again.

"True, but it's harder to go strict again for the season if I went too wild over the summer."

"Makes sense."

Devante's own appetite was rapidly shrinking. Eating in front of someone new was always a draining, risky affair, and Michael was the sort of thin and athletic that made it eight times worse.

Randor came back, order pad in hand, and raised his eyebrows in lieu of a question. "Um, chicken tenders, please," Michael said, after a quick look at Devante. "And can it be a double order of fries?" Devante relaxed slightly. Randor nodded and stalked away. Michael leaned forward across the table and when he spoke, it was in a hushed whisper. "Is he always so..."

"Rude?" Devante asked, feeling a grin of his own tug at his lips.

"I was going to say *taciturn*," Michael said.

"Either or," Devante said. "Yes, definitely, don't take it personally."

"Good to know." Michael winked, like they were sharing a joke. Devante's neck went hot under his collar. "Great shirt, by the way," Michael went on, breaking the tension between them and leaning back, one elbow slung over the back of his chair. "What was it you had on last week? Pineapples?"

"Good memory. And thank you." Michael's double order of fries had eased Devante's nerves somewhat, and the smell of his burger was starting to make his mouth water. "Do you mind if I…" he started, pointing at his plate.

"Please!" Michael said, gesturing for him to go on. "That looks good," he added, as Devante lifted the burger and bit into it. "No lettuce?"

Devante shook his head, chewing until he could swallow and say, "Never liked it. I'd get spinach, but they don't offer that here."

"Spinach on a burger," Michael said thoughtfully. "I'm gonna have to try that."

"It's surprisingly good," Devante offered.

Randor appeared, plunked a plate that was more French fry than ceramic in front of Michael, and disappeared. "You're not going to judge me if I use ketchup, right?" Michael asked, already reaching for the red bottle to the side.

"Not at a diner," Devante said.

Michael's grin, which was becoming all too familiar, flashed across his face for a heart-stopping second. "Fair enough."

Michael attacked and slowly but systematically conquered his plate of chicken and fries, and before Devante realized it, he had finished his burger as well. "God, that was good," Michael moaned, rubbing his stomach, and snatched at the two scraps of bill paper Randor had just placed down before Devante could even blink. "On me," Michael said, pulling out his wallet.

"You don't have to—" Devante started, but Michael held up a hand.

"Call it a blatant attempt at bribery," he said with a wink. "Any man who wears shirts like yours is a man I want to be friends with."

Devante's heart picked up the pace in his chest. "You don't have to bribe me to be your friend, Michael," he said, and immediately started second-guessing himself—had he sounded too earnest? Too eager?

"Well, if that's the case, then consider it an advance on our friendship," Michael said, pulling out a twenty and a ten and dropping them on the table. "You can get it next time."

Next time. Devante swallowed and nodded.

"Now, I know the bar is close, but I've only been there once and I haven't got my bearings yet," Michael said as they emerged into the sticky June evening.

Devante laughed. "It's this way."

They were the last ones to arrive at Mood, it turned out. Natasha, inexplicably, had commandeered the table top for an expansive game of what appeared to be Solitaire, and was resolutely ignoring Mike, who was telling a story about his lab. He broke off when Devante and Michael approached, and scooted down the bench. "Talking about your crabs again?" Devante asked, dropping down next to him.

Charlie hooted, and Mike rolled his eyes. "Crabs?" Michael echoed, sliding in next to Charlie.

"Horseshoe crabs," Mike said patiently. Devante snickered. Michael caught his eye, a glimmer of humor in his own. "I'm a grad student, and my lab works with horseshoe crabs."

"Ah," Michael said. "Are you guys all students, by the way?"

"All except Charlie," Natasha said, looking up from where she had just slapped the last king card onto the hearts pile and won her game. "He's an accounting peon."

"Right," Michael said. "So Mike's in biology, and Devante and Preeda are library science, which is just *so* cool, by the way," he added. "So what are you studying, Natasha?"

Natasha gathered her cards back into a deck and ruthlessly shuffled them together. "Journalism," she said. "God knows why, journalism's a dying field, but it's what I'm doing."

"Cool!" Michael said. "And I don't think it's dying, I think it just needs to reconsider what it wants to be."

That was as good as an invitation to Natasha, and she was off like a shot, her rant about paywalls and Brietbart flying out of her mouth with enough force to raise both of Michael's eyebrows. Devante sighed, the way only a man who has heard the rant seven and a half times already can sigh, and turned to Mike. "Here we go."

"He's new," was Mike's succinct response. "He'll learn."

Devante snorted. "How's your mom?" he asked. Mike called his family every Saturday morning like clockwork. When Mike had brought him dinner on Thursday, it had been with the news that his mother and both brothers had the flu.

"She's better," Mike said. "Keeping food down, anyway. Dad's got her hydrating like it's her job."

"Good."

Across from them, Charlie and Michael had moved on to figure skating. "A quad flip," Charlie was saying, "is that anything? I saw it on Wikipedia."

"It is a thing," Michael acknowledged, "although it's a lot harder than anything I can do right now. I've got two quads, and Sara, my coach, says I can try for the Lutz next off-season if things keep going well."

"Sick," Charlie said, apparently satisfied with the validation of his five minutes of research.

"Preeds, Dev, when do your classes start up again?" Natasha asked. She had moved on to doing tricks with her cards, making them jump from one hand to the other.

"Monday," Preeda said with a groan. Devante winced. "Don't *remind* us, Nat."

"Do you guys already work in a library, or are you just students?" Michael asked.

Preeda had a mouthful of wine, so Devante said, "Preeda works in the special collections library at Boston University. She's a cataloger. I'm at the Brighton Public, on the circulation desk."

"Oh, I pass the Brighton library every day on my run,"

Michael said. "Maybe I'll run into you there, Devante."

"Eyyy, *run*," Mike put in. Natasha rolled her eyes. Charlie guffawed.

Michael's eyes twinkled with amusement before he turned back to Preeda. "A cataloger, huh? Do you freelance? My books should be arriving any day now, and I never know how to arrange them."

"Wait till I get my degree," Preeda told him. "Then I can charge you more."

Michael laughed. "Totally."

The conversation moved on from there, until it was time to pay and go their separate ways. "Thanks for dinner," Devante found a moment to murmur to Michael on their way out.

Michael winked at him. "Anytime, Devante." Devante's name in Michael's voice made him shiver, which he resolutely ignored.

On Monday morning, settling in at the circulation desk at the public library, Devante pulled up his course pages for the summer semester. Starting with the class on resources for young adults, he pulled open the syllabus and started to peruse it.

Week Four: What to Do When a Middle-Schooler Asks You What Sex Is

"What are you reading?" Devante's supervisor asked, coming up to peer over his shoulder.

As quickly as he could, he closed the tab. "Classwork," he said, hoping she hadn't seen anything.

"Soon you'll be graduated and leaving us," she sighed dramatically, putting a hand to her forehead. "I don't know how we'll get on without you."

"Not until I find a job," Devante said, trying not to think about it. "You could have me for a long time yet."

"God knows that's true," she said frankly, and clapped him on the shoulder before going back to her desk.

Carefully, Devante pulled up the syllabus again and scrolled down to Week Four. *Handling sensitive, age-appropriate questions from young people*, the description read. "Sounds interesting,"

Devante murmured to himself, going back up to start at the beginning of the syllabus.

Most of the holds he'd placed in advance of this semester had come in over the weekend. During a slow period at the desk, Devante checked them out to himself, stowing what he could in his messenger back and pulling two plastic bags out of the box under the desk to double up for the rest. Most of them were children's books, middle grade through young adult, but there were a few theory books as well to keep things interesting.

The rest of Devante's shift passed relatively quietly. He spent his last half an hour shelving, earbuds in playing whatever Spotify decided he should listen to; today, inexplicably, was the *Pirates of the Caribbean* theme. When he finished, wheeling the cart back behind the desk, his supervisor thanked him and sent him on his way. Devante fetched his bags out of the staff room, made his way to the front door, winced at the baking sun, and stepped outside.

Chapter 5

DEVANTE TOOK A few steps out of the library and was immediately hailed, a melodious "Devante!" cutting through the air.

Michael jogged up to him and came to a halt, beaming all over his face. He was in a loose tank top and the shortest running shorts Devante had ever seen, a bright green sweatband at his hairline; for once, it was easiest to look at his smile. "Hey, man!" he said, breathing hard. "Fancy meeting you here."

"I work here," Devante managed, gesturing back at the library.

"Right, you said," Michael said. "How are you?"

"Pretty good," Devante said. "Just going in search of some lunch."

Michael lit up. "Oh, hey, I've been craving an iced coffee. Mind if I join you?"

Devante squinted at him. "Aren't you…in the middle of a run?"

Michael waved his hand. "I was just winding down," he said. "Could go for some air conditioning."

Devante wasn't sure he believed him, but the alternative was that Michael was interrupting his run specifically to have coffee with Devante, and that was clearly beyond belief. As Sherlock Holmes said, once you eliminate the impossible…"There's a Caffe Nero down the block," he offered.

"Great! Lead the way."

The air conditioning *was* nice, when they got there, even after the scant seventy-five seconds Devante had been out in the heat. Michael fanned his shirt out around him. "Hope I don't smell too bad," he said ruefully, looking down at the sheen of sweat on his arms.

He smelled warm and earthy, still like pine. The sweat made his skin look like it was glowing. "You smell fine," Devante said, immediately taking advantage of the opening in the line to hide from his own awkwardness.

He ordered a chicken caprese sandwich, and Michael behind him asked for an iced latte. "Together, please," Devante said to the cashier, gesturing to himself and Michael.

"Oh, that's okay, I have my card—" Michael started, but Devante shook his head.

"You said I could get next time," he reminded Michael. "This is next time."

"I did say that, didn't I?" Michael wrinkled his nose. "Alright then. Thank you, Devante."

Food and drink obtained, they made their way to the only open table in the cafe, tucked into the corner. "God, that smells good," Michael said, nodding to the sandwich as they settled into their seats.

"Do you want a bite?" Devante asked, his father's training overpowering his self-protective instincts.

"Do you mind?" Michael looked like he would absolutely be okay with Devante saying no, which made Devante scoot the plate a little closer toward him. Michael picked up half of the sandwich and took a small bite, his eyes rolling back in his head. "Okay, I'm *definitely* getting that next time I'm here. Thanks!"

"Anytime." *Take a bite, Devante. It doesn't matter that his mouth was just there.* What was it they called it in sorts of anime Devante couldn't picture himself admitting to watching? An indirect kiss? *Shut up and take the bite.*

Devante took the bite. It was a little overly large, but Michael didn't seem to mind.

"Hey, can I ask you a question?" Michael asked after a moment. "Sorry if it comes off a little weird."

Devante's hackles went up. "You can ask."

Perhaps reading the mood shift on Devante's face, Michael quickly said, "Nothing bad! Just...What exactly do you *learn* in library grad school?"

Devante relaxed, relief making him chuckle. "If you listen to Preeda, nothing at all," he said. Michael furrowed his brow. "She'd say it's a moneymaking scam for universities, designed to keep less privileged people out of libraries." He shrugged. "She has a point for herself; you don't really learn much about cataloging in library school, or at least not in our program."

"What do *you* think?" Michael asked. His brow was still furrowed, as though he were thinking hard.

"I think there's value in it," Devante said. "Maybe not as much value as they charge up-front, but I've learned a lot so far. Reference work, databases, professional ethics…It's designed for the more theoretical paths in libraries, not so much the technical stuff." He took another bite of his sandwich.

"Interesting," Michael said, and he sounded like he meant it. "So what sort of library work do you do?"

Devante swallowed and said, "I'm in circulation now, but that's not what I want to do long-term. It was just the only job I could find."

When he didn't go on, Michael prompted, a little smile on his face, "And what do you want to do long-term?"

Devante bit his lip, then admitted, "I want to work in a middle school library."

"Oh, wow," Michael said, his eyes going wide and… admiring? "Middle school specifically?"

"Well, any grade school," Devante allowed. "But yeah, middle school's the dream."

"Why?" Michael's face was open, curious but not disbelieving. Devante's heart started to beat a little faster.

"It's just…I remember being in middle school," he started. "It sucked, big time, and the only time I felt okay was when I was in the library. My school had a book club, and the librarian got to know me well enough during that time that she let me come in and spend my lunches there, as long as I did my actual eating at a table without any books around. But then I'd help her organize the books behind the desk, and she'd show me how to use a database or something, and it was just…nice."

"That's great," Michael said softly. "I hope you get to do that for someone else someday."

"Thanks," Devante said. He didn't usually go into all that whenever anyone asked him what he wanted to do, but Michael, it seemed, was a good listener.

A little embarrassed that he'd overshared, Devante cleared his throat and said, "What about you? You said you had a shipment of books coming from…"

"From Texas," Michael confirmed. "They should be here any day now."

"How many do you have?"

"About four boxes."

"Wow," Devante couldn't help but say. "For a one-bedroom?"

Michael grinned sheepishly. "What can I say? Gotta have my books."

Devante popped the last bite of his sandwich into his mouth, swallowed, and asked, "Which ones are you missing the most?"

"Oooh, good question," Michael said excitedly. "Definitely my Tolkien."

Goddamn it, why did it have to be Tolkien? "You like Tolkien?"

"I know, I'm a nerd," Michael started self-deprecatingly.

"No, I love Tolkien too," Devante hastened to say.

Michael grinned. "I knew you were a man of taste!" Devante flushed hot. "*The Hobbit* or *Lord of the Rings*?"

"Honestly can't choose," Devante said. "They're so different, it all depends what I'm in the mood for."

"Okay, follow-up question," Michael said, shifting in his seat to lean forward toward Devante. "For a sixteen-year-old girl who's read neither, but is slowly getting into fantasy as a genre, which would you recommend to start?"

"Your sister?" Devante guessed. Michael nodded. "I'd go *Hobbit*. Depending on her mindset, she might find it childish, but I think it's necessary context for *Lord of the Rings*."

Michael nodded. "I'm getting her both for her birthday, but wasn't sure which to tell her to start with. Thanks, Official Youth Librarian Devante."

"I like the sound of that," Devante admitted quietly.

Michael gave him a warm smile. "Have you done *The Silmarillion*?"

"Twice," Devante admitted.

Michael whistled. "Twice!"

"You?"

He shook his head. "I have to admit, it scares me."

Now it was Devante's turn to shake his head. "I get that, but it's honestly not that bad once you get into the flow of it. You just sort of have to be okay with not knowing exactly who everyone is the first couple of times you read it."

Michael looked disbelieving. "Knowing who everyone is, is kind of crucial for a novel, though, isn't it?"

Devante leaned forward too, warming to his favorite subject. "That's the thing," he said, trying not to sound too excited. "*The Silmarillion* isn't a novel."

"No?"

"No. It looks like a novel, but it isn't. It's an oral history written down, that just happens to be fictional. You can't look at it like reading a novel; you have to approach it like a long story told around a fire."

"Interesting," Michael said thoughtfully. "I'll have to give it another go."

Something small and brave seized hold of Devante's vocal cords, and he said, "You can always text me if you get confused."

"You'd have to give me your number for that," Michael said, mock-serious, a glint of amusement in his eye.

"Give me your phone," Devante said. Michael pulled it out of his pocket, called up a New Contact form, and passed it to Devante. Devante programmed his number in and sent himself a text. "There," he said, handing it back to Michael. "Now I have yours too."

Michael held it up. "Smile for the contact photo."

"No—" Devante said on instinct, and Michael instantly lowered the phone. "Sorry," Devante said, flushing hot. "You just took me by surprise. You can take one."

"Are you sure?" Michael asked. "I don't want to make you uncomfortable."

"It's fine," Devante said. Contact photos were small; it would only be of his face, and anyway the table was covering most of his stomach. And odds were Michael wouldn't look at it much anyway.

"Okay, smile," Michael said, holding up his phone again. Devante did his best; Michael seemed pleased when he lowered it again.

Devante opened the text he'd sent himself and saved the number under *Michael Lopez.* "Your turn?" he said, raising his phone.

Michael put the straw of his iced coffee in his mouth and gave Devante's phone a sardonic, playful look. Mouth suddenly dry, Devante took the picture and added it to the contact. "Thanks."

"So," Michael said, taking a sip of his iced coffee. "Devante Miller. Soon-to-be middle school librarian and Tolkien nerd. Tell me more about yourself."

Devante swept some crumbs off the table onto his finger and brushed them onto his empty plate. "What do you want to know?"

"For starters, where do you live?"

"Roxbury," Devante said. "I live with my dad." He braced himself for what he knew was coming next.

Michael nodded. "Where's your mom?"

There it is. "Died giving birth to me," he said.

Michael winced and reached out a hand to lay on Devante's forearm. "I'm so sorry," he said.

Devante gave the little head wiggle he'd perfected years ago for situations like this. "Thank you, but it's not like I knew her," he said. "And Dad made sure I never felt the lack."

"He never remarried?"

Devante shook his head. "Never even started dating again. She was it for him, you know?" Michael nodded. His eyes were the most solemn Devante had ever seen them, big and brown and sad. "I always wanted that kind of love for myself," Devante said, lulled into complacency by those soulful eyes, that intense gaze.

Michael's hand was still on Devante's arm, warm and comforting. He gave it a squeeze. "You will," he said, and when he said it, Devante almost believed it.

The moment stretched out into a peaceful quiet. "Your turn," Devante said, when it came to a close. "Tell me about your sister."

Michael smiled, a softer smile than his usual bright grin, so that Devante barely missed his hand when he took it away at long last. "Sixteen, and a terror," he said, chuckling. "Her name's Rosa, and she wants to be an environmental activist when she grows up."

"The world could use more of those," Devante said.

"Very true, and I can't wait to see what she does," Michael said. The love he had for his sister was evident in his voice. "She wants to go to Yale, although now that I'm here I'm going to make a case for Harvard or Brown instead." He shook his head. "She won't listen, she's too strong-willed, which is what I love about her, but as an older brother I have to try."

"Of course," Devante said. "You said she's getting into fantasy?"

Michael nodded. "She read *His Dark Materials* last year and loved it. Cried buckets at the ending. She really shipped Lyra and Will."

"If she's into environmental justice, she'll love Tolkien," Devante offered. "Tolkien was very big on anti-industrialism, and it shows in his work."

"Oooh, that's a good point," Michael said, realization dawning on his face. "And one I hadn't thought of. Saruman, right?"

Devante nodded. "The felling of Fangorn especially."

"Oh, awesome," Michael said, scrabbling for his phone. "Let me make a note of that so I don't forget."

"You live here in Brighton, right?" Devante asked while Michael typed into his Notes app. "Next to Charlie?"

"Mhm." Michael saved the note and set his phone back down.

"Then your local independent bookstore's the Brookline Booksmith, in Coolidge Corner," Devante said. "Take the 66 from Harvard Avenue. For her birthday present."

Michael dove back into his phone to make another note. "Thanks! Fuck Amazon, right?"

"I knew you were a man of taste," Devante quipped. Michael tossed his head back and laughed.

Devante's phone buzzed. *Devante, can you pick up a carton of eggs on your way home? Your father.* "It's my dad," he said, swiping the message open to get rid of the notification. "I should be heading back."

"Cool, cool," Michael said. "I should finish my run."

Devante looked at him suspiciously. "I thought you said you were finished."

Was that a blush on Michael's cheeks? If so, Michael was perhaps the most attractive blusher Devante had ever met. *Add it to his list of crimes.* "Yeah, well," he stammered, the first time Devante had seen him be less than utterly smooth. "Still gotta get home, you know?"

"Sure," Devante said, to let him off the hook. He stood, as did Michael, and they made their way to the door of the cafe. "Safe run," he said to Michael.

"Safe travels!"

Michael set off at a trot in the opposite direction of Devante's bus stop. Devante took a moment to watch him go, then turned and set off himself.

He picked up the eggs when he got off the bus, and a gallon of milk; they'd been on the dregs for coffee that morning. Carl was in the kitchen when he got home, making enough noise for three people. Whatever it was he was doing smelled amazing, though, so Devante just ducked in to put the groceries in the fridge and wave, and then went up to his room.

First day check in, he texted Preeda, dropping into his desk chair and dumping his bag of books on the floor.

She responded five minutes later. *Class seems interesting, at least. Makes up a little for having to take it.*

Almost done!!!!! he texted back, just to be annoying. She sent back a handful of throwing-up emojis.

Dinner turned out to be some sort of fragrant mushroom sauce over fluffy white rice, roasted broccoli and asparagus on the side. "Delicious," Devante said, digging in happily. Carl grunted, which was his way of accepting a compliment.

Devante did the dishes, scraping charred fragments of mushroom off the bottom of the saucepan, and wandered out into the living room to find Carl installed in his chair behind his paper. Devante carefully sat down on the couch and said, hesitation laced through his voice, "Dad, can I ask a serious question?"

Carl tilted the page of his paper down and looked at Devante over his glasses. "You only use that tone when you're about to ask about your mother," he rumbled. "Out with it, then, go on."

Devante smiled sheepishly, looking down. "I was just gonna ask…When did you *know*, with Mom? That she was the one, I mean."

"First moment I met her," Carl said without missing a beat.

"Really?" Carl was such a gruff, plodding, practical man, it was hard to imagine him getting swept up in love at first sight.

"First moment," Carl confirmed. "She shook my hand and smiled at me, and my whole head went white and my heart started pounding, and that was that."

"What about for her?" Devante asked. "Was it the same?"

"She said so," Carl said. "Not quite as immediate, but she always said she'd decided by the end of our first conversation that she was gonna marry me."

Devante smiled again, softer this time. "You guys only dated for what, eight months before you proposed?"

"*She* proposed," Carl grumbled. "She beat me to it. I already had the ring, though. Engaged at eight months, pregnant at ten, married at a year."

"A whirlwind," Devante remarked.

"Didn't feel that way," Carl said. "Felt like too damn long."

Devante nodded. "Thanks, Dad."

"It ain't a hardship talking about her," Carl told him. "You can ask anything you want."

"I know," Devante said quietly.

Carl nodded at him and raised his paper again. And then, a few moments later: "Anyone you want to tell me about, son?"

Devante shook his head slowly. "No, Dad. No one in particular."

It felt like a lie in his mouth. *It's not, though*, Devante told himself firmly. *It's just a stupid little meaningless crush. He's not the love of my life.*

Sure, said the voice in the back of his head. It didn't sound like it believed him either.

Chapter 6

IT BECAME A thing.

Devante could have written off Michael outside the library on Monday as a fluke, just two people in the same neighborhood running into each other. When Michael bumped into him after his shift on Friday, that, too, could have been a coincidence. Devante's end times on Mondays and Fridays were different, one P.M. and noon respectively, but they were close enough that Michael's usual run time could have overlapped with both of them. It was possible.

But the odds of Michael's running pace varying so little that he was at the door of the Brighton library again both times the next week seemed slim to Devante. And three Fridays in, when Michael turned up in his salmon shorts and a polo instead of running clothes—although still with the sweatband—that seemed suspicious too.

Devante didn't say anything about it, though. If he had, Michael might have stopped coming.

It quickly became apparent to Devante that, in addition to being generally warm and unfairly attractive, Michael had a wry yet expansive sense of humor, and seemed genuinely interested in learning everything there was to know about Devante, and was quite willing to answer any stupid question about figure skating Devante could think up. He'd gone to college, majoring in history and Spanish literature at the University of Texas, which was why, he said, his career in skating was only really picking up now, much later than it did for many other skaters.

His career, Devante discovered when he gave into his baser

urges and Googled him, *was* taking off. He'd come fifth at Nationals last year, and was projected to win a medal this year. He had also, last year, just missed qualifying for the Grand Prix Final.

Devante took that one to Michael, asking him about it over muffins in early July. Michael wrinkled his nose ruefully. "That stung," he admitted. "I was *so close* for the first time. But I'll try again this year, and maybe I'll make it."

"Not to sound like a newb," Devante said, making Michael laugh, "but what *is* the Grand Prix Final?"

The Grand Prix Series, Michael explained, was a series of six figure skating events all across Europe, North America, and Asia. Skaters were assigned up to two events each, and the top six in each skating discipline advanced to the Final in early December. "It's the second-most important competition in the season, the Final," Michael said.

"What's the first?"

"The World Championships," Michael said. His voice took on a dreamy air as he said it. "It's usually in March, after the European Championship and the Four Continents Championship."

"How high have you ever placed at the World Championships?" Devante asked, carefully folding his muffin wrapper for something to do with his hands as he tried not to look too lost in Michael's voice.

"Tenth," Michael said. "Not bad at all, but not great." He grinned. "Sara, my coach, has got high hopes for me this year, though. She's putting me through my paces. I'm going to get a lot busier come September, I can tell you that, and if I eat a muffin again after August first, she'll probably kill me."

"Wouldn't want that," Devante said. Michael twinkled at him.

Devante's Googling also turned up an Instagram account, *michaellopezfs*. Devante waited until he was alone in the house before opening it.

Lots of skating videos, and lots—*lots*—of selfies. Devante scrolled through and saw Michael's sharp, small face from almost every angle, and almost every angle looked good on him.

As he got further back in Michael's feed, a lot of his selfies were accompanied by the same, almost stunningly handsome white man, who appeared to be a figure skater too.

Michael had never mentioned a boyfriend, or a girlfriend, or a partner of any gender, but Devante realized with a sinking feeling as he scrolled, that didn't mean he didn't have one. One picture from last October showed the man, tagged as *georghummel*, planting a kiss on Michael's cheek while Michael looked scandalized at the camera. Devante's heart sank further.

Shaking himself, Devante scrolled back to the top of Michael's feed and clicked on his Story. Two skating clips, the first of a jump helpfully labeled *3A-1L-3T!!!!!*, which some quick Googling indicated was a triple axel-single loop-triple toe loop combination jump, and the second of a spin, Michael whipping around dizzyingly fast in a crouch, one arm extended up into the air. There was music playing, which after a moment Devante recognized as "Don't Cha" by the Pussycat Dolls. He tried not to read too much into it.

When Devante finally caved and followed him, Michael followed him back in under two minutes.

"I didn't know you had Instagram!" Michael chided him at their next coffee not-a-date. "I would have followed you ages ago."

"I don't use it much," Devante said. When Michael had followed him, he'd panic-scrolled through his own account to make sure there was nothing embarrassing, and what had been embarrassing was how little there was, just pictures of Preeda and their friends, and the occasional photo of whatever his dad had whipped up in the kitchen that day. Barely any of his face at all.

"I do," Michael admitted freely, laughing at himself. "Sara only lets me get away with it because it's good for fan engagement."

"Can I ask…" Devante started, trailing off. Michael nodded encouragingly at him. "That man in a lot of your pictures, Georg Hummel. Is he a friend?"

The hesitation before *friend* was, to Devante's ears, a massive vocal chasm, but Michael didn't react to it. "My best friend," he confirmed with a distant smile, no doubt thinking of Georg. "He's a German skater. We were in juniors together, and we've been friends ever since."

"He's very pretty," Devante remarked, trying to sound casual.

Michael cackled. "Don't let him hear you say that, his ego's big enough as it is. But yes, he was blessed in the face and the forearms departments."

Trying to sound supportive, Devante asked, "When will you see him again?"

Michael shrugged. "Not sure. Hopefully we'll get a Grand Prix event or two together, and ideally we'd both make the Final. But we're used to not seeing each other for long stretches at a time. It works for us."

Devante nodded. "That makes sense." It was evidence for Georg not being a boyfriend—would Michael be so cavalier about not seeing him if they were together? But then, plenty of people did well in long-distance relationships. Maybe Michael was someone who didn't need a partner around all the time. Devante took a bite of his sandwich and tried to think of how to change the subject.

He settled on, "How did you get into skating?"

"We lived three blocks away from an ice rink in Mexico," Michael said, leaning back in his chair. "We would go all the time, me and my parents, and then Rosa when she was old enough. There was a Novices coach who would come and scout at the public ice times, and he picked me out and convinced my parents to sign me up for a class." He grinned, teeth flashing white. "The rest, as they say, is history."

"I can't imagine it," Devante confessed. "Skating just looks so difficult, I can't imagine being able to do it as a little kid."

"Did you never go skating as a little kid?" Michael asked, taking a sip of his coffee.

Devante shook his head. "Not as a kid, and not anytime else," he said. "I've never been skating."

Michael's eyebrows flew up and he set his coffee back on

the table, sitting up straight. "Well then, Devante Miller, you have to come skating with me."

"Oh," Devante said, startled at the reaction his confession had caused. "I don't think that's a good idea."

"Nonsense!" Michael insisted. "It'll be fun, I'm a great teacher. I'll have you waltz jumping in no time."

"Michael," Devante said desperately, "what about me says *would be good at skating?* I'm a big, ungraceful fat guy."

"Nonsense," Michael said again. "Everyone can skate, and that includes you. Come on, say you'll come with me one day. I promise it'll be fun."

Michael's eyes were wide and beseeching, glittering in the afternoon light coming in the cafe window. His whole face was open, devastatingly earnest, and before he could catch himself, Devante caved. "Alright."

"Yessssss," Michael cheered, pumping his fist in the air. "You'll be a convert, I know it."

"Don't get your hopes up," Devante grumbled, sounding a little too much like his father for his own liking. Michael just laughed at him.

Michael was also a fixture at Saturday night drinks, sliding into the group with the same ease he used to slide into his finishing poses on the ice. He got on best with Charlie, but Charlie got along well with everyone; both of them had the same expansive, playful personalities. Natasha continued her pursuit of him for a few weeks and then, when Michael showed no signs of giving into her wiles, evidently gave up and built a friendship with him based on talking figure skating stats and comparing the Instagram videos of his competitors. Mike, to Devante's surprise, was a little standoffish, but he didn't make any trouble, at least. And Michael himself, at times, seemed a little reserved around Preeda, which also surprised Devante.

It might have just been Devante's crush-fueled imagination, but it seemed like Michael always had a special smile for him, a wink or a quick expression reacting to whatever story was being told around the table. No doubt he was doing it with everyone, but it warmed Devante through nonetheless.

"How're your classes?" Carl asked over dinner in mid-July. "Almost done, right?"

"Two more months," Devante said. "They're good. Very interesting." The ethics class made his brain hurt, but it was a good ache, like the few times he'd ever worked out and been sore afterward, and the young adult resources class was everything he'd wanted from his library degree in the first place.

"You job hunting yet?" Carl asked, spearing a potato with his fork.

Devante shuddered. "One thing at a time, Dad. Let me graduate first."

"Maybe I want you out of my house," Carl said, "ever consider that?"

"No," Devante said honestly. "You don't; you love having me here."

"Hmph," Carl grumbled, which meant *yes*. Devante laughed and went back to his beef. "How's your friend?" Carl asked suddenly, reaching for his beer to take a sip. "Preeda?"

Devante blinked, surprised. "She's good. Neck-deep in her own classes, but she's good."

"You used to talk about her a lot," Carl said. "Less now. Something happen?"

"Did I?" Devante didn't think he talked about Preeda any more than he talked about any of his friends—but then, it was true that he was talking about his friends to his father less overall these days. Talking about his friends would mean talking about Michael, and that meant risking saying more than he meant to. "Nothing happened," he said. "We're all just busy is all."

"Hmph," Carl grunted again, but he let it drop.

Mike was still bringing Devante dinner during his Thursday shifts, and the next time he and Devante ate Mexican food in the library staff room, he also brought up Preeda. "Still haven't made your move yet?" Mike asked, wiping his mouth with a napkin and balling it up.

"I wish you'd stop asking that," Devante said, a little irritated. "It's no concern of yours, and anyway I've never even said I *want* to. You're making assumptions."

"Hey, alright," Mike said, holding up a hand. "I'm just saying, she's clearly interested, and if you don't move fast, you might miss your chance." He took a bite of quesadilla and followed it down with a splash of Diet Coke. "Seems she and Michael are getting pretty chummy."

"What?" Devante asked, startled. "I don't get that at all." They were perfectly polite, Michael and Preeda, but it was all surface-level, to Devante's eye. Nothing like how Michael looked when he was talking to Devante. *Or Charlie, or Natasha,* he told himself firmly.

Mike shrugged. "Just saying what I see, man. First Natasha, and now Preeda…"

"You gotta learn to keep some shit to yourself," Devante said. Mike laughed and chucked his napkin at him.

Chapter 7

"ANY PLANS THIS weekend?" Michael asked over coffee and sandwiches one Friday at the tail end of July. He lifted the second half of his chicken caprese sandwich to his mouth and took a huge bite.

"It's my dad's birthday," Devante said. "So I'm cooking dinner on Sunday night."

Michael's eyes went wide, but his mouth was still full of sandwich. Several moments of mastication later, he swallowed and said, "That's great! What are you cooking?"

"Gumbo," Devante said. "It's his favorite. It's gonna take all day but it'll feed us for a week afterward."

Michael gave a little moan that set Devante's neck under his collar hot. "Mmm, delicious. How old is he turning?"

"Forty-seven."

He could see Michael doing the math. "He must have had you really young, then."

"Yup," Devante said. "He met my mom when he was twenty. Had me less than a year later." *Had me and lost her*, he thought, as he always did.

There was sympathy in Michael's eyes, but tactfully he just said, "Get him anything?"

"The day my father accepts a present from me is the day I take him in for a brain scan," Devante said frankly. Michael cackled, surprised. "He believes gifts should flow down, not up. He'll only accept homemade food, so I go all-out for his birthday."

"Nice." Michael's smile was wide across his face. "Wish him a happy birthday from me."

"I will."

Saturday was for prep, which mainly consisted of shopping. Devante had to schlep out to three grocery stores, stopping at home in between each to empty their grocery cart into the fridge and the pantry. Eventually both were full to bursting and Devante folded up the cart and stowed it behind the fridge before digging in the cabinet next to the sink and extracting the big soup pot. He wrangled it into the sink and gave it a preliminary wash; they rarely used it, it being so big, and there was a fine coating of dust on the outside.

Carl came in as he was drying it and grunted approvingly. "You're smart, kid," he said, reaching into the fridge for an iced tea. "Looking forward to dinner tomorrow."

"Yeah?" Devante asked, touched.

"Yeah." Carl gave a rare smirk. "Looking forward to all the ways you do it wrong."

"Oh, hush," Devante muttered, going back to running the dishrag over the pot's lid.

Carl had taught Devante how to make this gumbo when he was eighteen and about to go off to college. "Might have to impress someone while you're away from home," Carl had said, clapping him on the shoulder as they stood over the steaming pot. "If your mother hadn't already loved me, this gumbo woulda sealed the deal."

Devante had made it for Carl's birthday every year since then, and every year, Carl approached his first bowl like he was judging the Olympics, eyes peeled for any mistake or variation from his own version. If he'd ever found any, though, he hadn't let on, just made a serious face as he took his first bite and then thanked his son for the meal.

Devante woke the next day to a stream of texts in The Friend Group's chat.

MC: Say happy birthday to Carl!

CG: Happy birthday, Mr. Devante's Dad!

NM: Tell that fox I'm coming for him

NM: (And by that I mean happy birthday)

PC: Give my best to your dad too, Dev!

ML: Happy birthday!!!!!!

DM: Gross, Natasha

DM: And thanks, all, I'll tell him

Devante washed his face, dressed in a rare plain t-shirt, and went downstairs. Carl had an omelet waiting for him, sausage and American cheese and spinach, wheat toast well-buttered, and after polishing it all off, Devante washed the dishes and set to cooking.

Carl's birthday was the one day of the year when he was banished from the kitchen. He knew by now to text Devante anything he wanted from the fridge or pantry, and Devante would bring it out to him. He set himself up in his armchair with a thermos of coffee and the first of his daily papers, and Devante set to work browning the meat and cooking the okra.

It was punishingly hot in the kitchen before long, the vegetables cooking down in the roux. Devante threw the window open, cracked open an iced tea from the fridge, and kept going.

When he added the stock, meat, and okra to the vegetable mush in the pot, Devante allowed himself a break. He wiped his face on a paper towel and went out to the living room to flop on the couch. "How's it going?" Carl asked, turning the page of his paper.

"Fine," Devante said, pressing his third iced tea to his forehead.

"Need a hand?"

"No."

"Have it your way."

The traditional dialogue done, Devante pulled out his phone. "My friends all say happy birthday," he reported, pulling open his email to see if anything had come in while he was cooking.

"My thanks," Carl said, turning another page.

No new emails. Devante got up to test the boiling meat.

The gumbo simmered all day, Devante periodically getting up to taste it and add seasonings and stir. Toward the end, he added the seafood and put a pot of rice on the other burner. While the rice and seafood cooked, he set the table, bowls and placemats and silverware, bread knife and the crusty loaf he'd bought the day before in the middle to share.

Finally, Devante took a last taste, nodded to himself, and said, "It's done." With a flourish that was only for himself, he turned the burner off under the pot. From the living room he could hear his father's deep sigh and grunt as he got out of his chair and stumped into the kitchen.

Carl served himself first, steaming white rice disappearing under the thick brown stew. Devante followed him, setting his own full bowl onto his placemat and then fetching two beers from the fridge. Both of them finally installed in their chairs, Devante held out his beer and Carl clinked his against it. With bated breath, Devante watched Carl fill his spoon and take a bite.

Carl closed his eyes as he swallowed. "Thank you, son," he said. "You did well."

It was what he said every year, and every year it made Devante happier than almost anything. "Thanks, Dad," he said, rubbing the back of his neck. "Happy birthday."

They ate quickly and silently, both going back for seconds and thirds, until Carl took a final swig of his beer and leaned back, rubbing his stomach. "Good meal," he said succinctly. "I'll deal with the leftovers."

"You'll do no such thing," Devante said firmly. "It's still your birthday, and you're going to go out and digest in your armchair while I clean up."

"Alright," Carl said mildly. "Just thought I'd offer."

"Go on, out of my kitchen," Devante ordered. Carl cracked a half smile and went.

There were enough leftovers to feed them for ages, if they made a fresh pot of rice in a few days. The Tupperware filled a full shelf of their fridge, not counting the four servings Devante packaged away in the freezer. Quickly he washed the rice pot and their tableware, and then set the big soup pot in the sink to soak overnight.

Carl, predictably, was asleep in his armchair when Devante emerged from the kitchen half an hour later. Devante grinned to himself and took the couch, pulling out his phone.

There was a text from Michael. *How'd the gumbo go??????* Michael used more question and exclamation marks than anyone Devante had ever texted with.

Success, he typed back. *Dad ate himself asleep.*

Mark of a good meal!!!!! Michael sent.

On impulse, Devante wrote, *Want some? We've got plenty of leftovers. Just don't tell the others or they'll all want some.*

Omg yes!!!!! Michael wrote back. *My lips are sealed, if it means free Devante-cooked gumbo.*

Devante flushed hot. *I'll bring you some on Monday.*

See you then!!!!!

On Monday, after his circulation desk shift, Devante pulled the small lunchbox he'd stored in the staff fridge out and went to meet Michael just outside the front door. Michael was dressed in his salmon shorts again and a baggy green tank top, armholes cut halfway down his side. "Hey!" he said, straightening from where he'd been lounging against the wall when Devante came out. "That for me?" he asked, nodding to the lunchbox with a grin.

Devante handed it to him. "There's an ice pack in there, but you'll want to get it to a fridge as quickly as possible, in this heat," he said. "And I didn't put any rice in, so you'll have to make your own. It's better with fresh anyway."

"Sweet," Michael said, taking the lunchbox. Then, looking apprehensive, he went on, "Actually, with that in mind...I know we usually go to Caffe Nero, but would you want to have our lunch at mine today? It's not far, and I can get *this* into the fridge that much sooner. I have coffee, and turkey and cheese for sandwiches if you're hungry." He gave a nervous little chuckle. "God knows I am."

Devante was instantly divided between sudden nerves, and confusion as to why *Michael* seemed nervous about having Devante in his apartment. "Sure," he said, trying to cover the twisting of his stomach. "That'd be nice."

"Great!" Michael beamed at him. "Follow me, then?"

It was a short walk to Michael and Charlie's building. Devante fell into step beside Michael, who sent him another distant, nervous smile. Heart thudding, Devante smiled back.

Charlie's building was, as Natasha was fond of describing it, a shithole. Thankfully, Charlie, and therefore Michael, were only on the third floor, so they were able to bypass the elevator entirely. "Don't worry," Michael said as they emerged onto the third-floor landing. "I have air conditioning."

There was a pretty stick wreath hanging on the front of apartment 3C, and the door looked like it had been scrubbed clean recently, which was one up on Charlie's, 3B, next to it. Michael unlocked the door and let Devante in first, coming in behind him and shutting the door again.

Blessed air conditioning stole into Devante's lungs as soon as he was over the threshold, and he breathed in deep, then opened his eyes and took a look around him.

"It's nice," he said, meaning it as he took in the apartment. It was fairly small for a one-bedroom, but it still qualified as a one-bedroom, and so was one up on any of Devante's other friends' apartments. There was a tiny letterbox kitchen just off the front door that looked scrupulously clean, and opposite it a surprisingly spacious-for-the-apartment dining area. A short hallway ran in front of them; on the left was a closed door, which Devante took to be Michael's bedroom, and on the right was his living room.

Michael was toeing his shoes off next to Devante, so Devante followed suit, taking a moment to hope fervently that his feet didn't smell. "Come on through," Michael said. He put a gentle hand on Devante's back to guide him toward the living room, and

Devante promptly forgot all about his sweaty feet at the contact.

There was art all over the walls of Michael's living room, podcast posters and concert posters and art prints. No frames—it all appeared to be taped down by the corners. There was a short, overstuffed sofa that was barely more than a love seat, and a TV seated on top of a small cabinet with a bunch of cables running out of the back.

More to Devante's heart, there were *bookshelves*. There was only room for one unit, but it was stuffed full of books, mostly mass-market paperbacks, but with the occasional hardcover thrown in.

Devante took a step forward, eyes skimming over the titles. "You keep your romance novels out in public?" he asked, looking over his shoulder at Michael.

Michael shrugged, grinning. "I'm not ashamed of them," he said. "And I have another bookshelf in my bedroom, but it's much smaller than this one, so I don't really have any choice."

"Respect," Devante said, going back to his perusal. "You bought *The Silmarillion*," he said, reaching up one finger to run it lightly down the book's yellow spine. There was a whole Tolkien mini-section, arranged in internal chronological order— *The Silmarillion, The Hobbit, The Lord of the Rings*, and then at the end *The Tolkien Reader*, which surprised Devante.

"Well, after your recommendation, how could I not?" Devante could hear Michael's enduring smile in his voice. "I haven't quite worked up the courage to actually *read* it yet, but hopefully soon."

"After that we'll get you started on *The Unfinished Tales*," Devante said lightly, turning back to Michael.

"Looking forward to it," Michael said quietly. As Devante had predicted, he was indeed still smiling, and there was a long, heart-stopping moment where they just held each other's gaze and smiled dopily at each other. Michael broke it by looking down, inexplicably flushing a little pink, and saying, "I promised you food."

"You did," Devante said.

"Have a seat." Michael gestured to the couch. "There's not really room for both of us in the kitchen, but I'll make up a platter of sandwich fixings and bring it out."

"Sure I can't help?"

"No, no, just make yourself at home," Michael said. "I'll be five minutes tops." He disappeared back down the hallway and into the kitchen.

Devante lowered himself to the couch and pulled a book at random off the shelf. It was another romance novel, he noticed, about a figure skater to judge from the summary on the back cover. Devante chuckled to himself and put it back.

True to his word, Michael was barely five minutes before he came out bearing a large plate with turkey and three kinds of cheese, and another with rolls and tortillas. "One more sec," he said, placing them both onto the tiny coffee table, and disappeared again, this time returning with two knives and bottles of mustard and mayonnaise sitting on a stack of two plates. "Wasn't sure which you preferred," he said, setting it all down, "so I brought both."

"I'm a mustard man," Devante said. "You?"

Michael winced. "Don't judge me," he said, looking sheepish, "but I combine them." Devante carefully kept his face neutral. Michael laughed at himself. "Come on, dig in," he said, passing a plate to Devante and setting a tortilla on his own.

They assembled sandwiches, balancing dirty knives on the edges of their plates, and ate right there on the sofa. "I always feel like I'm doing something forbidden when I eat in a living room," Devante confessed, wiping a trace of mustard off his face with one finger and licking it clean. Michael's eyes followed his finger, and then snapped back up to his eyes. "Dad won't hear of it."

"No?"

Devante shook his head. "Meals should be eaten in the kitchen, at a fully set table," he recited, hearing it in his father's voice. "He'll allow small snacks in the living room, if eaten with a plate or paper towel directly under your mouth, and coffee. That's it."

"Is he strict?" Michael asked, popping the last of his wrap into his mouth.

Devante shook his head again. "Weirdly, no, he just has firm opinions about food and manners. But other than that, he's not strict at all. Barely has any rules ever since I got back from college, actually."

"He recognizes you're an adult," Michael said.

"Mhm." Devante took another bite of his sandwich.

"Wish mine did," Michael said casually, putting his plate on the table and leaning back against the arm of the sofa, facing Devante as he lounged.

"Your parents are strict, then?"

Michael made a face. "Not *strict*, they just…They don't get figure skating as an adult career, you know? To them I might as well still be in Novices. I think they'll recognize I'm an adult when I retire from skating and get a *real* job, but not until then."

Devante set his own plate next to Michael's and threw his arm over the back of the sofa. "Do you know what you want to do when you retire?"

Michael's eyes sparkled. "I haven't told my family this," he admitted, "but I want to go back to school, get my Ph.D." He quirked a smile. "I always wanted to write a dissertation on *The Lord of the Rings*, although I might do history instead. After that, I dunno." He sighed. "I don't want to be a pencil-pusher, stuck in a cubicle for the rest of my life. A lot of figure skaters write books, become TV or Internet personalities, but I don't know if I'm a big enough name for that." He shrugged. "I'll figure it out, I guess, and in the meantime, I'll keep skating as long as I can."

Devante nodded. Michael looked pensive for a moment, staring into the middle distance, then he came back to himself and met Devante's eyes again. "I wrote my undergrad thesis on Tolkien," Devante volunteered.

Michael perked up. "You never said! You were a linguistics

major, right?"

Devante nodded. "I wrote it on Khuzdul, the Dwarvish language. The *Hobbit* movies had just come out a few years before, so there was plenty of material to work with for an undergrad thesis."

"That's so cool," Michael said, grinning. "Can I read it?"

"It's up on the university website," Devante said. "I can send you a link."

"Please do! It sounds so interesting." Michael gently kicked his ankle. "How'd you do on the thesis?"

"B plus," Devante said. Michael nodded. "I don't understand why our theses were given letter grades and not just pass/fail, but hey."

"Doesn't make a lick of sense," Michael agreed.

They descended into another comfortable silence. Devante took a sip of water from the bottle in the messenger bag at his feet and returned it, then leaned back against the couch back and rested his head on his hand. "I really like your place," he murmured, catching Michael's eye and getting a little lost in his gaze.

"Thanks," Michael murmured back. "I decorated it myself." Devante snorted, which made Michael snort, and then there was silence again as they just stared at each other.

The silence was broken by a buzz from Devante's phone. He dug it out of his pocket. *This semester is killing meeeeeeeeeeee. Dinner b4 drinks 2morrow?* from Preeda.

The sight of her name made Devante flush cold, a weird shame filling his stomach. "I should go," he said, clicking his screen dark again and standing up. "Thanks for lunch."

"Is everything alright?" Michael asked, pushing himself to his feet.

"Everything's fine," Devante said. "Just, homework and stuff, you know?"

"Sure," Michael said easily, although there was still a layer of concern in his eyes. "Thanks for the gumbo. I'll text you my review once I've eaten it."

"I look forward to it."

Devante swung his messenger bag across his torso. There was an awkward moment where, if it were any other member of The Friend Group, Devante would hug them, and Michael seemed to be feeling the same urge, but at the last minute, Michael stuck out his hand. Devante took it and shook.

Michael's hand was warm and soft, only slightly smaller than Devante's. Devante all but fled the apartment.

Chapter 8

THAT WEDNESDAY, DEVANTE finished washing his lunch dishes to discover that his phone was ringing in the living room. He got to it right before it sent the call to voicemail, answering it before looking at the caller ID. "Hello?"

"Hey, Devante," Michael's familiar, airy voice filled his ear. "You busy?"

"No," Devante said honestly. "Just finishing up lunch."

"Me too!" Michael said brightly. "And I just had to call and give my review live."

"Your review?" Devante said, a little thrown. "Oh, you tried the gumbo?"

"*Tried* it?" Michael scoffed. "I *tried* it the way Adam Rippon *tried* the triple Lutz."

"Uhhh…"

"Devante, I *devoured* it. It was the most delicious thing I've ever eaten in my *life*."

Devante laughed, relieved. "I'm glad you liked it. I'll tell my dad the recipe's a hit."

"The recipe, the execution, the whole package," Michael said. "Absolutely superb. I have a year to figure out how to winkle an invite to your dad's birthday next year to have it fresh."

You could come if you were my boyfriend. What? "I look forward to seeing your efforts," Devante said instead, shaking himself.

"Speaking of efforts," Michael said, voice going sly. "What are your plans for this lovely, hot afternoon?"

"Why?" Devante asked, instantly suspicious.

"Nothing bad!" Michael said quickly. "Do you have plans, then?"

"No," Devante said slowly, reluctance drawing out the word.

"Great!" Michael chirped. "Then there's nothing stopping you from meeting me at the Warrior Ice Arena at, say, three?"

"Oh no," Devante said, realizing where this was going, "no, no, no."

"You said you'd come with me!"

"*You* said I'd come with you!" Devante objected. "I gave in under duress."

"Same thing," Michael said dismissively. "Come on, no one comes to Wednesday afternoon public ice time, we'll have it basically to ourselves."

"That's not better!"

"Oh, Devante, please?" Michael wheedled. "If you won't come for your own entertainment, then do it for me."

"What do you get out of it?" Devante asked. That pleading tone in Michael's voice, he was finding, went a long way with his stubbornness, but he wasn't out of the fight yet. "Besides watching me make a fool of myself."

"So far, the only people who have seen the choreography for my programs this year are me and my coach," Michael said. "But if you came to the rink this afternoon, you could see my step sequences, and maybe hold the camera for Instagram while I do a few jumps?"

"I don't know what a step sequence is," Devante said, his last bastion of resolve faltering in front of the idea of *seeing Michael skate in person*.

"I'll teach you," Michael said firmly. "Now say you'll come."

"I…" Devante tried, then gave in. "Oh, alright."

"Yesssss," Michael cheered. "Thank you, Devante, you won't regret it."

"I already do," Devante told him.

Michael laughed, the phone line between them making it sound a little tinny. Devante still swayed toward it. "See you at three," he said. "Dress warm!"

Five minutes before three saw Devante pull up to a halt in

front of the Warrior Ice Rink. The day was punishingly hot, but he had a sweater and gloves in his messenger bag, and he'd changed into thick socks before he left home. Sweating a little from the walk, Devante took a deep breath and went inside.

I'm here, he texted Michael, and within thirty seconds, Michael was in front of him, beaming fit to burst. "You came!"

"I said I would," Devante said.

"Come on, let's get you some rentals."

The rentals were awkward and bulky around his socks, and as Devante tottered from the bench where he'd put them on to the entryway to the ice, he couldn't shake the fear that the thin blades would snap under his weight. As promised, though, the rink was mostly empty, just a few college students twirling around the far end of the ice. Maybe he would get through this without too much public embarrassment.

In front of him, Michael stepped onto the ice, turned around gracefully, and held out his hand. "Come on," he said. Devante sighed and placed a blade onto the ice, and then the other.

He didn't instantly fall, but that was only because Michael seized his upper arms and forcibly held him up. "It's okay," Michael said. "Happens to everyone." He held Devante up until he steadied, then gave him an encouraging smile. "Let's try moving."

"Can't I just stay here and watch you?" Devante said pleadingly.

Michael shook his head. "Nope. I promised you skating, and skating you'll get. Now come on." He took each of Devante's hands in one of his, and glided a little way backward. "Come meet me."

Devante tried, and wobbled dangerously; only Michael's grip on his hands kept him up. "Slide, don't step," Michael said. "Try and angle your feet a little out, rather than straight on; it helps."

Devante tried again. He wobbled again, but he didn't fall, and the slide brought him very close to Michael, who didn't step away. "Good," Michael said, eyes trained upward on Devante's face. "Come on, let's get a little further out."

He slid backward again, still holding Devante's hands, and

this time Devante went with him. The space between them grew, but not by much; Devante could almost feel Michael's breath on his face. When Michael brought them to a halt, Devante stuttering to an awkward stop on his skates, he looked around and realized they were fully in the middle of the rink.

"Wow," he breathed.

Michael's grin was wide and beautiful. "I think you're ready for the next lesson."

"What's that?"

Michael's grin turned sharp. "Catch me." With a final squeeze, his hands slipped free of Devante's, and he was gone, a few yards away in the blink of an eye. The phantom grip of his fingers was still holding Devante's own, and Devante took off, waving his arms to keep upright as he set off after Michael.

Michael led him on a merry chase, halfway across the rink in fits and starts, letting Devante get close and then darting away again. "Catch me," he called again, laughing delightedly, and somehow Devante figured out how to put on a burst of speed, taking Michael by surprise as he barreled into him and sent them both crashing to the ice.

"Sorry," he gasped, pushing himself up so he wasn't crushing him, "sorry, sorry," but Michael was laughing again, his hands tight on Devante's arms.

"Happens to the best of us," he murmured. "I've taken worse falls than this."

He didn't seem inclined to let go of Devante's arms, and so for a long moment Devante stayed where he was, half-pinning him down onto the cold, slick ice. The laughter was still in Michael's face, his eyes were dancing, and the moment stretched out, long and languid.

If Michael were a woman pressed beneath him, Devante would have kissed her by now, no question. But Michael wasn't a woman, he was very much a man, and Devante was still confused about what that meant, so when the time came to kiss him or break the tension, he rolled to his side to let Michael up.

If Michael seemed a little disappointed as he got to his feet and held a hand out to pull Devante up after him, surely that was just Devante's imagination.

They skated a bit longer, Devante slowly growing surer and steadier on his skates. "You're getting the hang of this," Michael told him, any trace of unease or disappointment gone from his demeanor. "I was joking about the waltz jumps, but if we get you out here a few more times, I bet you'll be ready for them."

"What's a waltz jump?" Devante asked, mopping his brow with his gloves.

"This." Michael skated a bit away, then did something clever with his feet and leaped into the air, doing a half-turn before touching back down. He skated back over to Devante. "It's the easiest beginner's jump."

"No way I can do that," Devante said.

"Mmm, not yet," Michael allowed. "But soon."

Devante shook his head. "You promised I could watch you skate," he reminded him.

"I did," Michael said. "Let me get my phone." They had migrated back to where they started, so Michael was only gone from Devante's side for about thirty seconds to dart for their bags on the bleachers and return. Devante still missed him. "I want to get a video of my short program step sequence; that's just for me," Michael said, "and then I want a good clip of my quad Sal for Instagram. Would you mind?" Devante shook his head. "Great, thanks." Michael opened his phone's camera and passed it to Devante. "Wish me luck!"

"Luck," Devante said. Michael winked at him and skated away.

A step sequence, Devante discovered as Michael skated to the far side of the rink and began to move, was an on-ice dance, intricate foot- and arm-work as Michael's skates ate up the ice in long, elegant strokes. Devante couldn't quite follow every movement he was making, but he was entranced, only looking away long enough to ensure the camera was still trained on him. Off the ice, Michael was graceful and light on his feet, but when he skated, he turned into something else, something far more passionate and beautiful. Devante had no idea what song Michael would be skating this to, but he could almost hear phantom chords in his ears as he skated.

All told, the step sequence only ate up around thirty seconds of video, but Devante was breathing hard when Michael came to a stop. He pressed the stop button on the recording, blinking to try and restore his eyes' focus. "Now the jump," Michael called to him. "I'll try to line it up with where you are."

Devante flashed him a thumbs-up. Michael nodded and started moving backward on his skates, picking up speed. Devante quickly started a new video, and watched through the camera as Michael turned and then launched himself off the ice, spinning a breathtaking four times before landing on one skate.

"Did you get it?" Michael asked, reversing direction and skating toward him.

"I think so," Devante said, holding out the phone for him.

Michael took the phone and started the longer step sequence video. "Good," he murmured as he watched, "you've got a good eye, Devante."

"I just stood where you put me," Devante mumbled, embarrassed.

"And you kept me in focus and centered," Michael objected, squinting up at him with a frown. "Take the compliment, Devante."

Devante deflated. "Thanks."

Michael flashed him a smile and went to the jump video. "Okay, good," he said, playing it to a close. "I want a few more options, though; do you mind?"

"Not at all," Devante said, taking the phone back from him and readying a new video.

Michael wound up jumping the quad Sal four more times, until Devante could almost count the rotations with his own untrained eye. After the last, Michael put his hands on his knees and caught his breath before skating back over to Devante.

"Thanks," he said. "Ready for some hot chocolate?"

There was a small cafe, barely more than a hole in the wall with a few tiny tables scattered in front of it, off to the side of the rink. Michael insisted on paying, "as thanks for serving as my videographer," and they settled into chairs at one of the tables. "So," Michael said, taking a sip of his hot chocolate. "Skating, scale of one to ten. Go."

"A solid four," Devante said. He'd had a bit of fun in the end, chasing Michael around the rink, but his legs were aching, especially his knee from their fall. "Watching you is a ten, though," he added a little shyly.

Michael blushed. "Thanks," he said. "You liked my step sequence, then?"

"Very much," Devante admitted. "I don't know much about skating, but it was really beautiful."

"That makes it mean more," Michael said, devastatingly earnest and intense. "The technical side, the exact steps and forms, that's the sport. But when someone who doesn't know about all that says it's beautiful, that's the art, and that's what I care about most." He put his hand on Devante's arm. "Thank you, Devante."

All of Devante's senses were zoomed in to where he could feel the warmth of Michael's palm through his sweater, but he managed a strangled, "You're welcome," and hid his face in his drink until he had control of it again.

"How are your classes?" Michael asked. He gave Devante's arm a light squeeze and finally pulled his hand away. "How much longer is your semester?"

"Month and a half or so," Devante said. "And they're good. It's a lot of, you know, discussion board posts, but they're more interesting than some other classes I've taken online."

"You're in an ethics class, right?" Michael asked. Devante nodded. "I bet that gets some interesting discussions."

"Less than I expected, actually," Devante said. Michael raised his eyebrows. "I guess my cohort's all mostly on the same page. But there's been some interesting disagreements." Mostly about porn on public library computers, but Devante wasn't going to bring *that* up.

"Are you job hunting yet?" Michael asked, taking a sip of hot chocolate and leaving a brown liquid mustache on his upper lip.

"Don't you start too," Devante warned, and Michael threw his head back and laughed.

"Alright, I won't," he said warmly. "But I do have one very important question."

"Hit me."

"Are you planning to leave Boston?"

"No," Devante said instantly. "Boston's my home, and my Dad's here and will literally never leave, so I'm staying put if I possibly can."

"Good," Michael said firmly.

Devante's heart fluttered in his chest. "Good?" he repeated. "Why is that good?"

He regretted asking as soon as it was out of his mouth. *Too needy*, he told himself, but Michael just answered, cool as a cucumber, "Because I'd miss you."

"Would you?" Devante asked faintly. Michael nodded, lips pursed into the ghost of a smile. Devante looked down at his cup and took a long drink. "I'd miss you too," he said quietly to the hot chocolate.

"Then it's a good thing neither of us are going anywhere," Michael said. "Cheers." Devante looked up; he was holding out his Styrofoam cup. Devante tapped his against it and they both drained them.

Chapter 9

SEPTEMBER DAWNED, BRINGING with it the looming specter of term papers. Devante descended into study hell, emerging only for his shifts at the Brighton library and drinks with The Friend Group. Michael still met him for lunch on Monday and Friday, but they turned into working lunches, both of them bringing their laptops and setting up shop in Caffe Nero or Michael's apartment and working for an hour or so while they ate: Devante on his final papers and readings, and Michael on sponsor deals for the new season, or editing videos and pictures for Instagram.

It was tradition, in the final weeks of a semester, for Devante and Preeda to whine at each other over text whenever the mood struck. Preeda texted Devante as much as she ever had in those circumstances, but Devante found himself answering less and less, each text from her filling him with that same weird cocktail of shame and avoidance. She still plopped down next to him twice a week at Mood with a smile or a conspiratorial roll of her eyes, so Devante told himself she didn't mind, and that it was alright, and that it would pass.

The Saturday before their final papers were due, Devante was late to drinks, having missed his usual bus due to an impromptu nap on top of his computer. When he got there, Charlie, Natasha, and Mike were grouped around one side of the table, but only Preeda and a tumbler of whiskey waited for Devante on the other. She patted the bench next to her and he dropped in gratefully. "Where's Michael?" he asked the group at large. There was a half-drunk gin and tonic on the table, but no sign of the drinker.

Charlie, to Devante's surprise, cackled. "He was here for about five minutes, and then said he'd spotted his summer fling from two years ago at the other end of the bar and went to go chat them up. They're over there," he said, gesturing behind him with a wide sweep of his arm.

Devante squinted through the dim room and caught sight of them. Michael was leaning against the bar, facing away from the group toward a person of indeterminate gender but striking attractiveness, short red hair and what Devante could tell even from a distance was a complexion that could only be described as "creamy," who was laughing at something Michael had said. As Devante watched, Michael signaled to Katie behind the bar, then stepped up and took the stool next to the summer fling, leaning his elbow on the bar and talking animatedly.

Devante returned his gaze to his friends with a wrench, his stomach clenching in what was unmistakably jealousy. "Good for him," he muttered into his whiskey.

"God, I need to get laid," Mike moaned, sagging into Natasha's side.

She shoved him off. "Go get laid, then," she said, distracted by something she was typing into her phone. Her long nails clacked against the screen.

"What *are* you doing, Nat?" Preeda asked, taking a sip of her wine.

"Writing the next great Russian-American novel," Natasha said without looking up. "It's much more enjoyable than talking about Mike's penis."

"I mean it," Mike insisted over Charlie's hoot. "When was the last time any of us got laid?"

Devante felt Preeda's gaze on his face, and looked at her just in time to see her turn away, her cheek a little flushed. The twisting in his guts intensified. He took a gulp of whiskey.

"I have a full rotation of men and one enterprising woman on speed dial," Natasha said, clicking her phone off and setting it on the table. "My needs are satisfied."

"Wait, really?" Mike asked. "Who?"

"It's quite a long list," Natasha said smugly.

Mike rolled his eyes. "The *woman*, Nat."

In answer, Natasha looked over at the bar. As The Friend Group watched, she caught Katie's eye and winked; Katie smirked and winked back.

"Damn," Charlie hissed. "You landed *Katie*?"

"She pursued *me*, I'll have you know," Natasha sniffed.

"So are you, like, bi or something?"

Natasha shrugged. "Sure, I guess so. Doesn't really matter to me one way or the other."

Mike was looking at her a little more intensely than he had been before, and she noticed. "If you're having fantasies, you can keep them behind your eyes and none of my business," she warned, shoving one long-nailed finger in his face.

His gaze broke. "Well, I *wasn't*, but..."

"Ugh," Natasha said expressively, taking a long gulp from her glass. "This is why I don't tell you guys who I sleep with. You're all heterosexual and gross."

Not all, Devante both wanted and didn't want to say, still not sure if it was a lie or not. Next to him, Preeda shifted in her seat.

To distract himself, Devante looked past his friends to Michael and his fling, and instantly regretted it. The fling had their hand on his arm, and their heads were bent closer together.

Devante knocked his whiskey back in one go and stood. "Anyone for a refill?"

"Always," Natasha said.

"Yes please," Preeda said fervently, draining her wine glass and slamming it onto the tabletop.

"I'll help you carry," Mike said unexpectedly, wriggling his bulk out from under the table and coming to walk next to Devante. This was unlike Mike, but Devante did only have two hands and three drinks to carry, so he just nodded and led the way to the bar.

"One for me, Nat, and Preeda," he told Katie, who nodded and set to work filling glasses.

"Are you really sleeping with Natasha?" Mike, ever blunt, asked her.

"That's off-the-clock talk," Katie said instantly. "First rule of bartending: Don't discuss your own private life behind the bar."

"Fair enough." Mike turned to Devante, leaning his elbow on the bar. "What about you, Dev?"

"What about me?" Devante asked, already hating where this conversation was going.

"When was the last time you got laid?"

Devante squirmed. There was no harm in giving him a time span, he supposed. "Easter," he said reluctantly.

"Eyyyy!" Katie set three glasses down in front of them and Mike picked one up and toasted Devante with it. "Ringing in Jesus' resurrection in style."

"Not sure he'd approve," Devante said, picking up the other two and starting back toward the table.

"Well, I do." Mike clapped Devante on the shoulder. "Who was it?"

"None of your business," Devante said, trying to sound arch and carefree. He wasn't sure it worked, but Mike just laughed and went back to his seat, plunking the glass in his hand down in front of Natasha.

Devante passed Preeda her wine and retook his own seat. On the other side of the bar, he saw Michael and the fling stand up. The fling picked up their purse from where it had been slung over the back of their stool, and together they made their way to the door. Michael's hand was low on their back.

They had to pass The Friend Group's table to leave. Devante saw Michael catch Charlie's eye and wink, and then his eyes flicked to Devante. A complicated, indecipherable look passed over his face, and then he and his fling were out of view, disappearing through the door into the humid night air.

"Get it, sir," Charlie said once they were gone. Mike

hooted, and they high-fived between Natasha and her phone, where she was ferociously typing again. Devante felt Preeda look at him again and took a long pull from his whiskey.

Devante spent the rest of the evening, and most of the next day, in a funk. Every time he looked up from his final paper for his ethics course, or took a break from reviewing discussion board topics for his other course on young adult library resources, he saw in his mind's eye Michael's hand on the fling's lower back, and the look on his face when he accidentally caught Devante's eye on their way out.

He spent all of his Monday morning shift dreading the end of it, and was a bundle of nerves stepping out of the library into the thick noon heat. But then he saw Michael, straightening from a lounge against the stone wall and smiling at him, and all the tension in his body loosened, and his heart rate evened out, and he found himself smiling back.

"Hey," Michael said, coming up to him.

"Hey," Devante breathed.

"Lunch?"

Devante discovered that, under the anxiety, which was peeling away in Michael's presence, he was actually starving. "Lead the way."

Michael bought a muffin at Caffe Nero, and Devante nodded at it as they settled into their usual table. "Thought you weren't allowed to eat those anymore," he said, fanning the steam away from his own sandwich.

"Don't tell my coach?" Michael asked, a cute, wry expression stealing across his face. "It doesn't wreck my diet plan if I only have one every once in a while, and I had kind of a rough weekend. I could use the carb comfort."

Devante regarded him, unscrewing the cap of his water bottle and taking a long gulp. When he swallowed, he said, "Seemed like your Saturday evening, at least, was looking to be pretty nice."

Michael was pretty when he blushed. Devante already knew

that, but the pink flush that arced across his cheekbones made Devante have to hold back a dreamy sigh anyway. "Yeah," Michael muttered, picking at his muffin wrapper. "But nothing ended up happening."

Relief hit Devante like a tidal wave. "No?" he asked, trying to sound chill. "You guys looked pretty cozy. Charlie said they were your summer fling from a few years ago?"

Michael nodded. "Yeah, Rai. They were in town over the weekend. We went back to mine, but…"

Michael fell silent, worrying at his lower lip with his teeth. "But?" Devante prompted, completely unable to go on without knowing how that sentence ended.

Michael took a deep breath in and shrugged. "I couldn't do it," he said, finally meeting Devante's eyes. "I wanted to, or at least, I wanted to want to, but I couldn't."

"Oh." Devante paused, relief still coursing through his veins. "I hope they were okay with it."

"They were," Michael said. "Just laughed at me and gave me a hug and left."

"They *laughed* at you?" Devante repeated, a little outraged. "For not wanting to sleep with them?"

Michael, thankfully, seemed to revive a little under Devante's indignation on his behalf. "No, no," he said, popping a wedge of muffin into his mouth. "You'll think it's stupid, but…" He bit his lip. "There's kind of someone else I'm hung up on, and he's straight, and that's why Rai was laughing at me. It's not like me to get stuck on a straight boy, is all. I used to swear it'd never happen to me."

By the end of his explanation, Devante's heart was racing and his palms were sweating. He shoved a quarter of his sandwich into his mouth to buy time, chewed, swallowed, and somehow found the wherewithal to say quietly, "I don't think that's stupid."

"No?" Michael's gaze was searching.

Devante shook his head. "We all say we'll never do things we wind up doing. And besides," he said, mustering up a smile through his sudden jealousy of Michael's mystery crush. "Maybe he's less straight than you think."

"I hope so," Michael said softly. "Thanks, Devante. You always know what to say."

"Well, you're easy to talk to," Devante mumbled, shoving more sandwich into his mouth. Thankfully Michael just smiled at him and took another bite of his muffin.

Devante's heart was lighter after their conversation; so light, in fact, that four hours later, it took him a few minutes to realize the importance of the sentence he'd just typed into his final ethics paper. He'd finished up his other course on Sunday, submitting his final project and immediately texting Preeda; now, he finished his sentence, took a break to drink some water and check his phone for texts, and only then realized that the sentence he'd typed had been the last planned line of his conclusion.

He was done. Well, almost.

"Fuck," he said aloud, and then quickly scrolled to the top of the document. If grad school had taught him anything, it was that stopping this close to the finish line soured the whole experience. He forced himself to slow down and read carefully, catching a single typo and a misplaced comma, and then, without thinking about it too much, saved the file and uploaded it to his course page.

"Fuck," he said again, rubbing his hands on his thighs. He rubbed one across his forehead, then picked up his phone and put it back down. "*Fuck.*"

Bracing himself, he picked up his phone and opened The Friend Group chat window. *I think I just finished grad school,* he typed, took a deep breath, and sent it. The responses came in instantly.

CG: WOOOOOOOOOOOOOOOOOOOO

CG: Congrats, dude!!!!!!

NM: Hell yeah!

MC: OH WE GONNA PARTY THIS WEEKEND, well done Dev!

PC: Fuck you, I'm typing as fast as I caaaaaaaaaaaaan

PC: (Congrats, well done and all that, I'm just seethingly jealous)

ML: CONGRATULATIONS DEVANTE!!!!

ML: That's huge!!!!! What are you gonna do to celebrate????

ML: And good luck Preeda!!!!!

DM: I'm gonna make Dad clean up after dinner

DM: No other plans

MC: When's graduation?

PC: Two weeks, which is why I'm turning my phone off and finishing this FUCKING paper

MC: We're all going out to dinner after, non-grads' treat

CG: I agree

ML: Yes!!!!!!

NM: Don't spend my money, Mike Cooper

NM: But yes, of course

DM: Gotta go tell Dad. Thanks, guys!

Devante plodded his way downstairs, his phone still vibrating in his back pocket. His father, it turned out, wasn't home yet, so there was no one to see Devante pull a beer out of the fridge, crack it open, and take it to the couch. It was too late in the day for his soaps, so Devante just channel surfed, sipping from the can every now and again, and tried to take in the fact that he was now finished with the terminal degree in his field.

Carl came home half an hour later, stumping in the door with his usual heavy tread but carefully keeping the door from slamming behind him. "Why are you drinking beer before dinner?" he rumbled, toeing his shoes off. There was a good-smelling bag of food in his hand.

"I finished grad school," Devante said, making to stand. It was his turn to set the table.

"No, no," Carl said, shaking his finger at him. "That sounds like a good enough reason to let me set the table tonight. You stay put."

Devante lowered himself back to the couch and picked up the remote again. He could hear Carl walk behind the couch, and then there was a heavy hand on his shoulder, just for a moment. "Well done, son."

"Thanks, Dad," Devante said, turning to smile up at him. Carl nodded and made his way into the kitchen.

Dinner, which would have been delicious anyway, was made even better by the dual relief of Devante finishing school and Michael not sleeping with someone else. Devante didn't actually have it in him to ask Carl to do the dishes, but Carl shooed him out of the kitchen anyway, following him into the living room twenty minutes of clacking dishes later to sink into his chair and pick up one of his newspapers. "When's graduation?" he asked, snapping it open.

"Two weeks," Devante said.

"You get tickets from the school?"

"Yeah, but you don't have to come," Devante said. "It'll be really boring."

Carl lowered one side of the paper just enough to raise an eyebrow at Devante over it. "Course I'm coming," he said slowly. "You're my son."

"Alright," Devante said, touched. "Thanks." Carl harrumphed and went back to his paper.

Chapter 10

DEVANTE GRADUATED LIBRARY school in a cheap plasticky gown, a mortarboard on his head and a stole over his shoulders. To his great surprise, the dean who read out his name pronounced it correctly. He could hear Preeda, who had already received her degree, whoop from the crowd.

There was still half the alphabet to go after he walked, but it passed surprisingly quickly. His and Preeda's cohort was relatively small, and the buzz of *finally being finished with grad school* swept the rest of the ceremony by in a daze. Time didn't start moving correctly again until he came face to face with his father, after the graduates had dispersed to their families.

Preeda's family, being in Thailand, couldn't make it, so she was at his side. "Let's see, then," Carl said, crossing his arms. Devante slipped the ribbon from off his degree and unrolled it, turning the text side to face Carl. "Mmm," his father said, regarding it. "Looks official."

"It better be," Preeda said frankly. "God knows we paid enough for them."

"Worth it," Carl said. Devante flashed a smile at Preeda as he rolled it up and retied the ribbon.

Carl broke out the deep fryer for dinner that night, to which Preeda was invited—"No one should eat dinner the night of their graduation alone," Carl had said, and she'd given in without a fight—and made his famous fried chicken and French fries to celebrate. "God, these are amazing," Preeda moaned, tracing a fry through ketchup and popping it into her mouth. "Homemade is so much better than a restaurant."

"I dunno," Devante said, just to rile up his father. "That diner by Mood does a pretty good French fry." Carl scowled at him, and he laughed.

"Well, you eat those, and I'll come over and eat your father's cooking instead," Preeda said. When Carl wasn't looking, Devante stuck out his tongue at her. She stuck hers out right back.

"Well, you're welcome for dinner anytime," Carl said, to Devante's surprise.

"Thank you, Mr. Miller," Preeda said, sounding touched. She caught Devante's eye, a question in her gaze; he nodded, and she smiled.

After they'd eaten, Carl insisted on washing up again. Absent anything else to do, Devante and Preeda wandered up the stairs and into Devante's room. "So this is where the magic happens," she said, leaning against the doorframe and looking around the small, tidy room. "I've never been here before."

She was right, he realized; none of his friends had. Most of them had met his father, but they'd never gone above the first floor of their little house. "Not much magic," he said, ducking past her to drop down in his desk chair. She settled herself primly on the edge of his bed. "Lately, just a lot of paper-writing and sleeping."

"Looks good for sleeping," she said, bouncing slightly on the mattress. "Comfy, too."

"It is."

They fell into silence for a few moments, before Preeda cleared her throat and said, "Is anything on your mind, Dev?"

He furrowed his brow, confused. "What do you mean?"

"I just feel like something's been going on with you lately," she said. Her face was earnest, and slightly concerned.

Well, shit. Apparently he hadn't been as good at hiding his potential sexuality crisis as he'd thought. "Everything's fine, Preeds," he said, trying to sound reassuring. She didn't look reassured, though, just bit her lip and continued regarding him.

He couldn't lie to her, not with her face looking like that. "'Something on my mind' is a good way to put it," he said. "But it's nothing bad. Just something I've got to sort through."

"You know you can talk to me, right?" she said. "I'm a good listener, and I care about you."

That's the problem. The sad part was, if she weren't *Preeda*, if there weren't so much unspoken tension between them, he might actually enjoy talking to her about Michael. "I know," he said instead. "And maybe I will, once I've worked it out a bit more on my own."

"I hope you do," she said. "I'm here for you, whenever you're ready."

"Thanks," he said, then, more cheerfully, "What about you? Gonna start a new job hunt now that you've got your shiny new degree?"

"Ugh," she said, rolling her eyes and accepting the subject change. "I mean, I've been keeping an eye on the job boards for months, so I'll probably keep doing that. Might make a case to my boss for a raise now that I'm officially credentialed."

"Good luck," Devante said. "That sounds terrifying."

"Everything about capitalism is terrifying," Preeda said drily. Devante laughed.

After some frantic texting and exchanging schedules, The Friend Group settled on dinner Friday night to feast the new graduates. Natasha recommended the restaurant, a mostly-formal sit-down affair, and absolutely bulldozed anyone who suggested alternatives, so Friday afternoon saw Devante ironing his best (and only) plain white button-down, blazer, and slacks. In what was probably a coincidence but Devante liked to think of as a rare moment of racial sensitivity, the restaurant was in Roxbury and Black-owned, so Devante didn't have to worry about his cornrows, just washed them and let them air dry.

"Looking sharp," Carl offered as Devante passed through the living room on his way out.

"Thanks, Dad," Devante said. "Don't wait up." Carl grunted

in acknowledgment. Devante locked the door behind himself.

He didn't realize his mistake until he was at the restaurant; not until after he walked through the front door and gave his name to the host, who gave him a brief nod and stepped out from behind his stand to lead Devante to the table. He winded his way through the restaurant, and then Devante saw Michael seated at the table and immediately lost the ability to think about anything or anyone else.

He was dressed in a slim-fitting pink dress shirt and navy blue blazer, the combination of which made his skin look like it was glowing. His hair had clearly been freshly washed, and fell around his face in soft waves that just brushed his shoulders. He smiled widely when Devante appeared, his dark brown eyes glittering with evident delight, and nodded to the empty seat next to him. Without hesitating, Devante took it and sat down.

"Hi," Michael murmured, just for Devante's ears.

"Hi," Devante murmured back. Michael was wearing cologne, different from his usual scent, something soft and almost floral; it filled Devante's nose without the usual cologne sting, and made his head spin.

"You look great," Michael said. "Although I miss your usual shirts."

"I feel like I'm in drag," Devante confessed. Michael barked a short, surprised laugh and grinned sidelong at him.

It was only then that he noticed that Mike and Charlie were also there, dressed up in their Sunday best. Charlie was happily perusing the menu, and looked up when Devante finally noticed him to give him a smile and a wave. Mike, on the other hand, had a look on his face that Devante couldn't quite parse but seemed almost calculating, which slid off his mouth as soon as Devante caught his eye. "Hey, man," he said, easy smile taking the strange expression's place. "Some joint Nat picked out, huh?"

"At least we don't need ties," Devante said. Next to him, Michael chimed out a laugh and picked up his own menu.

Natasha and Preeda arrived together, five minutes later.

Natasha was in a stunning red gown that somehow set off her hair instead of clashing; Preeda was in the same wrap dress she'd worn to their graduation a few days before. "Hello, boys, the party has arrived," Natasha declared, sinking into the chair between Charlie and Michael. That left the empty seat between Devante and Mike for Preeda, who took it with a small smile for Devante, which he returned.

"So. Grads," Natasha said a few minutes later, after their drinks had been ordered and served, setting aside her menu and folding her hands on the table in front of her. "Let's get this out of the way so you don't have to talk about it again, at least not with us. What are your job plans looking like, now that you're credentialed?"

"I talked to my boss yesterday," Preeda said. "I can't get an off-cycle raise, but he said that next performance review season, I should expect a pretty sizable one. I think they want to keep me from running off for an official Cataloging Librarian position, now that I'm qualified to get one."

"Very nice," Natasha said, nodding. "Get that money, you deserve it. And our fair Devante?"

"I probably can't get a permanent position until next school year," he said. "I'll stick around my circulation job for now, maybe try and pick up some sub work. Dad's not going to throw me out, so I have time."

"Excellent." Natasha rapped her knuckles against the table. "Now that the boring adult talk is out of the way, who wants to hear about the date I went on Tuesday night? Because let me tell you, it was a *doozy*."

"I do," Charlie said. Natasha turned to him and started talking.

Next to Devante, Michael appeared to be listening too, so Devante turned to Preeda and said, "Congrats on talking to your boss. Sounds like it had a good result."

"Best I could hope for," she said, shrugging. "I'll keep an eye on the market in the meantime, but I like Boston. If I can stay here, I want to."

Michael, apparently, hadn't been paying as close attention to Natasha as Devante had thought, because at Preeda's words he said, "Would you have to leave Boston for your next job?"

"Cataloging jobs are few and far between, special collections-focused ones even more so," she said. "It's the sort of job where you have to go where the work is."

"I hope they give you enough of a raise that you can stay, then," Michael said sincerely. He threw Devante a look—pity? Devante squinted at him, confused, and after a moment Michael smiled at him and said, "I know *you're* not going anywhere, Devante."

"Not unless I absolutely have to," Devante confirmed. "Or Dad has to move to Florida for his health."

Michael gave a theatrical shudder. "Not Florida," he said. "Florida is actively detrimental to one's health."

"Says the Texan," Devante said, grinning.

Michael winked at him. "Texas isn't Florida. Florida is *humid*, and swampland, and fighting alligators to cross the street. Texas is a civilized, dignified sort of heat."

"No such thing as a dignified heat," Preeda put it. "Or at least, not a heat that you can be dignified in."

"I'll drink to that," Devante said, picking up his wine glass. Preeda toasted him.

Their server came by to take their orders then. When she left, silence fell around the table, until Mike sighed and said, "I need to move."

"Dude, why?" Charlie asked, outraged. "Your apartment is quality."

"Mike comes from money," Devante said sagely to Michael. "He can afford the finer things in life."

Mike kicked him under the table. "I do not come from money," he said. "I just got a good stipend from my grad program."

"That's what he says," Natasha said. "We know the truth."

"Whatever." Mike rolled his eyes. "I was thinking of going in on a place with someone, you know? Trying roommates again."

"Again, I ask, why?" Charlie asked. "If I had a place like yours and didn't have to live with roommates, you couldn't pay me enough to share a bathroom with someone again."

Mike shrugged. "Just thinking it might be nice to have some company around on the reg, you know? Someone to live with." He shot Devante another look, this one heavy and meaningful. Devante was starting to get sick of people giving him significant looks tonight. When Devante didn't respond, Mike went on, "Well, my lease isn't up until April anyway, so I have time to work it out."

"Depending on how big my raise is next review cycle, I actually might also move," Preeda said. "Invest in a slightly larger shoebox."

"*That*, we can support," Natasha said firmly. "You need an apartment you can't touch both sides of at the same time."

"I'd settle for enough space for a couch," Preeda said. "Spending all my time on my bed has wrecked my sleep hygiene."

"Well, you know we'll sling boxes for you whenever," Charlie said.

"Absolutely," Devante said. Preeda smiled at him.

"What, you'll offer to help Preeds move but not me?" Mike asked. "Rude."

"You can afford movers," Charlie said.

"Not that you'd need them," Devante asked. "Just put all your boxes on your shoulders and carry them to the new place."

"You like my shoulders, Dev?" Mike asked, grinning rapaciously. Devante, suddenly uncomfortable, coughed and reached for his wine to take a sip and hide his face. When he emerged, Mike had thankfully moved on and was arguing with Natasha about something, and Michael was giving him a curious look. Devante mustered up a smile for him, and Michael, apparently appeased, smiled back.

The food, when it finally came, was delicious, well worth the ironing Devante had done, especially when his friends came through on Charlie's word and refused to let him or Preeda spend a cent to cover their meals. "Congratulations, darlings," Natasha said to them on the sidewalk after the meal was over, giving first Preeda and then Devante a hug. "Couldn't be prouder of you."

"Thanks, Nat," Preeda said. Devante nodded his agreement.

Natasha peeled off to go catch her bus. Mike clapped both the new grads on the shoulder and made for the nearest Orange Line station. Preeda's bus was in the opposite direction, so she waved at the rest of them and took off, leaving Devante, Charlie, and Michael grouped outside of the restaurant.

"Is our bus stop on your way, Dev?" Charlie asked, pulling out his phone to look at a map.

"It's not far off," Devante said. "I'll walk part of the way with you."

"Sweet."

They set off, ambling slowly through the cool September evening. Somehow, their walking speeds put them in a triangle, Charlie slightly ahead of Devante and Michael, who wound up walking side-by-side. "It's nice to have a chance to dress up every now and again," Devante said, to fill the silence.

"I often feel that way about the banquets," Michael agreed.

"Banquets?"

"After every skating competition," he explained. "All the skaters get dressed up for a fancy function. There's a bit of dancing, but it's mostly to show off to sponsors. Mostly they're boring, but like you said, it's a nice excuse to get all dolled up."

"There's a lot of business in figure skating, isn't there?" Devante asked.

Michael made a face. "More than I'd like, now that I'm doing it as my career instead of just a high-stakes hobby during college. My coach picks up a lot of the slack, and I have a manager for the financials, but yeah, there's a lot of face work involved."

Devante jogged him lightly with his elbow. "Bet you're good at it." Michael just smiled at him sidelong.

"I think this is our turn," Charlie said from in front of them.

"It is," Devante said. "I'm that way," he added, pointing down the other side of the street.

Charlie clapped him in a one-armed Man Hug. "Congrats, man," he said. "You really kicked grad school's ass."

"Thanks, Charlie." Devante clapped him on the back and let go, and then, in a panicky rush of *déjà vu*, realized his second mistake of the night as Michael stepped up to him, arms open, a questioning look on his face.

There was no way out of it, and as Michael wrapped his arms around Devante, Devante's own arms coming up around Michael's back, he forgot why he'd felt that sudden rush of panic at the idea of hugging Michael. Michael's body was lithe and firm, warm where his chest pressed against Devante's, and that floral cologne filled his nostrils again, making his head swim. "Congratulations, Devante," Michael said softly, holding the hug for a moment longer before letting go and stepping back. "You should be very proud of yourself."

"Thanks," Devante said, just as quietly. "I am."

They looked at each other for a long moment, only to have it broken by Charlie saying, "I think I see our bus, Michael."

"Better go," Michael said brightly, tearing his gaze away from Devante to look down the street. "See you soon, Devante."

"See you!" Charlie called, already starting to jog toward the bus stop. With a final wave, Michael followed him. Devante watched as they ran down the sidewalk just in time to make their bus, and then continued his quiet, peaceful walk home.

Chapter 11

DEVANTE PICKED UP his job hunt in earnest as September slipped into October and the reality of his empty days, with no more schoolwork to fill them, loomed larger and larger. His initial impression was right, and all full-time school librarian positions had been filled over the spring and summer, but he kept his eyes peeled for substitute positions, and any part-time work he could fit around his public library shifts in the meantime.

Michael's schedule also got heavier and heavier, Devante found. He still made time to have lunch with Devante on Mondays and Fridays, but he ate less, and he showed signs of actually having been on runs when Devante met him outside the library.

Michael's first competition was Skate America, the second week of October. His Instagram filled with jump videos and preview clips of his routines. The night before his flight to Salt Lake City, The Friend Group chat blew up with well-wishes.

DM: Good luck Michael!

CG: Is it still break a leg for figure skating, or is that just theater?

PC: DON'T break a leg, how about that

CG: Where's the best place to watch??? Will it be online?

ML: You guys don't have to watch

NM: Of course we're going to watch, Michael

CG: Yeah!!!!

ML: I should warn you, I'm a little different on the ice to how I am in person

NM: Oh, I know, I remember from last season

DM: Different how?

NM: Let it be a delightful surprise, Dev

ML: It's fine, it's not a big deal, I just didn't want you guys to freak out

CG: Why would we freak out?

ML: My programs this year are a little…sexy

CG: Oh, dude, that's fine

CG: Not freak-out worthy at all

CG: You're a hot dude already

ML: Thanks, Charlie, that means a lot

ML: Best place to watch is NBC

Devante very firmly put aside the thought of how sexy Michael's performances were going to be. That was a problem for the future.

The future became the present that weekend, as The Friend Group packed themselves into Mike's apartment on the evening of the short programs. Charlie brought a couple six-packs of beer, and Mike was always good for nibbles, so the mood was high as the skating started, chattering and cheering cutting through the on-screen commentary.

Michael was skating in the middle of the group. His costume was a deep, mottled red, looking like the embers of a dying fire. His hair was slicked and tied tightly back, and he had dark red eyeshadow on. "Wow," Natasha said dreamily. "He looks amazing."

He did look amazing, Devante thought to himself, shifting uncomfortably on the floor at the foot of the couch where he sat. He took a swig of his beer as the music started, wincing at the hoppy aftertaste.

Sexy had been a good word for it, Devante reflected a few minutes later, as Michael took his bows, when Devante could form coherent thoughts again. He had skated across the ice like he owned it, like it was his own personal runway. The step sequence he had shown Devante months ago, when done to actual music, turned into a prowl, like Michael was hunting something, or someone. Devante was just distantly grateful that he was in loose pants, and that no one was looking at him.

"—raw, sexual power," one commentator was saying, "pure anyone-goes hunger."

"He's definitely a passionate skater," the other commentator replied. "He's almost animalistic when he really gets going."

"Damn," Charlie said from the couch, frowning. "That's fucked up."

Devante didn't know much about figure skating scores, and could only compare the number Michael received to the scores the skaters before him had gotten, but it was higher than most of them, and Michael and his coach, a white Latina woman with hair as tightly slicked back as Michael's, looked pleased. She hugged him around the shoulders, and he waved at the camera, his familiar bright grin beaming off Mike's tv.

His friends' chatter rose up again now that Michael's skate was over, but Devante didn't join in, just sat on the floor nursing his beer and thought. The skate had been attractive— Devante was still crouched over to hide the effects of just how attractive he'd found it—but it felt a little strange too, to see Michael like that. The Michael Devante had come to know over the summer was always careful, always respectful of his boundaries, always bright and shining; the Michael on the ice had been a burning fire, designed to reduce all boundaries around him to ash. He wondered how much of it was a side of Michael he just hadn't seen before, and how much was a performance.

After the skating was over, The Friend Group poured out of Mike's apartment with promises to be back in two days for the free programs. Devante pulled out his phone when he made it to the Orange Line and opened his private text chat with Michael. *Great skate!*

To his surprise, he got an answer as he was walking in the front door of his house. *Did you like it?*

Only one question mark? *Yes, I did*, Devante texted back. *You were great, and your costume is amazing.*

Thanks!!!! That was more like it. Devante relaxed a little. *I thought I was a little stiff, but the judges didn't seem to mind.*

I don't know much about skating, but you didn't look stiff to me.

Thanks, Devante <3 Gotta grab some dinner, talk later?

Devante replied in the affirmative, and fell asleep thinking about that heart emoji.

Michael was in third place after the short programs. Devante spent the intervening days before his next skate idly Googling analysis articles; apparently Michael was hot stuff, highly anticipated to do well in the free program and the series as a whole. He found a lot more adjectives too, "passionate" and "fiery" and "wild," and in one article "borderline slutty." He closed out of that article as fast as possible.

Michael updated his Instagram Story quite a few times, heavily-filtered photographs of Salt Lake City and selfies with the other skaters. Devante, on impulse, sent him a DM: *Aren't you meant to be skating?;)* He got a tongue-out emoji and a few more hearts to keep him up at night.

Natasha was the one supplying the drinks for the free programs, which meant Devante, once again on the floor, nursed a single avant-garde craft beer the whole night, sipping only enough to keep her off his back. Preeda's patterned-tights-clad legs dangled off the couch next to him, her sandals slipping off her feet.

Michael was skating late in the lineup, due to his third-place finish in the short programs, what Natasha called a "small bronze." The other skaters, those who had scored high enough to qualify, were once again good but indistinguishable from each other to Devante's untrained gaze. During one particularly boring skate, Preeda tapped him lightly with her foot. He flicked her ankle and took another sip of the nigh-undrinkable beer Natasha had provided.

Finally, Michael took the ice, dressed in a flowing green sheer top and clinging black tights, glitter painted around his eyes and across his cheeks. "Damn, that ass, though," Natasha said from the armchair. Devante privately agreed.

Michael's free program music was stately, almost boring in its repetition and melody, but the way he danced across the ice made it as effective a come-on as his short program had been. Devante could barely hear the music, so caught up was he in the way Michael's shirt clung to him as he picked up speed, the way Michael's feet twisted and turned around each other during what the commentators identified as his step sequence.

"Powerful," one commentator said as he hit his final pose and then dropped, hands on his elbows to catch his breath. "Lopez really knows how to work the ice and make it his own."

"As seductive as his short program," agreed the other disembodied voice. "Just what we've come to expect from a skater with Michael Lopez's background."

On the couch, Charlie whistled angrily and Natasha hissed a little. Devante just shook his head and pulled out his phone. *Well done,* he texted Michael, not expecting him to reply. *The whole group's here, we all thought you were great.*

To his surprise, he got a response while the last skater was performing. *Hang around for twenty minutes after the podium and call???? I wanna hear your guys' voices.*

"Michael wants us to call him twenty minutes after the medals," Devante said aloud to the group.

"Hell yeah," Charlie said affably, already returned to his usual good humor. The rest of them made affirmative noises, so Devante texted back, *Will do, lmk when you're ready for us.*

Michael had rocketed to the top of the leaderboard after his skate, but the final two skaters after him edged him out, knocking him to a final third place when the skating was done. "Woo, our boy got bronze!" Charlie cheered, pumping his fist in the air.

"Should have been second," Natasha said critically, "the silver medalist's axel was wobbly."

"Hey," Mike said suddenly, sounding like something had just dawned on him, "did anyone else get the sense the commentators were being a little racist?"

"Oh Mike," Preeda said pityingly. "So white."

"What?" he asked. "Was it really obvious?"

"*So* obvious," Charlie said. "But you got there in the end, and we're proud of you."

Mike humphed. "Pass me another beer, Nat."

Michael looked happy enough on the podium, clutching his bronze medal and beaming at the cameras. He was chatting with the other two skaters, making them laugh as they all posed and grinned with their medals.

Devante pulled Twitter open and searched for Michael's name during the wait to call him, fending off advances from Preeda's foot via more well placed flicks to her ankle. The stream of Tweets was largely supportive, a huge percentage calling out the American commentators for their bias in between praising Michael for his artistry and technical skill. Devante liked a few one of them to find later and show Michael when he got home.

Finally, twenty minutes had elapsed and he got a text: *Ready when you are!!!!* "Everyone shut up, I'm calling him," Devante said aloud, and the room quieted as he pulled up Michael's number and pressed *Call.*

Michael answered on the first ring. Devante put him on speakerphone. "Hey guys!" he said happily. The group chorused hellos. "What did you think?"

"You were *amazing*," Natasha said. "Should have been a silver, though."

Michael laughed tinnily. "That's what Sara said, she said

Kevin's triple axel was wobbly, but I'm happy with my bronze."

"Might need to find a new stream for your next competition, though," Charlie put in. "I don't know if those commentators on NBC were more racist or homophobic."

"Eh, it's usually a mix of both," Michael said, sounding unconcerned. "I play up to it a lot, though, so."

"What does that mean?" Mike asked.

On the line, Michael sighed. "It means that when the commentators, and more importantly the judges, see an out and proud Latino bisexual skater, they expect to see a slut," he said bluntly. "If I give them what they expect, I get more points."

"That's balls," Mike said.

"Yeah, that's fucked up," Natasha agreed. "You're totally right, but it's fucked up."

"It is what it is," Michael said. "I try not to think about it too much. It's fun, anyway, getting to be sexy while I skate. Once I get a bit more established, I'll try some new things, but for now I don't mind getting typecast a little."

"You're a stronger man than I would be," Preeda put in. "I couldn't put up with it."

Michael laughed. To Devante's ear, attuned as it was to all Michael's moods, it didn't sound like he thought it was funny. Then, "Haven't heard Devante's voice yet," Michael said, sounding a little tentative. "You there?"

"I'm here," Devante said.

"What did you think of my skate?" He still sounded tentative, and a little hopeful.

Devante bit his lip and said, "I thought it was a great performance. I'd have given you gold, but I can't wait to see your bronze in person." *With you attached*, he added in his head.

Michael's voice was warm and happy when he said, "Thanks, Devante. I'll be sure to bring it next time I see you."

"Good."

"Hey, I've got to run," Michael said, and Devante blinked, remembering suddenly that other people were on the call.

"Gotta clear the rink for the ladies this evening. It was great to talk to you all!"

"We'll see you in the gala tomorrow from Mood!" Natasha called.

"Ha ha, I'll do my best, then!" Michael said. "Talk to you guys later. Bye!"

"Bye!" they all chorused. "Bye, Michael," Devante said last, and pressed *End Call*.

"I'm gonna be sending some *very* angry Tweets to NBC tonight," Natasha announced.

"You're not the only one," Devante said. "I took a look earlier. People are *pissed*."

"As they should be," Preeda said. "I'll join you in the angry Tweeting, Nat."

"Thank you," Natasha said. "I'm only a lone white woman. The more voices the better."

"Is this the sort of thing I should use my privilege as a white man to help out with?" Mike asked, sounding like he genuinely meant the question.

"Stick to retweeting," Preeda advised. "Elevate the voices of others."

"Mmkay," Mike said, draining his third beer. "These are great, Nat, by the way," he added when he surfaced.

"Glad *someone* appreciates my taste," Natasha sniffed. "I'll leave you half of what's left."

"Cheers." With a groan, Mike pushed himself to his feet. "Now I'm throwing all of you out of my apartment. I have to clean it tonight."

"You couldn't clean it *before* we came and poor Dev had to sit on the floor for hours?" Preeda griped, getting to her feet.

Devante put both hands flat on the floor and pushed himself to his knees, then got one foot under himself and heaved himself up. He theatrically brushed his jeans off, and Mike laughed. "Sorry, Dev," he said. "I'll pay for your dry cleaning."

"Just get me a roll of quarters for the laundromat," Devante quipped. Mike laughed again, his cheeks a little pink from the alcohol. "See you all tomorrow?"

"See you!" they chorused, everyone getting their shoes on. Preeda and Devante hadn't taken theirs off, so they left first, walking down the hall together. Devante pressed the button for the elevator.

"Michael's really good," Preeda ventured as the elevator rumbled into life.

"He is," Devante agreed.

The elevator came, and they got in and pressed the button for the first floor. "You guys seem like you've gotten pretty close," Preeda said as the car began its descent.

Devante looked at her sharply, but she didn't seem to mean anything by it; her face was neutral, like she could just as easily have commented about the weather.

"I think we are," Devante said carefully. "He's a good friend."

The smile Preeda gave him was open and honest. "Good," she said. "You deserve more good friends. Sometimes I wonder if our group is as good to you as you deserve."

Surprised, Devante blinked. "I don't really have any complaints about The Friend Group," he said.

She just looked at him and said, "I know. That's what I mean."

His face must have registered his confusion, because she just patted him on the shoulder as the elevator doors slid open on the ground floor. Utterly befuddled, he followed her out of the building.

Chapter 12

SKATE AMERICA'S GALA performance was the next day, timed perfectly to fall within The Friend Group's usual drinks hour at Mood. Mike had promised to download the NBC app onto his phone in preparation.

Devante was surprisingly nervous about it, although for the life of him he couldn't pinpoint exactly why. Michael wouldn't actually be there in person to make Devante nervous around him, and as far as Devante knew, he'd never revealed what song he'd be skating to, or what he'd be wearing. There was no reason for the butterflies in his stomach, but there they were all the same, flapping around and making his dinner sit uncomfortably.

He washed the dinner dishes and went upstairs to change for drinks, flinging open his closet and running his hand down the row of brightly-colored, brightly-patterned shirts. His fingers caught on the first one he'd ever worn around Michael, the one with the pineapples. Without thinking too hard about it, he pulled it from its hanger, pulled his t-shirt over his head, and slipped it on over his undershirt.

"Don't wait up," he said to his father on his way out, the usual refrain. Carl, as per tradition, grunted from behind his newspaper, and Devante took it for assent.

"Looking sharp, Dev," Charlie greeted him when he arrived at Mood to find his friends all there already. There was his traditional spot open next to Preeda. He smiled at her when he slipped into it, the butterflies in his stomach picking up the pace.

"I love that shirt on you," Natasha said to him. "The color is just, mwah." She did the chefs-kiss fingers.

"Thanks," he said, surprised. Natasha rarely complimented anyone.

"It's starting," Mike said, tapping at his phone. He held it out across the table, angling it up so everyone could see the screen. Mike turned the volume all the way up, and Devante could hear tinny music over the ambient sounds of the bar.

There was a group opening performance, and then the third-place pairs team took the ice. Their performance was acrobatic and lively, the man actively throwing the woman into the air a couple of times. "Couldn't be me," Preeda said, shaking her head. "I'd like to see the man who could lift me."

"Bet I could," Mike said instantly. "Want to try? There's an ice rink in Brighton, I think it's where Michael skates."

"Warrior," Devante murmured, but no one seemed to hear him over Preeda's loud scoff.

Next up was the third-place ladies skater. "I love her," Natasha announced. "I have high hopes for her making the Final."

The skater, whose name Devante hadn't caught, skated to "Bad Romance," a punchy, aggressive performance that apparently had the audience on its feet, to judge by what the commentators said. "I see why you like her," Devante put forth. Natasha graced him with a rare smile.

Michael was next, and as he took the ice, Devante's hand tightened around his whiskey tumbler and he started to sweat. "Uh-oh, he stole your style!" Charlie crowed, grinning as he reached over to jostle Devante's arm. The rest of the group chuckled; thankfully, no one noticed that Devante didn't.

Michael's hair, usually up while he skated, was loose, artificial waves accenting his natural ones as it cascaded down around his shoulders. His eyeliner was winged halfway out to his temples, eyelids done up in a dark blue shadow. There were smears of glitter across his cheeks, making his cheekbones look even sharper. He was in leather pants that looked like they'd been painted on, stretching down over the boots of his skates, and on his torso, clinging to every curve and line, was a black t-shirt, sinfully tight, with a clip-art image of a pineapple on the front.

Blood was pounding in Devante's ears. What did it mean? What *could* it mean? Nothing, surely. Michael had more than once complimented Devante's style; no doubt he was just borrowing it for a performance. It didn't mean anything.

Devante was so busy arguing with himself that he missed the announcement of the song Michael was skating to, and its opening chords, but when the lyrics started, they cut through the haze in his head like a hot knife through butter.

"If I Had You," by Adam Lambert. Devante went dizzy.

Michael's gala skate was nothing like his two competition routines. Instead of a powerhouse of seduction, this time he was lighter, almost happier, a celebration in every movement of his arms and legs. The song was about longing, about wanting someone more than anything, but the music was upbeat, chipper, and Michael rose to the occasion. Whomever he was longing for made his life *better*, his skating seemed to say, and he was happy for the chance to want them.

With a fucking *pineapple* on his shirt. Potentially the most meaningful pineapple in the history of fashion.

Michael was out of breath when he hit his final pose, sweat clearly beading along his hairline and streaking past the glitter on his cheeks. Devante felt just as winded, and as Michael took his bows, Devante had to push himself to his feet.

"Where're you going?" Mike asked, looking up from the screen.

"Bathroom," Devante mumbled, stumbling away as his friends started to talk about Michael's performance. He didn't want to, he *couldn't* hear what they thought about it right then.

He made it to the bathroom in a daze, shoving past people on his way until the heavy door swung shut behind him and he could lean on the sink and catch his breath.

There was someone else in the bathroom with him, washing his hands, with the fuzzy-eyed look of someone who'd already had a few. "Everything alright, man?" he slurred, blinking in a friendly manner at Devante.

"I want the song to be about me," Devante said blankly, his brain still trying to power back online.

"Cheers, dude," the drunk man said. He patted Devante on the arm with one still-wet hand, realized what he'd done, and wiped both hands on his jeans. "I'm sure it is, my man," he added with a slanted smile, before making his way out of the bathroom.

Devante watched him go, then turned to face himself in the mirror. "I want it to be about me," he said, quieter, staring himself in the eye.

I want it to be about me. He wanted to be the one Michael wanted; *he* wanted to be the one who made Michael's life so happy. He wanted to affect Michael the way Michael affected him, wanted to fry Michael's synapses, make him short of breath, make butterflies appear in his stomach and his heart race whenever he saw Devante.

He wanted to be with Michael.

"I want to be with Michael," he whispered to himself in the mirror. "I want Michael to be with me."

There were tears in his eyes, he realized as they spilled down his cheeks. As he wiped them away, a sob shook him, and then another. The door to the bathroom creaked open, and in a flash Devante fled into the nearest stall and locked himself in, slumping against the wall with his face in his hands.

He wept; there was no other word for it. Sobs ripped through him, tears staining his hands with salt as he tried to keep quiet. Two people entered the bathroom; Devante could hear them chatting at the urinals. He clapped a hand over his mouth, trying to calm his breathing and get his tears under control, but pulsing under his skin, with every beat of his heart pushing blood through his arteries, was the realization: *He wanted Michael*, for real. He wanted him more than he'd ever wanted anything in his life; more than he'd wanted grad school, more than he wanted a job, almost more than he wanted to stop crying just then.

He wanted to kiss Michael, to date him, to sleep next to him and talk to him and laugh with him, and he wanted Michael to want that too. He wanted to know what Michael looked like without his clothes on; he wanted to touch Michael's hair and know if it was as soft as it looked; he wanted to know what Michael's face did during sex.

He wanted to have sex with Michael, lots of sex, and he wanted to take his own clothes off in front of him, to his own considerable surprise. Even when he'd lost his virginity at Easter, he hadn't taken more clothes off than had been absolutely necessary, but he wanted to strip bare in front of Michael and see what the sight of him did to the other man, if it did anything at all.

The rush of *wanting* ran Devante through, leaving him sagged against the wall of the stall, breath heaving and face wet. He pulled a wad of toilet paper off the roll and wiped his face as best he could. The two men at the urinals had long since left the bathroom again, and no one else had come in while Devante was having his breakdown, so he carefully undid the lock of the stall and edged back out to the sink and mirror.

Devante was lucky; his face never showed his crying much, even extended weeping like he'd just done. His eyes were a little puffy, but it was difficult to tell in the bad lighting of the bathroom. He splashed cold water on his face and the back of his neck and wiped it off with a handful of paper towels, and there was almost no physical sign left of the massive change he'd just undergone.

Summoning all the bravery he had in him, Devante left the bathroom, making his way back to the table where his friends still sat, grouped around Mike's phone. With Michael having finished, they were chatting more than watching any of the other performances, with the exception of Natasha.

Mike's eyes lit on Devante as he approached. "Everything okay?" he asked. "You were gone a long time."

"Everything's fine," Devante said, and he meant it. Everything *was* fine. He felt clearer-headed and surer of himself than he had in a long, long time, even beyond the peace that a good cry could give him. "What'd I miss?"

"All of the silvers," Natasha reported. "The gold medal ice dancers are about to go."

Devante sat and kept his eyes on the screen of Mike's phone, now more lackadaisically held out as Mike was drawn into conversation with Charlie about the state of his crabs. He didn't take in any of the other performances, though; his mind was still beating out the same rhythm: *Michael, Michael, Michael.*

The gala finished not long after he got back to the table, and his friends started packing up, shrugging jackets on and draining the dregs of their drinks. Devante pushed himself to his feet, feeling like if he'd pushed a little harder, he could have started floating off the ground.

"You sure everything's alright?" Preeda murmured to him. "You look a little dazed."

"Everything's beautiful," he said to her, heartfelt and meaningful. She scrunched up her face but didn't say anything more.

Devante honestly wasn't sure how he made it home that night. He did, though, blinking himself aware at the door to his house. He fumbled for his keys, but the door was unlocked, which meant Carl hadn't gone to bed yet.

Sure enough, when Devante got inside, Carl was still installed in his armchair. "Have a good night?" he inquired, turning the page.

"The best night," Devante said. *There's this boy, and his name is Michael, and he's amazing.* But of course, he couldn't say that. "A really good night," he repeated, instead.

"Good," Carl said. "Sleep well."

"You too," Devante said, making his way to the stairs and tripping up them to his bedroom.

He dropped heavily onto his back on the bed, making his mattress creak, and tugged his phone out of his pocket.

Adrenaline was still fizzing throughout his whole body. He pulled open his text chat with Michael. *Good skate*, he sent.

Michael's response was instantaneous, which made Devante want to giggle and press his phone to his face. *Devante!!!!! Thanks!!!!! It was great finally getting to skate it in front of other people.*

Devante tapped his phone against his chin, then, daringly, typed, *Great shirt,* and pressed Send.

This response took a bit longer to come through, but still not longer than thirty or so seconds. *Hope you didn't mind it*, with an emoji of a monkey covering its face with its hands.

Mind? Devante *mind* the shirt that had rocked his whole world? *I didn't mind it*, he sent back. *I loved it.*

Good <3, was Michael's reply. *You all still at Mood?*

No, we left when the gala ended. I'm at home.

Can I call?

Devante's heart thudded. *Yes.*

The phone rang ten seconds later. Devante pressed it to his ear with a hand that was, ever so slightly, trembling. "Hi," he breathed.

"Hi," Michael breathed. "So you watched my performance?"

"Of course." Absently, Devante wished for a corded phone, for something he could twist around his finger. "I wouldn't have missed it."

"I'm glad," Michael said. "I like knowing you're watching when I'm skating."

Thud, thud, thud went Devante's pulse. "You'll have a hard time shaking me, now that I've started," he said. "You skate beautifully."

"Thank you," Michael said softly.

There were a few moments of silence, both of them just listening to each other's breath on the line, and then a voice in the background on Michael's end called his name. "It's my coach," he said, sounding genuinely regretful even though neither of them had said anything for a good twenty seconds. "I have to go. It was good to talk to you."

"Good to talk to you too," Devante said. "Have a good rest of your evening."

"I'll see you soon?" Michael asked tentatively. "On Monday, right?"

"Right," Devante said. "See you on Monday."

"See you," Michael said.

"See you," Devante repeated. They both laughed. "Go," Devante said. "I'll talk to you later."

"Bye, Devante," Michael whispered, and then ended the call. Devante dropped his phone onto his chest and closed his eyes, counting the minutes until Monday until he fell asleep.

Chapter 13

"WHAT'S GOT YOU all in a good mood?" Ethan asked, the second time they caught Devante whistling to himself during his Monday morning shift.

"Meeting a friend for lunch," Devante said. He was a little too excited to be embarrassed, but he did stop whistling.

"Don't you have lunch with a friend every time you have a morning shift?" Ethan didn't usually work Mondays, but they did work during Devante's other two shifts. "And dinner on Thursday with what's-his-face, the beefy one?"

"Mike," Devante said. "And yes, but this friend's been away. Haven't seen him in a week."

"Aww, that's sweet," Ethan cooed. "What's this one's name?"

"Michael," Devante said, trying not to sound too dreamy.

"A Mike *and* a Michael. You've got an imaginative taste in friends, Devante." Ethan straightened from where they were leaning against the circulation desk as a patron approached. "One last check out and you're done."

There were still ten minutes on his shift, but Devante wasn't about to look a gift horse in the mouth. "Thanks, Ethan," he said. He clicked over to the circulation software from the job boards he'd been perusing and greeted the patron, who plunked five heavy books and a DVD down on the desk.

The patron also had holds which had been misfiled on the holds shelf, so it took a few minutes, but eventually they were off, a bag with their books and a printed due date receipt in their hand. Devante logged out of Chrome, clocked out, and stood up. "I'm out," he called over his shoulder.

"Have a good lunch," Ethan said, coming up to cover the desk until Devante's replacement came.

There were still three minutes until the official end of Devante's shift, but Michael was already outside, pacing in front of the library's entrance. He looked thoughtful, almost nervous as Devante went up to him, but then he caught sight of Devante and his face lit up.

"Hi," Michael breathed, moving in, and before Devante knew it he had Michael in his arms.

"Hi," Devante whispered back, giving him a squeeze and accepting one in return before letting him go. They looked at each other for a few seconds, and then Devante broke and grinned. "Hungry?"

"Starved," Michael admitted, chuckling. "Caffe Nero?"

The October air was a little brisk, and Michael was in a thin button-down with no jacket. He shivered a little as they walked. Devante had to fight the urge to put an arm around him. *We're not there yet*, he told himself, and compromised by shuffling a little closer and letting their arms brush.

They ordered their lunch, sandwiches and an extra cookie for Devante, and took to their usual table in the corner. "How was Salt Lake?" Devante asked, fanning the steam away from his sandwich with his hand.

"Beautiful," Michael said, smiling wide. "I didn't get to see much of it, but Sara let me do a little tourism on my off day after practice, and what I did see was lovely."

"You must get to see so many places," Devante observed.

"Mmm, sort of," Michael said. "Like I said, I don't usually get to do the full sightseeing experience when I'm there for a competition, but figure skating competitively is a great way to at least get a glimpse of a lot of the world. Europe, parts of Asia, and North America, anyway."

"I've never even been out of the country," Devante admitted. "I went to college out of state, but other than that I mostly just stayed put."

Michael swallowed his mouthful of food, smiled softly at him, and said, "Well, maybe I'll have to bring you to a competition or two with me."

"I'd like that," Devante said, feeling himself flush hot. That was more than friendship, surely? Michael wouldn't fly someone who was merely a *friend* to a competition, would he?

He went back and forth on the question for hours, tossing it over and around in his mind until he was almost sick of himself and resolved to stop, and then he would remember Michael's gentle smile as he said it and start all over again.

Michael flew out again a week and a half later, a much longer-haul trip to Tokyo for the NHK Trophy. The Friend Group farewelled him at drinks the Tuesday before he left. "So this is a big competition for you, right?" Preeda asked, sipping her wine. "Bigger than the last one?"

"Sort of," Michael said. "How I do in this one will decide whether I go to the Final or not, so the stress is higher, but it's the same level of competition, renown-wise."

"I couldn't *move* with that kind of stress, let alone skate," Charlie remarked. "God knows how you do it."

"It's not all bad," Michael said. "Georg will be there, he'll help keep me calm. Georg Hummel," he added, at Preeda, Charlie, and Mike's confused faces. "My best friend."

"Georg Hummel," Natasha said dreamily, draping herself over his shoulder. "The German Dreamboat. Will you get his number for me?"

Michael laughed. "You're not his type, darling."

"Drat," Natasha said, face falling. "Really?"

"Really," he confirmed, taking a swig of his gin and tonic. "He's been out almost as long as I have; where have you been?"

"With my head up my ass, apparently," Natasha said grumpily, settling back into her seat.

Georg Hummel—the pretty white boy from Michael's old Instagram pictures. Devante felt a stab of jealousy go up his spine and tried to drown it with a hearty swallow of scotch. It didn't work.

Michael left that Thursday; his Instagram Story turned into a chronicle of airports, and then a taxi, and then a nondescript Japanese hotel room over the course of the next day or so. Feeling a surge of masochistic curiosity, Devante looked up Georg Hummel's account and was presented with a clip of him and Michael, their cheeks pressed together in a tight embrace. *Back together with bestie <3*, the text on the picture read.

Mike couldn't host another gathering for the NHK Trophy, so he loaned out his NBC login and password. Devante watched from the comfort of his bedroom, a contraband bowl of popcorn on the bed next to him as he held up his tablet to watch the skating.

Michael and Georg were both slated late in the lineup, with Georg skating fourth-to-last and Michael second-to-last. As the competition wore on and drew closer to their slots, they started appearing in quick behind-the-scenes shots, mostly of them warming up separately.

Just before Georg went on the ice, though, the camera showed Michael standing rinkside, doing something on his phone. Georg came up behind him and wrapped his arms around Michael's waist; Michael lifted a finger, not looking up from his phone, and rested it on the far side of Georg's jaw. He finished whatever he was typing one-handed and then turned his head to beam at Georg, their faces very close together.

Next to Devante's bowl of popcorn, his phone buzzed with a text. *About to go on; wish me luck?*

Suddenly nauseous with a sick combination of envy and delight, Devante shoved more popcorn in his mouth and replied, *Luck!*

On the tablet, Michael looked back at his phone and grinned. Georg let go of him, patting him on the shoulder and going to take the ice.

The commentator reported that Georg would be skating to something classical, the title in German and instantly slipping out of Devante's head. He was clad in a tight purple t-shirt and black leggings, showing off every inch of his sculpted physique, and as the music started, he tossed his head with an air that was almost arrogant.

He skated well; that, Devante couldn't deny, however much he wanted to. He didn't have, in Devante's opinion, the ethereality or grace Michael was capable of, but his lines were elegant and his jumps were clean. He ended his skate in a respectable third place to date, and looked pleased enough with himself.

He ended his skate in third, but he ended the day in fourth, because when Michael took the ice, he blew Georg's skate out of the water. Devante hurriedly turned the sound down on his tablet when Michael hit his starting pose, because the commentators for this competition were the same as for the last and he didn't want to hear what they had to say again, but even without commentary or music, he could tell that Michael was in top form today. Devante had reason to be grateful that he was alone, because now that he knew exactly what he wanted from Michael, the seductive, passionate performance had an even stronger effect on him.

Michael ended the day in first place. Devante cheered aloud when his score was announced; on his screen, Michael seemed stunned. The camera cut to the other top-scored skaters; to Georg's credit, he was hollering as loudly as anyone in the crowd for his friend.

They were in very, very different time zones, so Michael didn't respond to Devante's *You were amazing* until Devante was already asleep. He woke up to a *Thanks!!!!!! Stunned!!!!!!* that made him smile all morning despite the less-than-thrilled look his father sent him when he caught him coming downstairs with the popcorn bowl.

"At least don't keep it up there overnight," Carl grumbled.

"Sorry, Dad," Devante said, beaming at him. Carl just looked confused.

Outside of Michael, Devante was starting to job-hunt in

earnest. He solicited recommendations for job boards from nearly everyone at the Brighton library, and checked them daily despite the email alerts he also set up. There was still very little posted in the field he wanted to go into, but he told himself that when one did appear, he would be ready.

"Why are you so all-fired to get a full-time job right away?" Preeda asked him the next time they were at Mood, the night before Michael's free program, when he admitted to her that he was starting to cast an eye on public and academic libraries as well as grade schools. "It's not like your dad is gonna kick you out. You have time to find the right job."

"Just want to feel like I'm contributing something real," Devante said. "Dad works so hard, I want to keep up my end now that I'm not in school anymore."

It wasn't the whole truth; the whole truth wasn't something that he could tell her, at least not right then. The whole truth was that, at some point between his realization about what he wanted from Michael and seeing Michael interact with Georg, he had more or less convinced himself to make a move on Michael when he got home from Japan. What's more, Devante was, based on Michael's choice of shirt in his gala performance, more or less convinced that he had a decent chance, despite Michael's touchy-feeliness with the German skater.

And if he made a move on Michael, and Michael *did* reciprocate…Well, the sooner Devante didn't live with his father, the better.

He used Mike's password again to watch the free programs at the crack of dawn the next day. Michael and Georg were as handsy as ever, the few times the cameras cut over to them in the run-up to their group's performances, only growing serious at the last minute. Georg did well, pulling an all-over bronze medal, but Michael did better: he touched the ice after one of his jumps, which kept him from first place, but with a silver medal, he and Georg both qualified for the Grand Prix Final in December.

Devante sent out his congratulatory text and promptly fell back asleep for three more hours, waking to a text that just read, *!!!!!!!!!!!!*.

The gala was later that morning, leaving Devante just enough time to eat a Carl-cooked omelet and wash the dishes before darting back upstairs. Carl definitely gave him a weird look as he raced past, but Devante paid it no mind, too focused on whether Michael would be wearing The Shirt again.

He was, to Devante's intense, possibly too intense, relief. He was skating later in the gala than before, having placed higher on the podium this time. Georg skated before him, a pretty pop number that had the crowd on its feet. The third-place ice dancers and ladies skater went next, and then Michael took the ice, sharp face gleaming with glitter, pineapple firmly stretched over his thin, muscular torso.

Thankfully, Michael's performance didn't reduce Devante to helpless sobs again, but then, he could hardly focus on the skate itself, mind racing to interpret every movement, every facial expression, and see if it could possibly be about *him*. Michael seemed to be in a great mood after his Final qualification, face alight and fierce with each step and spin and jump.

The group chat blew up with congratulations for him, once the rest of The Friend Group woke up and watched the recordings. *Thanks!!!!!!* Michael texted back that evening. *We're having a celebratory dinner at mine when I get back, details TBD but I'm cooking, so brace yourselves.*

Dinner at Michael's. Devante was going to have to iron his pineapple shirt.

Chapter 14

THIS SITUATION CALLED for an even more rigorous grooming ritual than originally meeting Michael had, Devante decided.

Michael's dinner party was finally scheduled, after much back and forth, to replace their Saturday night drinks a week after he returned home from Tokyo. Enchiladas were on the menu: Michael's mother's recipe, to be served with red wine and saffron rice.

Devante forced himself to sleep in the day of the big event, rolling over the first two times he woke up and burying his face in his pillow until he fell asleep again. Finally, he rose, accepted an omelet from his father, and washed the dishes, before returning upstairs to try and focus on his job hunt until no earlier than three P.M.

He did actually manage to apply for a job, a reference librarian position at Tufts University that he didn't want but could do if hired, and only then did he allow himself to turn his focus to grooming. He wrangled the ironing board out from its position next to the washer and dryer, and ironed his pineapple shirt, black jeans, and for good measure, his undershirt. He'd gone back and forth on whether to wear the pineapple shirt or not, waffling on if it was too obvious, but in the end had decided to go for it. It had obviously made an impression on Michael, a good one, and if his plan for tonight was to work, he needed to capitalize on that.

Next he showered, shampooing his cornrows through his hairnet before soaping up the rest of his body, from face to feet, and trying to let the hot water relax him even as it rinsed him clean.

As usual, he dried himself off in the bedroom, temporarily dressing in an oversize shirt and sweatpants to pad back into the bathroom once his scalp and hair had mostly dried to oil his head. He shaved, even more careful than usual not to nick himself, and gave his smooth face a firm nod in the mirror.

It was nearly five P.M. by that point, and dinner started promptly at 6:30 P.M. He dressed, fingers surprisingly steady on his shirt buttons, not a hint of shake to them despite the slow pump of nerves throughout his body. He slipped his wallet and his keys into his pocket, along with a tightly-folded satin bonnet he'd bought the day before, and went downstairs.

He'd saved the hardest part of his preparations for last. "I'm headed out," he said to his father, who was, as always, seated in his armchair. "Don't wait up—I might not come home tonight."

Carl looked up at Devante over his glasses, one eyebrow raised almost to his hairline. "No?"

"Yeah, dinner might go late, so I might crash in Brighton," Devante said. He didn't say, "At Charlie's," but he watched his father make the assumption with only a little twinge of guilt.

After a long moment, Carl nodded sharply. "Alright. Be safe."

"Thanks, Dad," Devante said. "See you probably tomorrow." Carl grunted. Devante took his leave.

He made it to Michael's apartment with time to spare, but he wasn't the first one there; Charlie, predictably, was already on Michael's couch when he let Devante into the apartment. "Hey, Dev!" Charlie called, waving. "You look sharp."

"You do," Michael said from just behind Devante's shoulder, making him startle a little. "Very nice."

"Thanks," Devante said, more to Michael than Charlie, but Charlie was already refocused on the cheese platter Michael had placed on the small coffee table.

"Can I help with anything?" Devante asked Michael.

Michael gave him a warm smile. "Would you mind setting the table?"

Devante almost laughed. "I'm good at that."

"Why didn't you let *me* set the table when I asked if there was anything *I* could do?" Devante heard Charlie say, around a mouthful of cracker, as he went into the kitchen for plates. Michael rolled his eyes fondly at Devante, stirring a bubbling pot on the stove.

Devante set the table for six, drawing on every lesson his father had ever given him about arranging a place setting. The table was only just big enough, and in fact Devante recognized two of the chairs clustered around it as having come from Charlie's apartment next door, but the unmatchedness of it all just made the place look homier, cozier.

Natasha, Mike, and Preeda filed in over the course of the next fifteen minutes, joining Charlie and Devante in the living room. "God, that smells amazing," Preeda said, angling her nose toward the kitchen.

"Five minutes!" Michael called back. "Don't fill up on cheese; there's a lot of food in my oven."

"Different parts of the stomach," said Charlie, who had eaten a full two-thirds of the cheese plate. "The cheese section and the Mexican food section are totally separate."

"Sure," Natasha said condescendingly. Charlie threw a cracker at her, which she caught and popped in her mouth smugly.

"Dinner is served," Michael said five minutes later. "There isn't room for a platter on the table, so grab your plates and come serve yourself in the kitchen."

The Friend Group filed first into the dining room and then into the kitchen. Devante took up the rear to let everyone else grab food first. "Wow, that's a lot of food," Mike proclaimed when he took the first place in front of the stove, where a steaming dish of wrapped bundles waited, freshly drenched in the sauce Michael had been stirring when Devante came in.

"I made enough for everyone to have four," Michael said, wringing his hands a little. "I hope that's enough."

"For Mike, it's just enough," Natasha said reassuringly, patting him on the shoulder. "For the rest of us, it's more than plenty."

"I resent that," Mike said, but he did take four bulging enchiladas from the pan before making his way back to the table.

There were still plenty left when Devante got there, but he limited himself to just two, and a heaping spoonful of rice. Too heavy a dinner made him sleepy, and that was the opposite of what he wanted tonight.

"My mother would make us say Grace," Michael said, settling down at the table after serving himself last. "But she's not here, and I'm hungry, so I'll just say thank you all for joining me to celebrate. I'm very glad I moved in next to Charlie and he introduced me to you all."

"To Michael," Natasha said, raising her wine glass. "May he smash the Grand Prix Final to pieces."

"Hear, hear," Devante said. Michael blushed.

They toasted him, drank, and set in. "Fuck," Natasha said feelingly after swallowing her first bite. "I know you said you were cooking, but I didn't know you were *cooking* tonight."

"You like it?" Michael asked a little anxiously. "It's the first time I've made it for people outside my family."

"It's delicious," Mike said around a mouthful. "You're, like, totally wife material."

"Mike," Natasha admonished.

"What? It's a compliment!"

"And I'll take it as such," Michael cut in, when Natasha looked like she wanted to argue. "Thank you, Mike."

"Seriously, though, how are you single again?" Preeda asked. Michael just laughed and didn't answer, although Devante thought, for a heart-stopping moment, that his eyes flicked to him for a moment before turning back to his food.

Not for long, Devante promised himself. *Not for long*.

The food was delicious, and none of them spoke much beyond noises of enjoyment and satisfaction. Natasha and Preeda went back for seconds, and even Devante, wary as he was of tiring himself out, helped himself to another serving of saffron rice.

As they finished eating, conversation sprung up, mostly about the Final. Charlie asked about Michael's competitors, and Michael went into a breakdown of the other five men's singles skaters' strengths and weaknesses, and the changes he was planning to make to his own routines to counter them.

Devante watched Michael more than he listened. Michael was in a slim-fitting green short-sleeve button-down shirt that showed off his toned, muscular arms and made his shoulders look broader than they were. The top button was undone, showing a tempting sliver of collarbone. He talked with his hands, sketching jump entrances and step sequences in the air as he described them; his hair, loose around his shoulders tonight, was slightly wavier and frizzier than normal from the heat of the kitchen while he had cooked.

His sharp, angular face was animated, expression changing constantly as he expounded about figure skating. Devante wanted him more than he'd ever wanted anything in his life.

The conversation went on for a long time, moving from the upcoming Final to Mike's crabs to the petty drama at Charlie's accounting firm. Devante stayed quiet for most of it, just watching his friends and laughing at the right places, and thinking about his plan for the rest of the evening. He was nervous, of course, but it wasn't as bad as he had been expecting. It felt inevitable, like he and Michael had been rocketing toward that night since the moment they met.

Finally, Natasha yawned and said, "I think I'm tapping out."

"Booooo," Michael said instantly, and then laughed. "Okay, okay. I know it's late."

"Yeah, I'm out too," Mike said, putting his hands on the table and pushing himself to his feet. "Gotta sleep off all that good cooking."

Everyone got noisily to their feet, Devante included. "Can I send anyone home with some leftovers?" Michael asked, walking backward into the kitchen. "There's plenty."

"I'll take some," Mike said, following him.

"Me too," Preeda put in.

Michael wound up sending leftovers home with everyone. When he started packaging up a serving for Devante, Devante took it, but said, "I'll stay and help clean up." Michael looked surprised, but thankfully pleased, and nodded.

Finally, the rest of The Friend Group filed out of the door, and Michael and Devante were left in blessed silence. "You wash, I'll dry?" Devante said to Michael.

Michael gave him a smile. "Sounds great."

Michael, shockingly for a Brighton apartment, had a dishwasher, so the plates and cutlery got rinsed and put into it. Michael popped a detergent pod in and started it, and then turned to the pots and pans. He was economical in his washing technique, scrubbing quickly and efficiently. Devante located a dishrag in the drawer Michael pointed him to and dried them as Michael passed them over, replacing them in cupboards where Michael directed him.

"We make a good team," Michael said when it was done, leaning against the counter and drying his hands. He looked at the clock on the wall. "It's late; do you have to be going?"

Here we go. "Actually," Devante said, "I was thinking I could crash here tonight."

"Could you?" Michael asked, thankfully amused rather than offended. "You're welcome to, although I warn you, my couch is too small for even Charlie to sleep on comfortably."

Devante took a step closer, heart pounding. "I was thinking, actually, I could sleep in the bed."

Michael bit his lip. His chest seemed to be rising and falling farther than usual, and he was staring at Devante's face with an almost anticipatory look. "Then where would I sleep?"

"In the bed. With me."

"Really." Michael braced his hands on the counter behind him, flexing his arms. "I should warn you," he said, tipping his head back and smiling lazily. "I only share a bed with people I've kissed."

Devante took another step forward. Adrenaline was humming through his veins. Michael's eyes were darting all over his face, from his eyes to his lips and back again. "Well then," Devante said, voice coming out lower and rumblier than he'd ever heard it before. "Guess you'd better kiss me."

Michael took in a deep breath, like he'd been waiting for something and it had finally come. Devante was close enough now that Michael could reach out and hook his fingers through Devante's belt loops. With a yank, he tugged Devante close, until their hips and chests were pressed together and Devante could feel the heat of him all down his front. "Maybe *you'd* better kiss *me*," he murmured. His eyes half-lidded, he tilted his face up, mouth a bare inch from Devante's, and there he stopped, eyes blinking up at him, waiting.

Devante didn't make him wait long. Without hesitating, without second-guessing himself even for a second, he leaned down and pressed his lips to Michael's.

Chapter 15

MICHAEL TOOK IN another breath, this one sharper, more surprised. Devante was just about to pull back and start apologizing when Michael's hands left Devante's belt loops to cup his hips, grip loose but firm, and his lips parted to slot in with Devante's, a soft, pleased sound leaving his throat.

The kiss lingered for a bit, and when it ended Devante went in for another, and another, and another. Michael's grip on Devante's hips tightened and he kissed back, mouth as eager as Devante's was to keep exploring each other. It was Michael's tongue that first broke the seam of their lips, slipping into Devante's mouth with a tentative touch to his own tongue. Devante took it, groaning softly and returning the caress. He lifted his hand and placed it lightly on Michael's jaw; Michael moaned and tilted his face into Devante's palm, without breaking the kiss.

They kissed for a long time, starting gently and growing firmer and more passionate, until Michael broke away and gasped for air. "Wow," he breathed, staring up at Devante, a delighted little smile on his face that Devante wanted instantly to kiss.

And he could, now, so he did, bending down to learn what that smile tasted like. He used his hand on Michael's cheek to move him, tilt him into a better angle, and when Michael gasped into his mouth he pressed his advantage, deepening the kiss, drawing Michael closer with a hand on his face and an arm slipping around his waist. Michael's hands flew up to clutch at Devante's shoulders and he moaned again, kissing him back just as fervently.

There was heat, now, and hunger. Michael took Devante's lower lip between his teeth, drawing it out; Devante growled and yanked him back in for another proper kiss, teeth almost knocking, tongues sliding together like a pairs skate. Michael's right hand left Devante's shoulders to wrap around the back of his head, careful not to snarl his cornrows, and his legs parted, allowing Devante to slip between them and pin them more firmly to the counter.

"Wait," Michael breathed, breaking away for a moment, "wait, did you mean you wanted to stay the night, or, uh, *stay the night?*"

"The latter," Devante assured him.

"Oh, thank God," and then they were kissing again, clutching each other close and attempting to devour each other by the mouth.

Devante pulled away from Michael's lips and kissed across his cheek to his ear, and then down his neck, Michael obligingly tilting his head back to allow Devante room to roam. Devante got his tongue into the hollow of Michael's throat, and then sent it along that strip of collarbone that had been tormenting him all evening before settling his teeth into the place where Michael's neck met his shoulder and nipping gently.

"Haaaaaa," Michael whined, his hips jerking against Devante's, which was a new and *extremely* delightful development. "I think," he panted, and then had to pause when Devante bent up and kissed him again. "I think," he repeated, eyes closed and breathing hard, "that we should move this to the bedroom."

"Genius," Devante said, "brilliant, yes, bedroom."

It took another minute for them to peel apart, but then Michael took Devante's hand and all but dragged him out of the kitchen and down the hall to his bedroom. There was a brief pause when Devante found it unbearable not to press Michael against the wall next to his door and kiss him breathless again; Michael threw his arms around Devante's neck and melted into it, one leg hitching up to press against the outside of his thigh. "Bedroom," Michael said again after a moment, "we're almost there, I promise."

Devante laughed and let him go, and in a flash the bedroom door was open and Michael was hauling Devante inside.

Devante had never been inside Michael's bedroom before, and the sight was arresting enough to distract him from his goal of reducing Michael to a puddle via kissing. He'd sprung for a queen-sized bed, Devante noted, a green sheet set and comforter, and there were movie posters on his wall—The Birdcage, Imagine Me & You, Big Eden. But then Michael closed the door behind them and was in front of Devante again, and there were much better things to be doing than examining his room.

After another few long moments of thrilling kisses, Michael pulled back, keeping a hand on Devante's jaw. "I should ask first," Michael said, breathing hard. "What exactly do you want to do tonight?"

"I don't know," Devante said, helplessly and honestly. "I've never, you know, slept with a man before, so I'm a little out of my depth. I just know I want you. I want to make you feel good."

Michael's eyes were burning. "That's a great place to start," he said. "I want to make you feel good too, Devante. So let's just go from there and see where it takes us."

"Alright," Devante said, a little breathless.

"To start," Michael said, half his mouth tugging up in a smile, "can I take your shirt off?" Devante nodded so fast he thought his head might fall off his neck. Michael laughed. "Thank you," he said, slipping his hand off Devante's face, down his neck to join the other at Devante's top shirt button.

Michael made quick work of the buttons, and before Devante had time to be nervous Michael was slipping the shirt off his shoulders and letting it drop to the floor behind him. "God, you're so beautiful," Michael said, running his hands down Devante's bare arms and looking him over with what looked like real hunger in his eyes.

"You too," Devante said. His voice was hoarse. "Your shirt too?" Michael nodded, and Devante set his trembling fingers to work.

Michael wasn't wearing an undershirt, Devante soon discovered, and when he let his shirt fall off his arms once Devante had finished with the buttons, there was nothing underneath but gleaming bare torso. "Jesus Christ," Devante said, feeling like he'd been punched at the sight of Michael's smooth, rounded pecs and washboard stomach.

Michael laughed, and Devante learned that his blush went all the way down to his chest. "Professional athlete," he reminded Devante.

"Yeah, but I mean, wow," Devante babbled. "Please say I can touch you."

"I wish you would," Michael said, breathless and earnest. Devante tugged him back into his arms and kissed him again, running his hands down the seemingly endless expanse of smooth, muscled back Michael possessed.

Michael's hands went to the hem of Devante's undershirt and he went stiff; Michael instantly let go, holding his hands up reassuringly before putting them onto Devante's shoulders and pulling him down into another deep, searching kiss.

"Please don't ask me if I'm sure," Devante murmured against Michael's lips.

Michael laughed. "I wasn't going to," he said, voice warm and deep. He licked along Devante's lower lip, slow and achingly hot. "You taste pretty sure to me." Devante had to kiss him again at that, and Michael moaned into his mouth.

"Okay," Michael said, when that kiss finally ended. "Action steps. Please don't take this the wrong way," he went on, a bashful smile on his face, "but I've kind of wanted to go to my knees for you ever since we first met."

There was a ringing in Devante's ears; he shook his head, utterly thunderstruck. "Is there a wrong way to take that?"

"Well, I don't want you to think I've been objectifying you this whole time—"

"Michael." Michael stopped talking. "It's fine," Devante said. "Me too."

"Oh," Michael said, looking relieved. "Then, can I?"

"Please," Devante said, trying and failing not to sound too eager.

Michael grinned and kissed him again. There were fingers fumbling at Devante's jeans button, and then his zipper, and then Michael's hand was in his boxers, long fingers brushing against his cock, which at this point was almost beyond hard. Devante gasped, the feeling better than his own hand had ever been.

Michael laughed against his lips. "Sit down?" he asked, gesturing to the bed.

Feeling a little awkward, Devante shuffled his pants and boxers off, kicking them aside, and sat on the edge of the bed. Michael removed his own jeans and went to his nightstand, returning with a condom. "Me putting it on you is a trick for another time," Michael said, passing it to Devante. "Would you mind?"

Devante didn't have a whole lot of experience putting condoms on himself, but he managed it well enough, with a minimum of fumbling. Unsure of what to do with the wrapper, he handed it to Michael, who tossed it into a trash can at the far side of the bed. Michael came back and knelt between Devante's spread knees on the floor, taking his face in both hands and drawing him into a deep, fervent kiss before he could feel too awkward at his exposed position.

"Tell me to stop if you need to," Michael murmured, pressing their foreheads together. "Even if you just want to. I promise I'll stop."

"Okay," Devante breathed.

Michael kissed him again, and then pulled away and bent down. Devante leaned back, his hands firmly planted on the mattress. Michael set to work, and Devante tipped his head back and groaned, deep from his chest.

Michael's mouth was heat, burning heat, and suction that started off too tight but gentled when Devante hissed in a breath. He seemed to know exactly what he was doing, exactly how to reduce Devante to a groaning, quivering wreck. "Can I touch your hair?" Devante gasped after a few minutes, aching with the need for more contact, more touch.

Michael pulled off long enough to say, "Yes, but don't pull," with a warm, happy smile, and then bent back to his task. Devante cupped a hand gently around the back of Michael's head, worming his fingers in among the strands. They were soft and thick, just as lovely as they looked, and Devante held on for dear life as Michael worked him closer and closer to the edge.

Before too long, Devante was gasping, "Michael, Michael, I'm gonna…" Michael didn't stop moving for a second, just hummed low in his throat and flashed him a quick thumbs-up before returning his hand to its grip on Devante's thigh. It was with a shocked, barked laugh that Devante tumbled over the edge, body arcing forward with the force of it.

Michael stayed exactly where he was until Devante was quivering with overstimulation. Devante had to gently unseat him by his grip on the back of Michael's head. Michael's lips were obscenely swollen and red, and without speaking he came when Devante urged him up, straddling Devante on the bed as Devante licked across those dark, bruised lips and sucked the taste of latex off Michael's tongue.

"Devante," Michael moaned, low and urgent, "Devante." Devante found himself struggling with Michael's briefs, shoving them to mid-thigh as best he could with his eyes closed. He had to break away from the kiss to look down and make sure his hand went where he meant it to go, and in a second he had it wrapped around Michael's cock.

"Oh shit," Michael gasped, falling forward and taking Devante with him. Devante kept his hand on him as he fell back, hitting the mattress with a thump. "Devante, please, please," Michael said between frantic kisses. He pulled Devante's hand off him by the wrist, brought it to his mouth to give a long, wet lick across his palm, and put it back where it had been. "Devante," he whispered.

Devante did the best he could. He'd never touched another man's penis, never even seen one, but he moved his hand along the familiar path. "Tell me how," he murmured into Michael's hair; Michael's face was pressed against Devante's shoulder, his back arched into the air.

"Tighter," Michael hissed, "and a little faster?" Devante obliged, and was rewarded with a chorus of moans and grunts and his own name, said in a voice that grew higher and higher until Michael gasped and shook and finished over Devante's palm and fingers.

Michael bent up and kissed him, breaking away after only a moment to catch his breath. "Wow," Devante said quietly, clutching him close with his free arm.

Michael chuckled, a warm, happy sound. "Wow," he agreed, falling to one side and propping himself up on his elbow. "Is that what you had planned for tonight?" he asked, grinning.

"I didn't really have a plan, past kissing you," Devante admitted. "I barely knew what I wanted after that. This was better than I could have imagined."

Michael kissed him, slow and deep. "I'll say," he murmured. Another kiss and he said, "Come on, let's get cleaned up before we get too sticky."

Devante felt remarkably unself-conscious as they padded, him still bare from the waist down and Michael entirely naked, into the bathroom. Devante washed his hands and disposed of the used condom in the bathroom trash can. Michael located a spare toothbrush and they brushed their teeth side-by-side in Michael's small bathroom, shoulders pressing together, giggling at each other in the mirror.

Once they were cleaned up, Devante went back into the bedroom and located his boxers, pulling them up over his hips. He bent to fish the crumpled bonnet out of his jeans pocket, and rose to see Michael watching him. "You don't actually need that," Michael said with an air of confession.

Devante cocked an eyebrow at him. Michael scrunched up his face, then went to the bottom drawer of his dresser and extracted something which revealed itself to be, when he unfolded it, a satin pillowcase. "Why do you have that?" Devante asked, starting to smile.

"Wishful thinking?" Michael tried, wincing. "Please don't think I'm creepy. I bought it just in case you ever changed your mind about being straight and decided you wanted me back."

Devante laughed. "Come over here," he said. Michael walked toward him with the air of someone expecting a castigation. Devante took the pillowcase, then took Michael's face in his other hand and kissed him. "Thank you," he said softly. "It was very considerate of you." Michael sagged against him. Devante hugged him, kissing the side of his head.

Devante replaced one of the pillowcases with the satin one, and he and Michael snuggled into bed. "Big spoon or little spoon?" Michael asked.

Devante bit his lip, then said tentatively, "Little spoon?"

"You got it." Michael flicked off the light and shuffled closer. Devante turned over and felt Michael press against his back, arm going over his waist. "Good night, Devante," Michael murmured, laying a kiss on the back of Devante's neck.

"Good night, Michael," Devante echoed, closing his eyes. He was asleep in moments.

Chapter 16

DEVANTE KNEW EVEN before he opened his eyes that he'd slept well, and that today was going to be a good day.

He was warm, tucked into an unfamiliar bed, with a heavy weight thrown over his waist that he drowsily realized was Michael's arm. Michael's hand was playing across his torso, tracing shapes in his undershirt or brushing along the back of his hand.

Devante sleepily slipped his hand around Michael's and brought it to his mouth for a kiss, then, with a deep sigh, rolled over to face him. Michael was propped up on one elbow, hair mussed from sleep. For all they'd had sex the night before, mind-blowing sex, the smile he gave Devante was tentative and shy. "Morning," he said, voice a little sleep-rough. "Any regrets?"

"None," Devante said instantly, shaking his head. He took a deep breath. "I'm gay," he said. "I'm gay, and I think I'm in love with you."

Michael was on him almost before he'd finished speaking, grabbing hold of his face and pulling him into a deep kiss that stole Devante's morning breath. He tasted like sleep and toothpaste; Devante chased it all throughout his mouth, the sounds of their kissing filling the still, silent bedroom.

Devante drew Michael down on top of him, until the other man was splayed across his chest, still kissing Devante slowly and languidly, like he could do it all day. Devante could too, and would have, had both their stomachs not given almighty growls, almost in unison.

Michael pulled his mouth free, laughing. "Hungry?" he asked, his eyes sparkling with amusement and what Devante fervently hoped was joy.

"Starving," Devante admitted.

Michael patted his chest before pushing himself to his knees. "Come on, I'll make breakfast. How do you like your eggs?"

"Scrambled, with milk," Devante said, following Michael out of bed. "You?"

"Don't laugh," Michael said warningly. "Over hard, with the yolks broken."

"I'm with you there," Devante assured him. "I never liked a runny yolk."

Michael beamed at him. "There, see," he said. "Another way we're compatible."

Michael went to his dresser and pulled out a soft-looking t-shirt and sweatpants. Devante, for lack of anything else, struggled back into his jeans and button-down. Michael hissed in a breath when he turned from getting dressed and saw Devante shrugging it on. "I'm never going to be able to look at that shirt the same way again," he said.

"I'll have to wear it even more often, then," Devante said. Michael gave him a hungry look and bit his lip, and then went to the bedroom door, pulling it open and beckoning for Devante to follow him.

Michael wasn't stingy with his eggs, cracking three into a bowl and whisking them with a fork while the coffee machine bubbled to life. "Will you make the toast?" he asked Devante, nodding to his fridge. "I only have whole wheat, I'm afraid."

"Whole wheat's fine," Devante said, extracting the bread from the fridge. Michael's toaster was tucked into the back corner of the counter, a luxurious four-piece model. Devante started feeding bread slices into it.

"Butter's in the bell," Michael said, pouring the egg mixture into the saucepan. "Cheese?"

"Yes please." Devante pulled the butter bell closer to himself and opened the dishwasher for a clean butter knife while Michael took the cheese out of his fridge.

They worked together in harmony, Michael scrambling Devante's eggs and then frying his own as Devante buttered four slices of toast. He put two on each plate of eggs and carried them to the table in the dining room, Michael following with two steaming mugs of coffee. Michael sat at the head of the table, Devante next to him, close enough that Michael could hook his foot around Devante's ankle as they ate.

After a few minutes of eating, Devante said, "Out of curiosity, did you just cheat on Georg Hummel with me?"

Michael choked on his eggs, swallowed, and laughed, throwing his head back. There was a mark on his throat, Devante noticed, a faint mouth-shaped bruise that made Devante want to attack him again. "No, no, nothing like that," Michael said, still chuckling to himself. "Georg and I are best friends who also have a no-strings-attached benefits situation, which I will be texting him today and ending. Assuming you want that," he added, suddenly sounding unsure.

"I do," Devante said quickly. "If you do?"

"I do," Michael repeated, just as quickly. He looked down at his eggs, and then back up at Devante. "It's just, every page of the gay handbook says not to get serious with a boy just out of the closet, but every instinct I have is screaming fuck that, I want to be your boyfriend."

"Fuck that," Devante said. "The handbook, I mean. Boyfriend. Yes."

Michael kissed him, the butter from his toast still slick on his lips. Devante licked it off his own when they parted. "Okay," Michael said, grinning. "Boyfriends. I'll text Georg and let him know. He'll be thrilled; he's been telling me to ask you out for months." He took a sip of coffee. "Do you want our friends to know?" he asked, almost casually.

"Yes," Devante said after a moment's thought. "I should…" Michael waited patiently, watching his face as he took another bite of egg on toast. "I should talk to Preeda first," Devante finally finished. "But yes, after that I'll drop it in the group chat, if you're comfortable with it."

"I am," Michael confirmed. Then, a little more hesitantly: "*Did* something ever happen with Preeda?"

Devante sighed. "We had sex, around Easter," he said. "We never spoke of it again."

"That bad, huh?"

Devante wrinkled up his nose. "Neither of us came, we just sort of...stopped, and got dressed again, and I left."

Michael whistled. "It's a wonder she's still so clearly fond of you."

"It wasn't anyone's fault that it was so bad," Devante said. "We were a little drunk, and there was less chemistry than we thought at the time. For obvious reasons," he added, and Michael gave a little acknowledging nod. "But I should tell her first about you, I think."

"I think that's smart, and kind," Michael said. "Two of my favorite things about you." Devante dropped his face into his hands to hide his blush. Michael laughed. "If you're going to be my boyfriend, you're going to get affection, Devante Miller," he said, mock-serious. "You'd better get used to it."

"Oh no," Devante said into his palms, "how will I cope?" He was rewarded with the chiming sound of Michael's giggle.

They finished their meal, and cleaned up, and then Devante said regretfully, "I should go. I have to go home and change before I talk to Preeda."

"It certainly would make a point if you just rocked up in last night's clothes," Michael said. "But I take your point. I'll walk you out."

Michael walked him to the door, and then came a long period where he pressed Devante *to* the door and kissed him stupid, and when he finally pulled away Devante chased him, and there was more kissing. "When can I see you again?" Michael whispered against Devante's mouth before taking his lower lip between his teeth.

Devante laughed. "You'll see me again tomorrow, for lunch," he said, stealing in for a swift kiss of his own. "Unless you're planning on standing me up now that we're officially boyfriends."

"Never," Michael declared. In Devante's mind, that deserved another kiss, and another, and another. Finally, though, Devante thumped his head back against the door. "I really have to go."

"Alright," Michael said, regretful. He stepped back and ostentatiously tucked his hands into his pockets.

"I'm really happy," Devante told him, suddenly struck by the urge to make sure Michael knew.

Michael favored him with a soft, adoring smile. "That makes me really happy to hear, Devante," he said. "I am too."

"Good." Devante took one final look at him, then escaped out the door before he could do something stupid like pick him up and bear him back to the bedroom.

Devante spent the bus ride home in a happy daze, rubbing his finger over his lower lip, bruised and swollen from kissing.

Carl was in when Devante got home, installed in his chair with his papers. "Good night?" he rumbled, looking up when Devante came in.

"The best," Devante said rashly, but Carl didn't ask, just nodded and went back to his newspaper.

Devante went upstairs and changed, whistling to himself. The whistling stopped, however, when he finished dressing and pulled out his phone. He took a moment to steel himself, and then opened his texts with Preeda.

DM: Hey

DM: Something I have to talk to you about. Can I come over?

PC: Sure. Good or bad?

DM: I think it's good

PC: That's good. I'm at home, come on over

"Going out again already?" Carl asked when Devante came back downstairs.

"I'm going to Preeda's," Devante told him. I'm dating a boy, a wonderful boy, and I have to tell her about him, he did not say.

"Give her my best."

"I will."

A bus ride and a short walk put him in front of Preeda's building. He called her on the intercom and she buzzed him in. A short elevator ride later, he was knocking on her door, and she was opening it with a smile and letting him in.

"So," she said, when she was perched on the edge of her bed, patting the spot next to her. "What's up?"

Devante sat down, stared at his hands for a long moment, and then decided just to spit it out. "I spent the night with Michael last night."

She went very still next to him. "In a, you slept on his couch kind of way?"

Devante shook his head. "In a, we had sex and I'm gay kind of way."

"Oh." There was a moment of silence, and then her hand was on his back, warm and comforting. "Dev, look at me." He looked at her, braced for anything, but what he got was a reassuring smile. "Thank you for telling me," she said. "You're right, that is a good thing, as long as you're happy and he's happy."

"I am," Devante said, "and he is, or he told me he is, and he seemed like he meant it."

"Then I'm happy for you both," she said firmly. "I understand why you felt like you had to tell me in person, but I'm honestly, genuinely thrilled for you, if a little surprised."

"I'm sorry it was so bad when we…" He trailed off. "I guess now we know why."

"It wasn't all your fault," she said, and then hesitated. "I guess if you've been brave, I should be too."

"What do you mean?"

She took a deep breath. "I think I was about as genuinely into you, as you were genuinely into me."

"Oh." Devante thought for a second, and then said again, "*Oh*. You mean—"

"I don't have a label or anything," Preeda said. "I'm not there yet. But, yeah, more or less."

"Okay," Devante said. "Thank you for telling me."

She smiled at him. "So, tell me about him," she said, nudging him with her shoulder. "I want deets."

Devante laughed, relief still coursing through his body. "I just…I like him so much, Preeds." She nodded encouragingly at him. "The first time Charlie brought him to drinks, it was like my whole body just said *yes*, and we've just gotten closer since then, and he's funny, and so good-natured, and charming—"

"And hot," Preeda put in.

Devante groaned. "He's *so hot*, Preeds, I can barely stand it sometimes. And then he wore that fucking pineapple t-shirt in his gala and I just knew I had to try."

"So, what, you seduced him last night?"

"Sort of?" Devante said, shrugging. "More like, I told him I wanted to stay over, and he said he only cuddled with people he'd kissed, and it just sort of…went from there."

"Damn," she said, nudging him again. "Our Dev, the playboy."

"Gay playboy," he said. "Gayboy."

She snorted. "Are you going to tell The Friend Group?"

He nodded. "I just wanted to tell you first."

She patted his knee. "Well, you're very sweet, and I appreciate it. And I know the rest of our friends will be happy for you, although you might knock a few of them for six with the announcement." She grinned. "Natasha is going to be *seethingly* jealous."

Devante threw his head back and laughed.

He left Preeda with a hug, a nice warm one that had none of the awkwardness their hugs had had since Easter. On the bus ride home, he opened The Friend Group chat. His messages had a slew of responses in minutes.

DM: I have an announcement to make. Well, two announcements

DM: 1) I am gay 2) Michael and I are dating

DM: Don't tell my dad yet, and don't make it weird, please?

PC: Congrats!!! Happy for you both

CG: What The Fuck

CG: In like the best possible way, I'm totally happy for you, but What The Hell

CG: How long has this been going on????

NM: Extremely happy for you, Dev. If I couldn't snag him I'm glad one of us did

ML: Literally just since last night, Charlie, simmer down

CG: Sorry

ML: And Natasha and Preeda, thank you!!!!!!

CG: I don't mean to be accusatory or whatever

CG: Just surprised

CG: And happy for you!

CG: Totally happy for you

NM: This is possibly the best coming out message I've ever seen, btw, Dev, well done

PC: Very chill and to the point. I approve heartily

CG: Wait

CG: Were you guys having sex on the other side of my wall last night???

DM: Michael, don't answer that

ML: Don't worry, I wasn't going to

CG: I keep sticking my foot in my mouth, so going to shut up with a final: seriously, genuinely happy for you, Dev

CG: I hope Michael knows he's a lucky, lucky guy

ML: I do. Believe me, I do <3

Devante locked his phone when he got off the bus. There were no messages from Mike yet, which worried him slightly, but then, Mike had a shift with his crabs today. But then again, Mike having a shift with his crabs usually meant he was glued to his phone.

It was lunchtime when Devante got home. Still in a good mood despite Mike's conspicuous silence, he volunteered to make grilled cheeses, which Carl accepted with a grunt and a nod. Devante whistled to himself as he fried bacon and broke out the good cheeses, layering them together with turkey and avocados.

Devante called Carl into the kitchen when they were done, doling out two iced teas from the fridge. "You're chipper," Carl observed, plunking down into his seat at the table.

"It's a good day," Devante said.

"Mmm. So I should expect you to be spending more nights out in the future?" Carl asked, casting a gimlet eye at Devante over his glasses.

Devante squirmed a little, but it was true, so he had to say, "Probably."

"Hmm," Carl said, turning his attention to his sandwich. "Hope you bring her home sometime." With that, he picked the sandwich up and bit into it, while Devante tried to do the same over the guilty twist to his stomach.

When he checked his phone after lunch, Mike had finally responded: a single thumbs-up emoji. Devante sighed and sent one back. If it was going to be a problem, it wouldn't be the biggest one he had.

Chapter 17

"DOES THIS COUNT as our first date?" Devante asked over takeout pasta in Michael's apartment, the day after they officially became boyfriends.

Michael shook his head. He was draped over one side of the sofa, arm flung over the back to face Devante full on. Occasionally he nudged Devante's foot with his own. Devante was unreasonably pleased about it. "If we're counting these as dates, we have to go back to the beginning," Michael said. "This would be our couple-dozenth or so date." He had a Styrofoam container of chicken and salad in his lap, which he was attempting to cut up with the cheap plastic knife the restaurant had provided. Devante was enjoying laughing at him.

"Hmm," Devante said, loading up a forkful of pasta Alfredo. "I like the idea of us having been on dozens of dates already," he said, and then took the bite. When he'd swallowed, he went on, "But I also like the idea of us going on a first date. An official one."

"I agree," Michael declared. "I'm going to go get real silverware, one second." He put the Styrofoam container on the coffee table, levered himself to his feet, then took Devante's face between his hands and kissed him, quick and sweet. "I'll miss you," he murmured. Devante rolled his eyes, fighting the fond grin that was, despite his efforts, spreading across his face.

Michael kissed Devante again when he came back, tasting like the spice mix on the chicken and vinaigrette dressing. He settled back into his spot on the sofa, metal knife and fork in hand, and picked up his food again. "So, a real date," he said, sawing off a piece of chicken. "Meal or activity?"

"If I say activity, are you going to make me go skating again?" Devante asked suspiciously.

Michael laughed. "No, not if you really don't want to," he said. "Although I had a great time when we did, and I suspect you did too."

"Hmm," Devante said, sounding far too much like his father for his own comfort. "Let's say meal."

"Alright," Michael agreed easily. "There's a restaurant I've been meaning to try in Allston. Russian food."

"I've never had Russian food," Devante said. "Let's do it."

"Let's do it!" Michael cheered. He fished his phone out of his pocket to check his calendar. "How does Thursday evening work for you?"

"Thursday evening words perfectly," Devante said. He speared a chunk of broccoli on his fork, then said, nervous, "I don't mean to invite myself over, but I *do* have a library shift a block away from here Friday morning…"

"Then you should spend the night," Michael said instantly.

They grinned at each other. "Great," Devante said.

"Great," Michael echoed, still grinning.

Devante took a few more bites of his lunch, but his appetite for food was quickly waning. Michael seemed to agree; when Devante put his food on the table, Michael did too, and reached for him. They met in the middle, Michael's hands on Devante's face and Devante's on Michael's waist, the kiss starting as smoothly as though the last one had never stopped.

Michael tipped himself backward, pulling Devante with him by the mouth and face. It was difficult to be aware of where his arms and legs were when Michael was kissing him, but he did his best, trying to wedge his knee between Michael's leg and the back of the couch, although the couch wasn't really big enough for that. "Devante," Michael whined, tugging on his shoulders. "Come *here*."

"I don't want to crush you," Devante said.

Michael kissed him again, arms stealing down to wrap around his waist and yank Devante closer to him. "But what if I ask," he breathed, "very, very nicely?"

"Oh." Devante felt punch-drunk, out of his mind on the feeling of Michael's body pressed all along his, *under* his. "In that case…" He lowered himself down, inch by careful inch, until his nearly his full weight was pinning Michael down.

Michael moaned and took his mouth again, arms flinging about his neck. Devante lost himself in the sweet heat of Michael's mouth, the way Michael's body pulsed and writhed against his own. He got his mouth onto Michael's neck again and spent a long time mapping it, teeth and tongue plotting out the sensitive places, the spots where his pulse beat just below his skin. Under him, Michael moaned softly and tilted his head to give him space.

The heat advanced by degrees: Michael hooked one leg around Devante's hip, grinding him closer, so Devante slipped first two fingers, and then, encouraged by Michael's noise of pleasure, his whole hand beneath Michael's shirt, caressing the hot skin of his waist. Michael's kisses grew sharper, more urgent, so Devante slipped his hand slowly up Michael's chest, stopping when he met a nipple to run his fingers around it until it pebbled and stood erect.

"Here, lean up," Michael murmured. Devante leaned back and Michael took hold of the neck of his shirt and pulled it off, tossing it away somewhere, anywhere, Devante didn't care where it went as long as it was no longer covering the soft, cut dips and planes of Michael's chest.

"Yours too?" Michael asked softly. Devante nodded, starting on his top buttons. Michael started at the bottom, and they met in the middle, fingers tangling for a second before Devante wrestled the shirt off his shoulders and away. "Undershirt on?" Michael confirmed. Devante nodded, flushing hot. "It's okay," Michael assured him, "it's okay, come back here."

The kissing was even better without their shirts, even with

Devante's undershirt still on. He could feel the heat of Michael's hands on his back so much better through just the thin cotton, could feel Michael's nipples catch on the fabric. His own hands skimmed up Michael's sides and down his stomach as their kisses grew hot and sloppy.

Devante only realized they had been grinding their hips together when Michael broke away from his mouth to gasp, "Shit, Devante, please, I need…"

"What do you need?" Devante murmured against his chin.

Michael laughed, a breathless, giggling sound that instantly became the center of Devante's existence. "I need to either slow down or, uh, keep going," he said. His chest was heaving, his mouth red and slick. Devante had raised another mark on his neck, this one higher and a little darker, and the sight of it made Devante hungry.

Devante knelt up as best he could on the narrow cushions. He put his fingers to Michael's jeans button and, at Michael's frantic nod, undid it. Michael's hands were on his own jeans a heartbeat later, and then, after a moment of wrestling denim, Devante had Michael's cock in his hand, and was gasping into Michael's neck as his fingers closed around Devante's in turn.

It was dry, and the angles were awkward, but it was still the best thing Devante had ever felt. "Your couch is *not* big enough for his," he laughed into Michael's cheek—Devante had one foot on the floor, body half-off the couch to give them room to work their wrists.

Michael's eyes were closed, one hand on the back of Devante's head and the other working in the gap in his jeans. "Reason number one to buy a new couch," he gasped, panting. "To have better sex with my hot boyfriend on it." Devante nipped at his jaw and he swore. "Please, please, a little faster, Devante, it's so good, I'm so close…" Devante sped up his hand, sucking at the join of Michael's jaw and neck, and with a shocked, wrangled cry, Michael came, jerking against Devante's palm and spilling heat between them.

He never let up on the rhythm of his own hand, even through his aftershocks. As soon as he could, he tugged Devante up to kiss his mouth, tongue hot and slick between Devante's lips, and it was only a few moments before Devante followed him over the edge.

They clutched at each other with their clean hands, Devante's face tucked into Michael's neck as they caught their breath. "We are," Michael said finally, and Devante could hear the smile in his voice, "really good at that."

Devante smiled and pulled his face free to kiss him. "We are," he agreed. "But now I'm really uncomfortable."

Michael cackled, wild and free, and Devante's heart swelled in his chest. "Alright, up," he said, patting Devante on the shoulder. Devante levered himself to his feet and held out his clean hand for Michael to follow.

After they'd washed their hands in the kitchen sink, and made out for a good long while against the kitchen counter, Michael slung his arms around Devante's waist and said, "I have a very serious question for you."

"Alright," Devante said, grinning down at him. "Hit me."

"How do you feel," Michael asked solemnly, "about pet names?"

Devante grinned wider, amusement flaring in his chest. "I've never used pet names before," he admitted.

"Because I kind of love them," Michael went on. "And if you're amenable, I'd like to suggest a trial period."

Devante carded his fingers through the hair at Michael's temple, completely unable to stop himself smiling like a crazy person. "Alright," he said. "I'm *amenable* to a trial period. Did you have any in mind?"

"As a matter of fact, I did," Michael said. "I think I would like for you to call me *baby*."

"Baby," Devante murmured, earning himself a sweet, slow kiss. "I could do that."

"And what about you?" Michael asked. His fingers were toying with the belt loop at the very back of Devante's jeans.

"Which pet name would you like to trial?"

Devante made a face. There *was* one that had immediately popped into mind, but the thought of sharing it…"I don't know." Michael just blinked up at him, eyes wide and innocently curious. They made Devante want to be brave. "Maybe *sweetheart*?"

"Sweetheart," Michael purred, and something in Devante's chest loosened up. Trusting him had been the right choice. "I like that. You have a very sweet heart."

"Thank you," Devante managed, completely tongue-tied. "I like yours too." Michael laughed, and Devante un-tangled his tongue by putting it into Michael's mouth instead of trying to talk more. Michael, to judge by the way he sighed and tightened his arms around Devante, approved.

Devante ran into Charlie on his way out of Michael's apartment a few hours later. "Hey, man," Charlie said, holding out his hand for one of those bro-high five-slash-handshakes he loved. "Hey, I guess I'll be seeing you around a lot more, huh?"

"Guess so," Devante said.

"Sweet." Charlie grinned. "Could always use more Dev in my life."

"You're sweet," Devante said, blushing a little.

Charlie just laughed. "I won't keep you. Give my best to Carl, alright?"

"Oh, hey," Devante said, remembering something. "If you run into my dad and he mentions all the nights I've been spending out of the house in Brighton—"

"Gotcha," Charlie said, winking and making a finger gun with his hand. "Crashing at my place. No prob."

"Thanks, Charlie," Devante said gratefully. "I hate to make you lie to him…"

Charlie shook his head. "You do what you gotta do around the closet, man. Straight as an arrow myself, but I get it."

"Right," Devante said. "Can I hug you?"

"Bring it in," Charlie said instantly, opening his arms. He

was shorter than Devante, less built than Mike, but his hugs were good, firm and solid. "Have a good rest of your day, Dev," he said, patting him on the back and letting go.

"You too, Charlie."

Devante checked his phone on the bus back to Roxbury. One text from his dad: *Devante, you coming home tonight? Just checking. If you are, dinner's in two hours. Love, your dad.* Devante snorted, heart swelling with fondness, and replied, *On my way back now.*

He also found an email, from the reference librarian job he'd applied to a week ago on a whim: a request for an interview, that week if possible, with several potential time slots. He sat up in his seat, startling the person next to him.

I'd love to come in for an interview, he wrote, having to fix several typos from the bouncing of the bus. Thursday morning would be best for me, although I can also do Wednesday afternoon if Thursday is no longer available. Thank you, and looking forward to meeting you, Devante Miller.

Thursday would give him enough time to do his research and interview prep—and he'd have the prospect of his first official date with Michael that evening to look forward to if it went badly. *Got a bite on the job hunt,* he texted Michael. *Interview this week.*

!!!!!!!!! came the instant reply. *What's the job?????*

Reference librarian at Tufts, he sent back.

Congrats!!!!! But I thought you wanted a grade school????

Ideally, yes. But I might have to take what I can get.

Well, I support you either way. I bet you'll crush it!!!!! Let me know if I can help at all???? <3 <3 <3

Devante replied that he would, then realized how far the bus had gone along its route and quickly pulled the cord.

Carl was in the kitchen when Devante got home, poking at something in the slow cooker. "Dinner in an hour, hour and a half tops," he called into the living room as Devante closed the door behind him and toed off his shoes.

"Thanks, Dad," Devante said, padding into the kitchen for an iced tea. "Smells amazing."

"Thanks," Carl huffed. "Good day?"

"Great day," Devante confirmed. "Got a request for an interview for a job."

"Hey now," Carl said, voice as close to excited as it ever got, which was slightly less gruff than normal. "That's something."

"I don't know if it's the job I want, but it's something," Devante agreed.

"No rush, kid," Carl said. "I'm not throwing you out anytime soon. I want you in the right job, not the first job."

Devante hugged him around the shoulders, earning himself a reluctant grumble. "Thanks, Dad. I appreciate it."

"Yeah, yeah." Devante just grinned and hugged him again.

Chapter 18

DEVANTE DRESSED FOR his interview on Thursday morning with the same care he had for his seduction of the man who was now his boyfriend.

Library job interviews didn't require suits for women, but the general advice he'd gotten in library school was to stick to suits if you were a man, so he pulled out his dusty undergrad baccalaureate suit and got it dry-cleaned on Wednesday. He washed his hair, shaved, and ironed his white button-down. He even shined his shoes, borrowing his father's shoe polish and brush. He went back and forth on whether to borrow one of his father's ties as well, but in the end decided to show a bit of personality in his look, opting for the one with a subtle pattern of tacos.

He opted for a cab to Tufts' campus, not wanting to rumple himself on the bus or train, calling his Lyft with plenty of time to spare. He had a phone full of encouraging texts from Michael and The Friend Group, which he reviewed in alternation with his review notes on Tufts' mission statement and the library's collecting areas.

He was ready.

Devante took the walk from where the Lyft dropped him off to the library to be grateful that he was interviewing in the fall-almost-winter, and not the heat of summer. It meant he was still crisp and clean when he got to Tisch Library, instead of a melting sweaty mess.

He'd expected to have to go to the circulation desk to check in for his interview, but there was someone waiting just inside the door, who made eye contact as soon as he got inside. "From the suit, I'm guessing you're Devante?" she asked.

"Guilty," he said, putting on his best smile.

"Great," she said, holding out her hand. "I'm Ronnie, we talked over email. Nice to meet you."

He shook it. "Nice to meet you too."

"If you'll follow me, you'll be meeting with our search committee, a small group of people who would be your peers, and our library director," she said. "It's a long day, so if you need a break at any point, for the bathroom or some water or just to stop talking for a few minutes, just say, okay?"

"Can do," Devante told her, resolving inwardly that he never would.

"Great." She gave him a big smile. "Let's get started."

Afterward, he wouldn't remember much of the interview. In between undergrad and grad school, he'd held a job that he'd had to interview for, a mindless data entry grunt position, very different from library work, but he found he still had many of the skills he'd needed then. The search committee had all been very friendly, and Devante could be charming when he needed to be, so although he stumbled a bit on the questions about why he wanted to break into reference librarianship—"I don't" not being a suitable response—overall, he thought it went well.

He remembered a bit more of the meeting with the library director, if only because they vaguely intimidated him, standing a full three inches taller than his own six foot two, broad-shouldered, with a handshake to match. But then they smiled at him and the fear broke a little, and he was able to talk about his experience in library school and how his time with the Boston Public Library system would help him in this job.

He emerged from the library three and a half hours after he went in, sweating slightly and hand still aching from the director's parting handshake. *Done*, he texted The Friend Group. *I think it went well?* He got back a bunch of congratulatory texts, Michael's *Great job, sweetheart!!!!* taking his primary focus.

In the Lyft back home, Devante could barely keep his eyes open. There were a good six hours before his date with Michael that evening; a nap was definitely called for after the morning's exertions.

At Michael's request, he called him as soon as he got home. Carl was at work, so Devante had the house to himself and didn't have to worry about anyone hearing his opening of, "Hey, baby," when Michael picked up.

"Mmm, I still love the sound of that," Michael said happily. "Pet names were a good choice. The interview went well?"

"I think so," Devante said, shrugging out of his suit jacket and hanging it up. Awkwardly pinning the phone between his shoulder and ear, he started work on his shirt buttons. "The director was even taller than me."

"A giant!" Michael proclaimed. Devante laughed. "Well, I know you're ambivalent about this job, so I hesitate to say I hope you get it, but I hope they at least saw the value they'd be getting in you."

"Thanks, baby." Devante stripped out of his shirt and hung it up next to his jacket. "You have training this afternoon, right?"

"I have to leave in fifteen minutes," Michael confirmed. "Sara's not letting any slack in the line this close to the Final."

"Are you nervous?" Devante stepped out of his suit pants; they went on the pants hanger next to his shirt and jacket.

"Yes," Michael said, laughing at his own bluntness. "It's my first time in the Final, and I'm older than most first-timers. But Sara thinks I have a good shot at medaling, although I don't have enough quads for a shot at the topmost spots."

"Older and more mature, and stronger," Devante said. "I saw some of the other people who qualified; they look like they'd break under a strong wind. Except Georg," he added. "He's appropriately sturdy."

Michael snickered. "I'll tell him you said so, he'll be delighted," he said. Then, a bit more seriously, he said, "I've been meaning to talk to you about Georg."

"Go ahead." Devante pulled a soft pair of sweatpants on and sat on the edge of his bed. "I'm listening."

"So, as soon as you left on Sunday, I called him and told him about us," Michael said. "He was thrilled, I told you he would be, and our friends-with-benefits stuff is totally over, no concerns there. But our friendship might not look very different on-screen to how it was at the NHK."

"How do you mean?"

Michael sighed. "We were only sleeping together for about a year, but we've been friends for close to a decade, and we've always been touchy-feely. It's honestly pretty much instinct at this point. I talked to him and we agreed to try and keep our hands to ourselves, so to speak, but—"

"Don't worry about it," Devante interrupted him, surprising himself. As he thought about it, though, he agreed with his instinctual response. The jealousy he'd felt watching Michael and Georg interact on-screen felt like a distant dream when he cast his mind back, compared with the way Michael looked at him now that they were together. "I trust you."

"Are you sure?" Michael asked plaintively. "We can try, at least."

Devante shook his head, even though Michael couldn't see him. "I don't want to get in the way of your friendships, Michael. It's fine, I promise."

"Promise you'll tell me if it's not," Michael said. "The last thing I want is to make you uncomfortable or unhappy."

"I promise," Devante said. "Tell you what, we'll compromise. You and Georg act normally at the Final, and I'll see if it bothers me. But I really don't think it will."

"Okay," Michael said. "I like that better, a trial period."

"Then that's what we'll do," Devante told him.

"Great." Michael sounded relieved. "I—you're great, Devante."

Devante smiled to himself, heart fluttering. "You're great too, Michael."

"I have to run to practice," Michael said, voice still warm and affectionate. "How will you spend your afternoon?"

"Asleep," Devante proclaimed. "That interview took it out of me."

"Good," Michael purred. "I want you well-rested for tonight." Devante's whole body flushed hot, and maybe Michael could hear it, because he laughed, sounding delighted. "Sleep well, boyfriend. I'll see you this evening."

"Bye, boyfriend." Michael laughed again and hung up. Devante crawled under the covers, set an alarm for four hours just to be safe, and was asleep in moments.

It turned out to be a good thing he'd set the alarm, because he woke up to it, a little groggy and reacting to some *very* interesting dreams. *Maybe I didn't sleep as well as I thought last night*, he thought, rubbing his face with one hand and throwing the covers back with the other. He looked down at his lap, sighed, and firmly put *that* thought away for later that night.

He met Michael at Cafe St. Petersburg in Allston exactly two hours later, dressed in a sweater that always made him feel snuggly and his usual dark jeans. Michael was back in his green short-sleeved button-down and slim-fitting khakis. They were both wildly overdressed for the restaurant, but that just made Devante feel warmer and happier, that they'd both cared enough about their first date to make an effort. From the amused, adoring look in Michael's eyes, he agreed.

They ordered, borscht for Michael and the chicken Kiev for Devante, and sat down at a table by the window. "How was your nap?" Michael asked, tucking his foot around Devante's ankle under the table.

"Apparently much needed," Devante answered. "Slept for four hours."

Michael's eyes twinkled. "Guess I'll have to wear you out again before bedtime."

One side effect of dating Michael, Devante was coming to realize: all the blood in his body constantly rushing between his face and other, lower areas. "Guess you'll have to try," he said back. Michael winked at him.

Devante asked after Rosa, and Michael lit up. "She's great," he said. "Her senior year's going well, she's been on four college visits already, and she texted me last week that she's finally giving Tolkien a try."

"What did she start with?" Devante asked. "*The Hobbit* or *The Lord of the Rings*?"

"*Lord of the Rings*," Michael said. "So far she loves Aragorn."

"Who doesn't love Aragorn?"

"No one who's seen the movies," Michael said. Devante had to agree.

Their food came, and turned out to be extremely delicious. In between bites, they discovered that they disagreed about Eowyn's ending in the final book, and Devante spent the whole meal trying to convince Michael that Tolkien hadn't written it to be anti-feminist, but anti-war. "I get that," Michael said as they left the tip on the table and wandered out into the cool night air. "I'm just saying, when it's your only major female character, it's not a good look."

"Fair," Devante conceded.

"What *I* always wanted," Michael went on, "was more Galadriel. I bet she was up to some killer shit in Lothlorien that we just didn't get to see." Casually he pulled his hand out of his pocket and let it dangle between them.

"Oh, she was," Devante said, reaching out just as casually and slipping his fingers through Michael's. "And now I have to convince you to read *The Silmarillion*, because odds are she killed some elves herself."

Michael's happy smile at Devante taking his hand dissolved into a look of interest. "Oh? I haven't gotten to that part yet."

"You started it?"

Michael winked at him. "Well, my boyfriend really likes it, you see."

Devante felt a grin bubble over his face. "He sounds like a man of taste."

"Oh, I don't know," Michael said, mock-solemn. "He likes

me, after all."

"Definitely a man of taste, then," Devante said. Michael squeezed his hand and smiled at him.

The mood between them, light and affectionate, shifted almost as soon as they were in the front door of Michael's building. With walls and a ceiling around them, suddenly Michael's hand in his was hot, electric, a current of desire coursing back and forth between them. They raced up the stairs to Michael's apartment, and were on each other the moment the door was closed.

"God," Michael gasped as Devante kissed down his neck, putting both hands on Devante's ass to haul him closer until they both stumbled into the nearest wall. "I want you so much, like, all the time, it's *insane*."

"Same," Devante breathed, slipping his mouth over his jaw to catch his mouth. Michael parted instantly, moaning low and hungry from the depths of his throat, hands squeezing where they rested on his backside. "But then," Devante said, pulling back and pressing their foreheads together, a wicked vein of humor rushing through him, "people who read *The Silmarillion* are hot."

Michael cackled, throwing his head back, and pulled his hands from Devante's rear end to grab hold of Devante's arm and tug, slipping out from under him to pull him down the hallway. "Bed," he said. Devante, of course, followed.

They undressed each other between kisses, Michael stripped bare and Devante down to his undershirt and nothing else. "I," Michael said, towing Devante back toward the bed by his face, "want to blow you again."

Devante licked his lips. "Is it boring if I also want to do that to you?" he asked, as he ran one hand down Michael's chest to rest on his hip.

Michael shuddered under his touch. "Not boring," he babbled, "not boring, are you sure?" Devante nodded, and Michael kissed him, tongue sweeping into his mouth to rub against his own for a heart-stopping, blood-pounding moment.

"Do you mind going first?" Michael asked. "Only if I try to blow you after hearing that, I might go off without a touch and rob you of your chance."

Devante shook his head. Michael kissed him again and clambered over the bed to the nightstand, extracting two condoms from the drawer. Devante noticed the yellow copy of *The Silmarillion* on top and, as if giving truth to his joke, it was his turn to shudder with arousal.

He liked the act, he found; not as much as Michael evidently did when it was his turn, but enough to want to do it again—he liked knowing how much Michael enjoyed what he was doing, feeling the proof of it on his tongue, and in the way Michael's hands scrabbled at his shoulder and fisted into the bedsheets as Devante worked.

Even better was the way Michael barely took a moment to catch his breath before diving onto Devante in turn, and the blissed-out happy smile on his face when he was done reducing Devante to a wrung-out dishcloth of pleasure and crawled back up the bed to drape himself over Devante's chest and kiss him, both their mouths still tasting of latex.

"One day," Devante murmured, already halfway toward sleep, "I'm gonna spend two hours on your thighs." Michael had lovely thighs, thick and muscular, and Devante had barely spent any time with them so far. It was a crime of missed opportunity.

"Mhm," Michael hummed drowsily, tracing figures on Devante's undershirt, his head pillowed on Devante's shoulder. "Only if I can spend two hours with *yours*."

"Deal," Devante said. "Although I'm not sure why you'd want to."

He heard Michael mumble something about, "crush my head like a watermelon," before Michael evidently dropped into unconsciousness. Devante tried to keep his chuckles to a minimum so as not to disturb him, and closed his eyes to follow him down.

Chapter 19

DEVANTE HAD HAD a boyfriend for less than two weeks when said boyfriend kissed him goodbye and got in a cab for the airport, to fly to Windsor, Canada, for the Grand Prix of Figure Skating Final.

The Friend Group gathered at Charlie's to watch this time, Mike begging off hosting due to a busy crabs schedule and therefore no time to clean his apartment. Charlie didn't have cable, but he did have a TV, and he did something clever with a bunch of cables and a set of Bluetooth speakers to get the NBC coverage to play on the bigger screen. Preeda provided the drinks, four sizable bottles of red wine, and Natasha brought four boxes of microwave popcorn.

"You ready to see your man, Dev?" Charlie asked, nudging him with his shoulder.

"Always," Devante said distractedly, not looking up from where he was typing out a cover letter draft into the Notes app on his phone. With a few more words, he finished the draft and locked his phone. "Is the microwave free?"

His popcorn popped, and some extra butter melted to drizzle over the top, Devante retook his place on one of Charlie's two couches and pulled out his phone again, this time to take a group selfie. "Everyone smile," he said, angling the phone out to catch all their faces. Photo taken, he sent it to Michael. *Good luck, baby*, read the caption.

My favorite face, and some other good ones too <3 was the reply. Devante smiled at his phone and put it away.

There were six men's singles skaters total in the Final. Georg was skating fifth, Michael fourth, based on how well they'd done in the rest of the Series compared to the other finalists. The sixth-place skater went, unremarkable to Devante's eyes, and then it was Georg's turn.

"Nat, your pretty boy's up," Charlie called down the hall to where Natasha was in the bathroom. She washed her hands in a hurry and came running back to jump on the second sofa next to Mike.

Georg mostly did well, one nasty fall on a quadruple Salchow aside. "That's gonna cost him," Nat said sagely, mouth full of popcorn, and she was right; his score came in just under the other skater. The camera cut to Michael, who wrinkled his nose at his friend's score, said something to his coach, and then took the ice.

"Time to turn down the volume," Charlie said, reaching for the remote.

"No, don't," Devante said, holding his hand out. "I kind of want to hear it this time." Michael had played him videos from his last training session, and even he could see the difference between them and how he had skated in the Series. He wanted to hear if the commentators noticed it too.

If anything, the differences were even more pronounced in Michael's performance today; his movements were sharper, his seduction targeted instead of wide-ranging; Devante could see that Michael was thinking of him and only him with every minute movement of his face, although it could just have been wishful thinking on his part. But then Charlie jostled his shoulder, crowing. "Your boy's *hot*, Dev, look at him go!"

Michael finished with a crisp slide into his ending pose, sweat gleaming on his temples and in the hollow of his neck. "Definitely a change in Lopez's skating this time around," the commentator said. "We'll see if the judges like it."

"Ugh," Preeda said, throwing a piece of popcorn at the screen. "He was *better*, admit it, you bigots."

The judges, thankfully, *did* like it; Michael's score was significantly higher than the last two had been, and if Devante remembered correctly, a full five points higher than it had been in Japan. "That's more like it," Natasha said grumpily.

Michael was sitting in first place after his scores were revealed, and he stayed there up until the very last skater, Anton Tsarkov, who knocked him down to second. Natasha started talking as soon as Tsarkov got his scores. "It'll be tough," she said, "but he's got a good shot at third place overall."

"Not silver or gold?" Preeda asked through a mouthful of popcorn.

Natasha shook her head. "Tsarkov's free program is *good*, as is Weldon's. They're both one quad up on Michael, too, which isn't going to help him any. Assuming no one fucks up tomorrow, Michael's best shot is a bronze."

"Assuming no one fucks up," Charlie said. Natasha acknowledged his point with a nod of her head.

"Hey, Dev," Mike said, loud and sudden, looking up from his phone. "Have you checked Instagram lately?"

"No, why?" Devante pulled out his phone.

"Your boy is, like, all over Hummel," Mike said.

Devante pulled up Instagram and checked Michael's Story: a selfie of him with his head resting on Georg's shoulder, *Reunited!!!!!* as the caption; a blurry shot of Georg on the ice, captioned *Good luck bestie!!!!!!*; a video taken by someone else of Georg and Michael playing some sort of clapping game backstage after their performances, that ended with Georg seizing Michael's hands entirely and both of them dissolving into laughter.

"I mean, that's fucked up, right?" Mike asked. "He shouldn't be doing that shit, not now that he's with you."

"Eh," Devante said, shrugging. "We talked about it before he left. I don't mind; it doesn't bother me." It didn't, truly; seeing Michael and Georg together, all he felt was happiness that Michael could spend time with his friend again. No jealousy at all, as he'd predicted.

"It doesn't bother you to have your boyfriend all over some other dude?" Mike asked disbelievingly. "Some other *hot* dude?"

"No," Devante said, bristling. "Michael promised me that part of their friendship was over, and I trust him."

Natasha shoved her foot into Mike's thigh. "Way to imply our Devante isn't hot enough for Michael, dude."

"I didn't mean *that*," Mike objected. "Obviously Dev is fine-looking—"

"*Fine*-looking?" Preeda hooted. "Keep digging, man."

"Or stop," Devante said, stung. "You can stop talking anytime you want, Mike."

"No, look, come on, Dev," Mike said, leaning forward. "Don't be mad, okay? I'm not saying anything about how *you* look, I'm saying Hummel looks like he was made in a factory, and if it were my girlfriend, I'd object to her being so close to someone that…symmetrical."

"So far you've said that my boyfriend is clearly cheating on me because I'm not hot enough for him," Devante said. Anger, the sort he rarely felt, was lurking between his temples and under his stomach, and he didn't like the feeling. "Maybe stop before you say anything else."

"Are you mad at me?" Mike asked plaintively. "Don't be mad, Dev, I didn't mean it like that. I'm sorry, okay?"

"Okay," Dev said. "Whatever." He stood up and brushed his jeans off. "I'm gonna head out, Michael's gonna call me any minute. Thanks for hosting, Charlie. I'll see you all tomorrow."

"Dev," Mike said, but he was drowned out by Natasha, Preeda, and Charlie chorusing their goodbyes to Devante. Devante put his bowl of popcorn on the table and left.

The cold December air on his face dissipated some of his anger a bit, cooling what remained into a bitter irritation. How *dare* Mike? It was Devante's call whether he was jealous or not, and he wasn't.

A text from Mike lit up his phone. Devante ignored it in favor of answering the call that came in a moment later. "Hey, baby," he said, putting the phone to his ear.

"Hey, sweetheart," Michael said. "You sound irritated,

what's up?"

"Nothing," Devante said, sighing. "Just Mike trying to start some shit about you and Georg."

"Oh no," Michael said, sounding worried. "What happened?"

"Just Mike being a jerk," Devante told him, trying to sound reassuring. "He told me Georg was too hot for you to be friends with, and that he didn't believe I wasn't jealous."

Michael sighed, the sound tinny over the phone. "I was afraid of that," he said. "I'll talk to Georg, we'll tone it down—"

"No," Devante said firmly. "Mike's full of crap. I *wasn't* jealous. I want you to have the sort of friendships that make you happy, Michael. I don't want you toning yourself down on my behalf."

"And I don't want you hassled by our friends," Michael said.

"I won't be, not after today," Devante said. "The others kind of tore him apart anyway, and if he tries it again I'll, I don't know, shout at him or something until he stops."

That got a small laugh out of Michael. "I'd like to see what you shouting at someone looks like. I don't think I've ever even seen you angry."

"I was angry just now," Devante admitted. "But it's fine. I'll make him apologize tomorrow, and it'll blow over. I promise."

"Okay."

Michael still sounded uncertain. Devante said, "But we should be talking about you, Mr. Small Silver. Well done! You skated amazingly."

"Thanks," Michael said, thankfully shifting toward sounding pleased. "Sara's really proud of me; she said I hit a new level today."

"You did," Devante said. "Even those horrible commentators couldn't think of anything negative to say about you. They sounded pissed off about it, too."

Michael laughed. "Hey, pissing off the NBC commentators is a win in my book." Devante chuckled. "Oh, hey," Michael went on. "Did you want to meet Georg tomorrow?"

Instant nerves filled Devante's stomach. "Over FaceTime?"

"Yeah! He wants to say hi to the man I've been talking about for six solid months. I thought I could call you before you leave for Charlie's. Just for five minutes."

Michael sounded so earnest and eager, Devante couldn't stay nervous. "Sure," he said. "I'd love to meet him."

"Thank you," Michael said sincerely. "It means a lot."

"Of course." Devante turned the corner and saw his bus stop. "I'm about to get on my bus, baby, I've gotta go. You did amazingly well today. I'm really proud of you."

Devante could practically hear Michael's blush. "Thank you, Devante," he said. "I'll see you tomorrow?"

"See you."

Michael texted Devante later that night. Even if Devante hadn't been there when Michael packed for the Final, he would have been able to tell what book he brought from the text's contents.

ML: So Finrod/Maedhros, am I right?????

DM: You mean Fingon?

ML: Fuck, these NAMES

ML: Yes. Fingon. That rescue from Morgoth's place was super romantic

ML: Would you sing a duet with me and then cut my hand off above the wrist to save my life?

DM: Without hesitation, baby

ML: See, that's love!!!! That's romance!!!!!

DM: It gets better

DM: Maedhros is a redhead

ML: OH HO HO

ML: I love it

DM: Finrod's boyfriend's name is Turgon

ML: I would have read this a lot sooner if anyone had told me how gay it was

Georg, Devante learned within seconds of the FaceTime call connecting, was the *perfect* best friend for Michael, and by that, Devante meant, "borderline hyperactive and extremely cheerful." "Hi!!!" Georg chirped, as soon as Devante could see his face. He could almost see the multiple exclamation points after the word. "It's nice to finally meet you, Devante!"

"It's nice to meet you too, Georg," Devante said, not trying to fight the instinctive smile that spread across his face. "I've heard so much about you from Michael."

"Oh, me too," Georg said, waggling his eyebrows. "He hasn't shut up about you since May."

"Hey!" Devante heard Michael object from offscreen. "I didn't set this up for you to *slander* me, Georg—"

"Oh, hush," Georg said. "I'm talking to your boyfriend." He turned back to Devante. "You are just as handsome as Michael said!" he said brightly. "I knew this from Instagram, of course, but it is better in person!"

Devante couldn't help but laugh; Georg's high energy was, he was discovering, extremely infectious. No wonder Michael couldn't help draping himself all over him all the time—Georg was made to be hugged. "Thank you," he said.

Georg beamed as though Devante had complimented *him*. "I will try to skate better today," he said. "I have to impress Michael's boyfriend."

"I was impressed yesterday," Devante told him. "You're very good." He tried to remember what Natasha had said about Georg's short program yesterday. "Your Ina Bauer is very elegant," he offered.

"Thank you!" Georg beamed brighter, and turned to Michael offscreen. "You did not tell me he knew skating!"

"I don't, not yet," Devante said. "But I'm trying."

"That is good," Georg said. "Now Michael is making faces,

threatening faces, so I will give him the phone. It was lovely to meet you, Devante!"

Devante laughed. "You too, Georg."

"*Thank* you," he heard Michael say, and then Michael's face came into view. "Absurd," he said, shaking his head. Georg's face came back into view just long enough for him to press a smacking kiss onto Michael's cheek. Devante just laughed again. "Ridiculous," Michael told him, and then turned back to Devante. "It's good to see you," he said, more seriously and more warmly. "Are you going over to Charlie's soon?"

"Leaving in about twenty minutes," Devante said. "Are you nervous?"

"Yes," Michael said, chuckling a little at himself. "Second place is a long way to fall from."

"I bet you won't fall," Devante said. "I bet you'll do great."

Michael twinkled at him. "Thank you, sweetheart." Offscreen, Devante heard Georg coo. "I've gotta run," Michael said regretfully. "Warm-ups start soon. Can I call you after the medals ceremony?"

"Of course," Devante said. "I'll talk to you then. Good luck, baby."

With a warm, happy smile, Michael said, "Thank you, sweetheart. Bye," and the call ended. Devante took a moment to just feel the giddy fluttering of his own heart before getting up to get ready to leave.

When he got to Charlie's Mike was already there, as was Natasha. Mike stood when Devante came in, and for a moment they just stood facing each other like two cowboys at a duel. "Say you're sorry," Devante said finally.

"I'm sorry," Mike said instantly. "I was just trying to look out for you, but it's none of my business, and I shouldn't have got so fired up about it."

Not great, as apologies went, but Devante wasn't good at being angry. "Thank you," he said. "Let's move on." Mike nodded thankfully and sank back onto the couch he had been sitting on.

For diplomacy's sake, Devante took the cushion next to him.

The free programs unfolded exactly as Natasha had predicted. No one fucked up, and Michael, at the end of the day, had a shiny bronze medal hung around his neck for his efforts. "Well called," Preeda said, toasting Natasha.

On screen, Georg, who had come in a respectable fourth place, was throwing his arms around Michael, both of them jumping up and down. Devante spared a sidelong look at Mike, who was studiously typing away on his phone, not sparing a glance for the TV.

Michael called before Devante left Charlie's, so Devante put him on speakerphone. The group chorused their congratulations, and Michael laughed delightedly on the other end of the line. "Thanks, guys!" he said, when they quieted down. "It was a good day."

"Your triple axel was clean as hell," Natasha hollered at Devante's phone. "Sexiest thing I've seen all week."

"Why thank you," Michael purred, before bursting out laughing again. "Seriously, though, I worked hard on that entrance."

"It showed," Preeda said. Everyone in the room turned to look at her in surprise. "What, Nat's the only one allowed to know anything about figure skating?" she asked. "I'm learning."

"I'm proud of you, Preeda," Michael said.

"Thank you." She toasted the phone with her wine glass before taking a long pull from it.

"Not to break up the party," Michael went on, "but would you guys mind giving me a moment alone with my boyfriend?"

Charlie cooed. "I was just on my way out," Devante said, fighting back a smile and picking up the phone. "See you guys around." He made his escape in a cacophony of joking jeers and genuine goodbyes, and turned speakerphone off when he made it outside, pressing the phone to his ear. "You still there?"

"I am," Michael confirmed. Devante could hear the smile in his voice. "Listen, sweetheart, I need you to do me a favor," he said, his voice getting a little low and sultry.

"I can already tell I'm going to like this favor," Devante said.

Michael laughed. "I need you to be waiting at my apartment when I get home," he said.

"Oh yeah?" Devante pressed the phone harder to his ear and looked around to make sure no one was nearby.

"The thing they don't tell you about winning a medal at the Grand Prix Final," Michael said, almost conversational were it not for the fact that his tone was still pitched deep and wanting, "is that it makes you want sex. *Lots* of sex."

Devante grinned, blood starting to pump a little faster. "Sure you want to wait until you get home?" he said teasingly. "After all, Georg is right there with you."

"Devante, sweetheart, right now there's only one man I want inside me, and it isn't Georg."

Devante tripped over his own feet, only catching himself at the last minute. "Sweet fuck, Michael."

"Good or bad?" Michael asked, dropping character a little bit in his concern. It made Devante miss him more sharply.

"Good," Devante assured him, "just, give a man some warning first."

"This is me giving you warning," Michael said. "My flight lands at Logan tomorrow at five o'clock. I want you there when I get home. Assuming," he added, suddenly sounding a little unsure, "you know, you want to. Do that."

"Oh, I want to," Devante said. "I'll be there."

"Good." Michael sounded satisfied, which was *doing things* to Devante. "I'll let you go for now," he said. "Think of me when you get home."

"I'm always thinking of you," Devante said, which was perhaps more honest than was called for this early in their relationship, but Michael just made a growling noise, which Devante took for agreement. "See you tomorrow, baby."

"See you tomorrow," Michael said, and it had the weight of a promise.

Chapter 20

MICHAEL GOT BACK to his apartment at exactly 6:02 P.M. the next day. Devante knew that, because he'd been camped out outside Michael's door since 5:30 P.M., and had been watching Michael's Lyft speed ever closer on his phone.

He must have decided, with all of his luggage, to risk the elevator, because Devante heard it rumble to life moments after the Lyft ride ended. Devante pushed himself to his feet, brushing his jeans off and trying not to fidget. Finally, *finally*, the elevator ground to a stop and the doors opened to reveal Michael, two suitcases in hand as he stepped out of it.

Devante opened his mouth to say something about Michael risking his life in the elevator, but the blazing look Michael gave him made him close it again. He came forward and took one of the suitcases instead, leaving one of Michael's hands free to unlock the door. He pushed the door open and then fisted his free hand into Devante's shirt, dragging him and both suitcases behind him into the apartment.

As the door closed behind them, Michael tossed the suitcase he was holding away, grabbing onto Devante's shirt with both hands now and pulling him into a deep kiss. Devante wrapped one arm around his waist and put the other hand on his jaw, cradling his head as he deepened the kiss. He felt Michael deflate against him, a long breath sighing out from his nose against Devante's cheek as a load of tension seemed to melt off his shoulders. "There," he said, when the kiss finally ended. "Now I'm home."

"You're home," Devante said. He pressed another brief kiss to

Michael's mouth and then pulled back. "I bet you want a shower."

"I do," Michael admitted, "and then I want you." He blinked up at him. "Do you still want to…"

Devante nodded quickly. "If you do."

"I do," Michael said, just as quick. He put a hand on the back of Devante's neck and kissed him again. "Ten minutes," he murmured against Devante's lips.

Devante wrangled the suitcases into the bedroom while Michael showered. He didn't know yet where everything in them went, but he unzipped them, revealing clothes, skating costumes, and Michael's skate bag. Then, at a loss, and nerves about their plans for the evening starting to crawl into his stomach, he undressed down to his undershirt and boxers, carefully folding his shirt and jeans and putting them on top of Michael's dresser.

He was sitting on the edge of Michael's bed when the shower stopped, a confusing mix of petrified and aroused. Then Michael came out of the bathroom, haphazardly dried off, his hair hanging wet around his face and sending tendrils of water running down his chest to absorb into the towel wrapped around his waist, and Devante lost all his fear, a powerful desire replacing it.

With a smirk, Michael let the towel drop. "Get over here," Devante said, his voice a harsh rasp. Michael was on him in three steps, straddling his legs on the bed and catching his head in a powerful, hungry kiss.

Most of the next hour devolved into flashes of bright sensation: the snap of the nitrile glove onto Devante's right hand; the squelch of the lube as it came out of the bottle; Michael's high, breathy gasps as he taught Devante how to stretch him; the tight grip of Michael's hands on Devante's shoulders, twisting the straps of his undershirt as he lowered himself down; the salt of Michael's skin as Devante licked up his throat. Devante buried his face in Michael's neck, completely overcome as Michael petted him, murmuring soft words of encouragement even as he bit off swears of his own.

They moved together like they were made to do it, like they'd been doing it for years; Devante couldn't remember a time when he hadn't been surrounded by Michael, encompassed by Michael, drowned in Michael.

It finished in a burst of feeling, Michael following Devante off the ledge when Devante accidentally sank his teeth into Michael's shoulder with the pulse-pounding thrill of his conclusion. They fell back together, Michael on Devante's chest, Devante still inside him. Devante wrapped his arms around Michael's back, holding them as tightly together as he could, catching his breath.

"Wow," Michael murmured into his skin, a few minutes later. Devante loosened his grip enough to let Michael elbow himself up, resting a hand on Devante's chest. "Thank you, sweetheart," he murmured, moving his hand to trace a finger down the slope of Devante's nose. "That was perfect."

"It was, wasn't it?" Devante asked, still a little out of breath. "It was perfect."

"It was," Michael confirmed, smiling softly down at him. "Just what I wanted."

Devante reached up and swept a lock of hair behind Michael's ear. "*You're* just what I wanted," he whispered. "Everything about you is just what I was looking for, and I didn't even know it."

"Oh, sweetheart," Michael said, voice just as quiet as Devante's. "Me too." He bent down and kissed him, slow and thorough, and then rested his head in the crook of Devante's shoulder and sighed happily.

Hunger drove them out of bed eventually. They ordered pizza, too lazy and tired to cook, and ate it tucked up together on the couch. "Can you stay tonight?" Michael asked sleepily, half-dozing on Devante's shoulder.

"Mhm." Carl hadn't said anything when Devante told him he probably wouldn't be home that night, just grunted his assent. Devante was going to have to start coming up with a cover story to explain his nights away; surely Carl wouldn't just take it on faith for much longer. "I'm all yours until tomorrow."

"Mmm, good." Michael buried his nose in Devante's neck. "Don't want to let you go." Devante tightened his arm around Michael's shoulders and hummed to himself, primally satisfied.

Somehow they found the energy to stand up and shuffle to bed before falling deeply asleep, Michael's arm thrown over Devante's waist and his nose buried in the nape of his neck. Devante dreamed of Michael, flashes of him visible in dim light, gone before Devante could caress or kiss them. The chase was thrilling rather than frustrating, though, leaving Devante breathless and full of desire.

He slid from his last dream into wakefulness as easily as breathing, coming to consciousness over the course of a smooth, unhurried ten seconds. Michael was clearly still asleep behind him—he whistled softly through his nose while he slept, and his arm was lax where it hung over Devante's chest. He had wriggled one leg between Devante's own in his sleep; Devante could feel his warm, moist breath on the back of his shoulder.

He lay there, luxuriating in the feeling of being held by Michael, for what must have been at least fifteen minutes, before his bladder made itself known. He carefully disentangled himself from his boyfriend, smiling softly when Michael grumbled and glommed onto Devante's satin-covered pillow in his absence, and made for the bathroom.

The sound of his flush and the sink running didn't wake Michael, so Devante decided some light cooking probably wouldn't be too disruptive either. He may not have known where Michael kept all of his clothes and skate gear in his bedroom yet, but he knew the layout of Michael's kitchen back to front.

He put a pot of coffee on, listening to it bubble as he browned some of the sausage from Michael's freezer. He set it aside and started cracking eggs into Michael's best frying pan, a healthy pat of butter underneath to smooth the way.

Michael wandered out as Devante was finishing up the first omelet, clad in a fresh pair of briefs and Devante's button-down, which hung loose around his torso, the sleeves falling past Michael's hands. "Mmm, I could get used to waking up this way," Michael murmured, sleep still wrapped around him in an almost visible haze. He pressed close to Devante, kissed him lazily, and accepted the mug of coffee Devante handed him. "How long have you been up?"

"Only around half an hour," Devante said. "Only out of bed for about ten." Michael hummed into his coffee, leaning back against the counter. "I like you in my clothes," Devante admitted quietly, earning himself a smile that hit his eyes like the rays of sun through the window.

"You should leave some here," Michael said. "So you won't have to carry a change of clothes every time you spend the night, and I can wear them when I miss you."

"It's a good idea," Devante said. He cracked more eggs into the pan, whisked them, and sprinkled the sliced-up sausage throughout the mixture. "I've been trying to think of a cover story for Dad," he went on. "To explain why I'm spending nights away all of a sudden."

"I had a thought about that," Michael said. He was perking up the more coffee he drank, and set the mug aside to hoist himself onto the counter, legs dangling among his cabinets. "You could say you're tired of the morning commute to the library, and you're going to start crashing at Charlie's the night before so you can sleep in a little longer."

Devante considered it. "That might work," he said. "Are you okay with me spending Sunday and Thursday nights here? I don't want to crowd you."

"I'd be okay with you spending more," Michael said wryly, "but those are the only nights I can think of a reasonable explanation for." He kicked out his leg to tap his foot against Devante's knee. "I'm not going to get sick of you, Devante," he said with a smile, leaning his head against the upper cabinet behind him. "I promise."

A little breathless, Devante could only say, "I'm not going to get sick of you either."

They ate clustered together at Michael's table, knees knocking underneath it as they smiled at each other between bites. "So," Michael said, a little too casually. "I know you just met Georg, and you're probably meeting-my-people-ed out, but…"

"But?" Devante prompted.

"But I promised Rosa I'd call her today," Michael said, "and if you can stay, I'd love you to meet her too."

Devante flushed. "She knows about me?"

"She does," Michael confirmed, cutting off another piece of omelet with his fork. "I haven't told my parents yet, but aside from Georg, she had to listen to me talk about you the most, and she can keep a secret." He looked sidelong at Devante, nervous. "Is that okay?"

"It's okay," Devante said, putting a hand on his arm. "It just surprised me, that's all. I'd love to meet her." Michael beamed at him. A few minutes elapsed, in which Devante finished his omelet and grew steadily more and more shameful, and then he said cautiously, "I *am* going to tell my dad about you, I promise. I just have to figure out the right way."

"Oh, no, hey, Devante," Michael said. It was his turn to put a hand on Devante's arm. "I didn't tell you I told Rosa to guilt you, okay? I don't mind when you tell your dad, I promise." His face was beseeching, open and earnest. "I'd like to meet him eventually, as your boyfriend, but I know coming out to parents is complicated, and I'd never want to rush you."

"I know," Devante said. He covered Michael's hand on his arm with his own, needing to feel the warmth of his skin. "You will meet him. Soon."

"Whenever," Michael said. He scrunched up his face adorably. "I'm not going to say I'm not a little nervous about it, so really, I don't mind waiting."

Devante chuckled, the tension in his chest easing a little.

"Dad's not scary, I promise. Not like Rosa."

Michael barked a laugh, surprised and pleased. "She is terrifying, I'll give you that. But she'll like you. She already likes you, from everything I've said about you."

It was still early in Boston, so Rosa in Texas wasn't awake yet, leaving them a few hours to themselves. They spent the time kissing on Michael's couch, the heat level never rising above sweet and easy. Devante could kiss Michael for hours on end, and had, a few times; there was always more to learn of the give and take of his mouth, the shape of his lips, the push of his tongue, and that wasn't even getting into the way the skin of Michael's neck felt between his teeth. Devante took care not to leave any visible marks, mindful of the fact that they'd be calling his sister soon, but Michael let him slide one shoulder of Devante's shirt off and bite a trail from his shoulder to his neck.

Eventually, Rosa answered Michael's text, and they hurriedly dressed before settling back onto the couch again. The call connected, and Devante blinked; the face on the other end was a carbon copy of Michael's—same sharp features, same bright eyes, same smile on her face. Her hair was curlier, though, and her eyebrows were more naturally wry. "Morning," she said. "Congrats on the medal!"

"Thanks," Michael said, smiling at her.

"Now, to business," she went on. "Where's the boyfriend?"

Michael laughed and tilted the phone; Devante snuggled closer into his side so he could be seen. "I'm here," he said.

She grinned. "Nice to finally meet you, Devante! I feel like I know you a little bit already, with how much I had to listen to my brother pine for you."

Michael groaned. Devante just laughed. "Nice to meet you too, Rosa."

Her face turned sharp and serious. "Now, I have a very important question for you, Devante, and it's one that will color our whole relationship."

He blinked. "Okay."

"Bagginshield or Legolas and Gimli?"

He almost laughed with relief. "Legolas and Gimli."

"Interesting," Rosa said. "Explain yourself."

"Have you read the Appendices yet?" She nodded. "Gimli followed Legolas off the edge of the world, in a boat Legolas made himself," Devante said. "You don't get love truer than that."

"But the *drama* of Bagginshield," Rosa said. "The betrayal! The last-minute forgiveness! The gold sickness! The mithril shirt!"

Devante shrugged. "That's all well and good, but it's not what I look for in a love story," he said. "Give me the slow and steady devotion any day."

She scowled, but he could tell she was fighting a smile. "I guess I can't argue with that," she said. "It's the right answer for someone dating my brother, anyway." Devante grinned at her. Michael, out of sight of the camera, wormed his free hand into Devante's, linking their fingers together.

Chapter 21

DEVANTE FLOATED THE idea of spending Sunday and Thursday nights in Brighton to his father when he got home that afternoon. Carl gave him a look that was clearly suspicious, but all he said was, "Sounds reasonable. My best to Charlie. Kid still got two couches?"

"Yup," Devante said, guilty and relieved in equal measure. "One's big enough for me, too, so all the better."

"Well, alright then."

That Thursday, Devante carted a backpack in addition to his messenger bag to his shift in the afternoon. At dinner, Mike noticed the extra baggage in the staff room. "You moving somewhere?" he asked, nodding to it.

"Keeping some things at Michael's place," Devante said. "Clothes and stuff. I'm gonna start spending nights, so he cleared out a drawer for me." Mike had no poker face, and clearly had opinions, but maybe he was still skittish from their fight during the Grand Prix Final, because he just nodded and dug into his quesadilla with a little extra relish.

Michael had training late Thursday evenings, so he got to his apartment at the same time Devante did. "Hey, sweetheart," he said, pausing in his fumble for keys to turn his face up for a quick press of lips. "How's that timing, eh?"

"Pretty good," Devante said. Michael let them into the apartment and, once they were inside, pulled Devante into a proper kiss.

Michael showered, and they clambered onto his couch, Michael sinking into Devante's arms with a tired sigh. "I really do need a bigger couch," he murmured, trying to tuck his feet onto the seat and failing. "I'll have a look at IKEA this weekend."

"I'll help you put it together," Devante volunteered. "I'm good with flat-pack stuff."

"Yeah?" Michael beamed up at him. "My handy man." Devante kissed the tip of his nose, because it was there and he could. Michael squirmed happily in his arms.

"How was practice?"

Michael groaned. "If I ever say another nice word about Sara Teasen again, know that something's wrong with me," he said, voice adorably grumpy. "She's working me like a dog."

"When's your next competition?"

"Early January. Nationals. And then the Four Continents in February, and Worlds in March."

Devante put his nose into Michael's hair, breathing in his pine-scented shampoo. "Sounds like you've got a lot still ahead of you."

Michael sighed gustily. "Yes, and she's right to work me this hard, I can't slip this far into the season just because I medaled at the Final. But I'm tired, and my feet hurt, and I want to whine."

"Whine away." Devante kissed the top of his head.

Michael made a high-pitched whining sound, digging himself further into the crook of Devante's arm. Devante tipped his knees over to cover Michael's thighs, which he seemed to appreciate.

Michael, for all his moaning about his terrible schedule, was still in bed when Devante left for work the next morning, scrolling mindlessly on his phone. Devante kissed him goodbye and locked the door behind himself on the way out.

Michael still met him for lunch that day, and the Monday after, and they settled into their new routine with an ease that almost surprised Devante; would have surprised him, if he hadn't known, hadn't been able to *feel* how well they worked together. They saw each other at their Friend Group drinks on Saturday, then Devante spent Sunday night, they had lunch Monday, then a few days off until he spent Thursday night at Michael's, and they had lunch on Friday. It wasn't enough—Devante wasn't sure he could ever have *enough* of Michael—but it was good.

They kept in contact on days they couldn't see each other, texting and calling. Before long they had a standing Wednesday evening phone call, which Devante took in his bedroom. Michael's next load of laundry included a couple of Devante's shirts and undershirts; when Devante put them on again, they smelled like Michael, and sent him off to work almost giddy.

They made love mostly on Sunday nights or Friday mornings, oftentimes both. Michael was a seemingly endless font of ideas when it came to the sexual realm, and Devante had more kinds of sex with him in the month of December than he had previously known existed in the world. He liked nearly everything they tried, and everything else he wanted to try at least once more to get the hang of it before making a ruling.

His favorite, though, was midway through the month, when Michael had been in the shower and something in Devante had snapped, and Michael had come back into the bedroom to find Devante pulling his undershirt over his head. Devante tossed it aside, meeting Michael's eye nervously; but his nerves disintegrated under the hungry, grateful expression that was on Michael's face as he raked his eyes over Devante's newly-exposed torso.

Michael crossed the room in a flash and kissed him, a hard bite to it that set Devante's blood racing. He laid Devante out on the bed and kissed his way down his chest, and left little bite marks across his stomach, before taking Devante into his mouth. He almost forgot to put the condom on, he was so single-minded. When Devante looked down at him, he had to look past his own flesh, and for once he didn't mind it.

"You make me feel beautiful," he murmured, when Michael was done and he'd reciprocated and they lay in each other's arms, both breathing hard.

"You *are* beautiful, so that's good," Michael said.

"Not like you," Devante said, unable to stop himself.

Michael propped himself up on one elbow. "No," he said slowly, "you're beautiful like *you*, which is much better. I thought so the first time I saw you."

"You thought I was beautiful?" Devante asked.

Michael made a face. "Well, almost. What I thought *exactly* was, wow, he's hot as fuck." Devante barked a surprised laugh, and Michael grinned. "I didn't think you were *beautiful* until I faked a run by the library a few days later and saw you in the sunlight."

"I *knew* you were faking that run," Devante crowed. Michael blushed and hid his face in Devante's still-naked chest. "Seriously, though," Devante said, stroking Michael's hair. "You were attracted to me right away?"

"Mhm." Michael's voice was muffled until he turned his head to rest his ear against Devante's heart. "It was like I saw you and my whole body just went *yes*." Devante hummed and held him tighter.

In between his times with Michael, Devante spent December kicking his job search into high gear. To his surprise, he was offered the job at Tufts. After a brief conversation with his father, and a much longer talk with Michael, Devante decided to turn it down. "I appreciate the offer," he told the hiring manager, "but I don't think it's the right move for me right now."

"Fair enough," she said. "We're sorry to lose you, though. Best of luck in your search."

Devante abandoned his half-hearted forays into public or academic libraries, focusing instead on school library jobs. He cast his net as far away as Providence, although the prospect of a two-hour commute didn't thrill him.

He kept Michael updated on his job search, but there was one job he didn't tell him about, a substitute K-8 librarian position for schools in Brighton. It was almost *too* perfect, on paper; part-time but with great pay, near Michael, and willing to consider an entry-level candidate. He spent three hours one Saturday on his application, resolving not to think about it again once he'd sent it off.

That resolution didn't need to last long; they called him the following Wednesday. "You got your application in just under the wire," the school principal told him with a smile in his voice. "Your cover letter was great, I don't mind saying."

"Thank you," Devante said. His fingers, behind his back, were crossed so tightly his knuckles were going white.

They scheduled an interview for the following week, on Monday afternoon. "I have to cancel our lunch tomorrow," Devante told Michael regretfully on Sunday night.

Michael made a sad face. "Why?"

"I kind of have a job interview."

"Devante!" Michael said, face instantly changing to one of excitement. "Why didn't you tell me?"

"Because I really want it, and I don't want to jinx it," Devante said all in a rush. "I'll tell you about it after the interview, once I know how it went, but for now…"

"Of course," Michael said. "I'll miss you tomorrow afternoon, but I'll be thinking of you." Devante kissed him, his gratitude for Michael's understanding and excited nerves about the interview making it a little sharper than he had intended. Michael responded instantly, and the rest of the evening was spent without words.

Devante spent his Monday morning shift researching the school he'd be interviewing with. He'd done his research already, of course, but re-researching kept him calm. He'd brought his suit to the library with him, and changed in the bathroom before calling a Lyft to the school.

Four hours later, he called Michael from his Lyft home. "How'd it go?" Michael said instantly, answering on the first ring.

Devante closed his eyes. "Really well," he admitted, clenching his fists with the force of it. "Really, really well."

Michael cheered. "That's amazing! Now will you tell me about it?"

Devante kept his eyes closed, trying to focus on the sound of Michael's voice. "Substitute school librarian position," he said. "Part-time, so I could still keep my shifts at the Brighton library, and on-call. They have a permanent librarian with a chronic health condition, so they said I'd likely get a lot of work. Really good pay."

"Where?"

"Also Brighton," Devante said.

He heard Michael suck in a sharp breath. "Sweetheart, that sounds *perfect*," he said slowly.

"I know," Devante moaned, leaning his head against the window. "And the interview went *so well*. They liked my tie, and I wasn't nervous at all once I met the committee, and we just…*vibed*."

"I'm crossing every finger and toe I have for you," Michael said. "Any idea when you'll hear?"

"They said a couple of weeks," Devante said. "They're still interviewing candidates, I was one of the first they got in."

"That's probably a good sign."

"Don't," Devante begged. "We can literally never speak of this job again or I'll go insane."

Michael laughed. "Alright, sweetheart, alright. But keep me posted, alright?"

"I promise."

Carl had also known about the interview, due to Devante's ironing of his suit shirt, but he took one look at Devante's face when he got home and wisely didn't ask.

Two weeks before Christmas, Michael asked Devante on another official date. Devante knew full well what was coming when he said yes, and gamely wore his warmest jacket and gloves to the outdoor ice rink. "I haven't done this in months," he warned Michael, strapping on his rental skates.

"It's like riding a bike," Michael told him.

"I don't know how to do that either."

However, Michael proved to be correct; Devante wobbled a lot on the first few steps, nearly taking them both down, but regained his ice legs in under fifteen minutes. "There, see?"

Michael asked, doing a little twirl in front of him. "Easy as pie."

Devante grumbled at him, but held out his hand. Michael took it. They were both wearing gloves instead of mittens, and so could interlace their fingers as they skated side-by-side between other couples and families who had had the same idea. Devante mostly had to keep his eyes in front of him to stay upright, but he spared a few glances for Michael next to him, who was practically glowing in the warm light of the lamps around the rink.

"You really love skating, don't you?" Devante asked.

Michael looked at him, a soft smile on his face. "I really do."

I love you rose unbidden to Devante's tongue, and it was only with an effort that he kept it behind his lips.

He hadn't said it; not since waking in Michael's arms for the first time, all those weeks ago. He'd meant it, then, and he meant it now; but it seemed a bit too soon to say it again, for real this time. He could wait, and let Michael go next. He wasn't under any doubts that *love* was where they were going, and he could be patient.

"Go on," he said to Michael, giving his hand a squeeze and then letting go. "Go show off."

Michael flashed him a bright smile before skating off to the center of the public rink. He built up speed and launched into the air—two rotations, a double something Devante still couldn't identify. There was a burst of applause for him, which Devante joined. Michael bowed theatrically and did a split jump on the way back to Devante.

"What brings a talented skater like you to a dinky little outdoor rink like this?" Devante asked as Michael slid back into place next to him.

Picking up on the game, Michael gave him a sidelong, sultry look. "Oh, you know," he said, over-casual. "Can't pick up a boyfriend only skating on private ice."

"Looking for a boyfriend, are you?" Devante asked. "I can't imagine you don't have people knocking down your door, with moves like that."

"Mmm," Michael allowed. "Not the right ones, though."

"What's the right one like, then?"

"Tall," Michael said instantly. "Much taller than me, and broad-shouldered and -chested. Handsome, obviously. Dark eyes, a sweet smile. The best taste in novelty patterned shirts."

"Sounds like he might be hard to find, with a list that specific," Devante observed.

"Oh, I don't know," Michael said lightly. "I actually have a candidate in mind who ticks all those boxes."

"Oh?" Devante couldn't keep down a grin. "Must be quite a guy."

"He's the best," Michael said, dropping character to turn soft and earnest. Devante slipped his hand back into Michael's, and they skated on.

Chapter 22

DEVANTE WAS SHAKEN out of his trance, where he'd been staring blank-eyed at his phone for who knew how long, by the phone itself ringing. He answered it on instinct. "Hello?"

"Hi, sweetheart!" Michael's voice ran out over the line. "Were you watching?"

Watching?

Shit. Nationals. "Shit," he said aloud, fumbling for his laptop, where the stream was still running, tinny music coming out of his earbuds, which were lying beside the computer on his bed. "Shit, Michael, I'm so sorry, I meant to, I swear, I had the stream up and everything—"

"Take a breath," Michael said. Devante obeyed, sucking in a huge gulp of air. "It's okay if you didn't watch, Devante. I won't be mad." He sounded a little hurt, though, and like he was trying to hide it. "I just remember you said you were going to."

"I was," Devante said, wincing. "And I will, as soon as it's up on YouTube. I still have the stream up, I just…"

"You just?" Michael prompted.

"I got a phone call," Devante said, and then the contents of that phone call, the only thing that would have made him miss Michael's performance, came back into his panic-fuzzy brain. "Michael, baby, they offered me the job."

"What!" Michael shrieked, loud even through the phone. "Are you serious?" He didn't sound hurt anymore, just excited. Devante loved him agonizingly in that moment. "They offered you the job?"

"They did," Devante said, a little breathless at the memory.

"And they called at just the wrong time, you were just about to go on the ice, but I couldn't miss the call—"

"Sweetheart," Michael interrupted. "It's fine. Obviously you had to take the call! My feelings were a little hurt, but now I understand, and they're not anymore, okay?"

"Okay," Devante said. His fingers were twisted into the fabric of his comforter; he had to exert real will to loosen them. "I bet you were great."

"Why are we still talking about me?" Michael asked, laughing, and the genuine delight in that sound broke through the last of Devante's guilt. "You just got a job offer! Did you take it?"

"They told me to take a few days to think about it," Devante said. "There's no benefits or anything, it's part-time, but I think they could tell I was a little out of it by the end."

"That was good of them," Michael said. "They want your honest, clear-headed acceptance. Are you going to say yes?"

"I mean, how can I not?" Devante asked. "It's the perfect first-step job in my career. This is a *career* job, Michael," he repeated, still not quite believing it himself.

"I know," Michael said, warm and fond. "Is your dad home?"

"Yes," Devante said, a little startled at the change of subject.

"Okay. So here's what I want you to do when we hang up: I want you to go downstairs and drink a big glass of water, and then I want you to tell your dad you got a job offer, and talk it over with him. I've never had a real, proper job, just college student work and then some part-time food service while I got my figure skating career off the ground, so I can't offer you any real advice, but your dad can."

"Okay," Devante said. "That's smart. You're smart, Michael."

"You're smart too, sweetheart," Michael said patiently. "And capable, and competent, and you care a lot about people, and that's why they want you to work for them."

"Right," Devante said faintly. Gathering himself, he said, "Glass of water. Talk to Dad. Then find a video of your skate and watch it three times."

Michael laughed again. "Sounds like a good plan." He hesitated, like he wanted to say something else, and finally settled on, "I'm proud of you."

I love you. "Thank you," Devante said instead. "I think I'm proud of me too."

"Good," Michael said firmly. "Now go on. I'll talk to you later."

"Bye." *I love you.*

Devante made it down the stairs and into the kitchen, where he pulled the biggest glass from the cabinet, filled it from the sink, and drained it dry. The water *did* help; the act of swallowing was somehow focusing for his mind, and the cold water made him feel more settled in his body.

Carl was in his armchair, newspaper folded on the armrest, eyes fixed on the television. "Everything alright?" he asked when Devante came into the living room, turning his focus from the wrestling match to his son. "Thought I heard a commotion upstairs."

"I got a job offer," Devante said bluntly, dropping onto the couch.

Carl blinked, and then a smile broke through his habitual frown of concentration. "Well now. That's something." He studied Devante for a minute. "You don't sound happy," he observed.

"I am," Devante said. "I am, honest. It's just..." He waved his hands fruitlessly. "Big. It's a career-starter, you know?"

"Yeah." Carl shifted in his chair. "I never had that," he said unexpectedly. "A career-starter."

"No?" Devante looked at him, curious.

"No," Carl said. "I just knew I had to get a job when I met your mother, a real one, not those part-time no-money time-wasters I'd been doing before. So I applied to everything I could find, and the only one that took me was the Reggie Lewis, as a so-called facilities manager. Scrubbing bathrooms, mainly, and track equipment," he added wryly, and Devante laughed. "It paid the bills, enough for me to start putting some money aside for the first time in my life. Made a name for myself, and someone higher-up took a chance on me when the assistant trainer job opened up a few months later." He shrugged. "I guess I've had a career, but I never knew what the next step on it was gonna be. Just started climbing, first for your mother, and then for you."

"You did well by me," Devante said quietly. "I know how hard you've worked all my life."

"Yeah, well, I had help," Carl said. "Your mom had an inheritance, enough for the down payment on the house. But that's not the point," he went on, growing a little more serious. "Point is, I never had a plan for myself. Your mother was the best two years of my life to that point, but she was still only just two years. Less than, even. I figured I had time to make a plan, with her, and then I didn't, and then the plan was keeping food in your mouth, and nothing else. But you're not like that."

"I'm not?"

Carl shook his head. "You've got a plan. You've always had a plan, long as I can remember. You know what you want out of life, and you've got a good idea what it'll take to get it." He fell silent for a moment. "I'm real proud of you, son. Always have been, but especially now. You've got your plan, and you're gonna follow it, and if it doesn't work, you'll make a new plan. No doubt about that."

Devante looked down at his knees. "Thanks, Dad."

"Ain't gotta thank me," Carl said. "You're my son." Devante nodded, still not able to look at him directly. Carl cleared his throat. "So tell me about this job," he said, voice a little gruffer than it had been. "You gonna take it?"

"I think so," Devante said. "Part-time substitute librarian for a public school system in Brighton. Good pay, and they promise a lot of hours, but I should still be able to keep my public library job, or most of it, anyway."

"Health insurance?"

Devante shook his head. "No, no benefits, but I'll be able to afford a marketplace plan once I'm booted off yours." Now that they weren't talking about Carl's emotions, he could turn and face him again. "It's not much on its own," he said, "but it's a good first step."

"Sounds like it," Carl said. "Sounds like the sort of thing that could set you up nicely for your next job."

Devante nodded. "That's it exactly. Get some years of experience, earn some good references in my field."

"Good." Carl nodded, rubbing his hands on his thighs. "How long did they give you to think about it?"

"A few days," Devante said, "but I won't need it. I'm gonna sleep on it, and then call them back tomorrow."

"Good," Carl repeated. "Proud of you." Devante smiled at him and got up.

A recording of Michael's skate was on figure skating Twitter by that point. The group chat was lit up talking about it; Devante put his phone face-down on his comforter to focus on the performance.

It was, as usual, breathtaking, and Devante said as much to Michael in their private chat before switching over to The Friend Group's thread.

NM: Silver for sure, although you've got a good shot in for gold, I say

ML: No way, but thank you for your confidence in me

NM: It all depends on Carter's triple axel in the free

DM: Well, I'd give him gold

CG: Yooooo, Dev, where you been?????

CG: Did you miss your own boyfriend's skating live?

ML: Don't tease him, he had a good reason

PC: Does that mean what I think it means?????

DM: Probably

DM: I was on the phone getting offered a job

CG: YOOOOOOOOOOOOOOOOOOOOOOOOOOO

PC: I KNEW IT, I could sense The Vibes in the air

NM: Are you going to accept?

DM: Gonna sleep on it, but like 99% yes

CG: CONGRATS

CG: First round's on Dev when Michael gets back

NM: Don't spend other people's money, Charlie

DM: It's fine, I'll be able to afford it

PC: Oh ho ho, that good of an offer, is it?

MC: Congrats, Dev!

Michael came home from Nationals with a shiny silver medal to go with his Grand Prix Final bronze. Devante bought the first two rounds of drinks at Mood that Saturday, still high off the feeling of calling his contact at the public school back and accepting the job, compounded by having Michael pressed all along his side, fingers twisted around his own under the table.

"So what's next for you in the season, Michael?" Preeda asked, daintily sipping her second glass of wine.

"The Four Continents Championship, next month," Michael said, leaning his torso back to cuddle Devante more effectively. "It's in South Korea this year."

"That's a long flight," Charlie said.

"Yup," Michael said, popping the final p. "Not looking forward to that part."

"Will Georg be there?" Mike asked. Devante shot him a look and he held his hands up. "Just asking."

"No," Michael said regretfully. "He's European, so he's excluded from the Four Continents. He already had his continental competition last week."

"How'd he do?" Preeda asked.

"Pewter," Natasha and Michael said together. Devante

could see the edge of Michael's grin at her from where he was wrapped around Michael's back and side.

"Pewter's...fourth?" Charlie tried. At Natasha's nod, he pumped his fist in front of his chest triumphantly.

"Enough about figure skating," Michael said airily. "I want to hear about all of you."

"*I* want to hear about Devante's *job*," Natasha said, leaning forward across the table toward them. "You said the pay's good, right?"

"Yeah," Devante said, "like, surprisingly good."

"Wonder if that means the job's a nightmare," Natasha said wisely.

Charlie elbowed her. "Don't put the man off," he said. "I'm sure the job's fine, Dev," he told Devante. "What are you gonna do with all that money, though?"

"Save up, mostly," Devante said. "Student loans are coming due in a few months, and I want to have a little cushion before then."

"So practical," Preeda said, rolling her eyes, but Devante knew she meant it fondly. "Are you gonna move out of your dad's place?"

Devante felt Michael grow very still against him. "Eventually," he said, trying to sound casual. "It's in the plan."

"God, I need to move," Mike said loudly, putting one elbow on the table and the other on the back of the bench behind him.

"Again, I ask, fucking why?" Charlie said, shaking his head. "You've got a plush setup now, my man. Where would you even go?"

"I was thinking Brighton," Mike said. His eyes flicked to Devante, who looked down at his drink.

"Why?" Preeda asked, sounding skeptical. "Brighton's nowhere near your lab. It would, like, double your commute."

"Brighton's nice," Mike said defensively. "Good place to live." He sent Devante another glance, this one heavier and more meaningful. Devante fought the urge to roll his eyes, and tightened his arm around Michael.

"Moving's the pits," Michael said loftily, reaching for his gin and tonic. "I've never been to your place, Mike, but from the sounds of it, Brighton's not good enough to give it up. And a short commute's nothing to sneeze at." He took a sip from his glass. "Back in Texas I had a super long one to the rink, I couldn't even run it. A short distance from my rink is what I mainly looked for when I was apartment-hunting here."

"Well, if *you* don't think I should move..." There was a small but very evident trace of nastiness in Mike's tone; Devante bristled, and without looking up from her phone Natasha reached over and smacked him in the chest. "Ow!" Mike yelped, rubbing at it. "What was that for?"

"You're being a dick," Preeda informed him.

To his credit, Mike looked abashed at the news. "Sorry," he said to the table at large. "I think I've had too much."

"You're getting old," Natasha said. "Can't hold your shitty beer anymore." She picked up her drink and drained it. "I'm done too," she announced. "Got a paper to write tomorrow, and I need my wisdom sleep."

There was a general commotion around the table as everyone got up and shuffled into their jackets. Devante had told Carl he would be out tonight too, so he took the bus back to Brighton with Michael, squeezing onto a two-seat bench together. Devante wanted to put his arm around Michael, but outside the walls of Mood the action felt much riskier. Perhaps Michael sensed his dilemma, because he slid a little closer and, under the cover of their coats, let his hand rest on Devante's leg. Devante smiled at him, and in the crappy fluorescent light of the bus, Michael smiled back.

Chapter 23

TWO WEEKS BEFORE his new job started, Devante woke one Tuesday morning to the smell of frying bacon and a low rumble of what sounded like many voices coming from the kitchen.

Confused and bleary-eyed, he threw a hoodie on over his undershirt and sweatpants over his boxers, and stumbled downstairs to see what all the commotion was. He found Carl, frying the bacon on their griddle while two pancakes cooked on the stove, what sounded, closer up, like NPR coming from his phone. "Morning," Devante said over the hosts' smooth, careful voices.

Carl tapped one blunt finger on his phone until the voices stopped. "Morning," he said. "Blueberry or chocolate chip?"

"Chocolate chip," Devante said. Carl nodded and moved to the pantry to grab the little yellow Nestle bag. "What were you listening to?"

"Kid at work told me about it," Carl said. "Called a podcast. Gives you the news but you don't have to have a radio."

"I know what a podcast is," Devante said. "Why were you listening to it so loud?"

Carl pointed his spatula at the sizzling bacon in answer. Devante nodded and went to the coffee machine.

Carl spent breakfast talking about his new crop of trainees at the Reggie Lewis. Devante half-listened to him, attention caught between him and his food. "One kid, poor brat, 's got a bad case of duck foot," Carl said. "His form's all a mess because no one ever taught him to run right, just tried to get him to hold his feet straight."

"Can you work with duck feet?" Devante asked, sipping his coffee.

Carl nodded. "Can work with anything; it's just a matter of tweaking the form. But he's in for a hard road re-learning how to run."

"Poor kid," Devante said.

Carl shrugged. "He loves track, and he loves running; he'll be alright in the end." He had a look on his face that could almost be fondness; when he caught Devante looking, he winked and turned his attention to his stack of pancakes.

Devante did the dishes, thinking about his father's crop of trainees. It was typical of Carl to get attached to the so-called hopeless cases; the worse the runner's form when they came in, the more Carl liked them by the end. It was just how he worked.

Carl was in his chair when Devante was done, as he always was. He had his newspaper in front of his face, but his phone was still playing NPR from its spot on the armrest, in front of Carl's elbow. Devante looked at the tableau for a few hard, painful moments, and then said abruptly, "Dad, I've gotta talk to you about something."

Carl lowered the paper, looking surprised, but he obligingly poked at his phone and paused his podcast. "Something wrong?" he asked, looking Devante up and down.

"No," Devante said. "Yes. No." He went and sat on the couch, and found that his leg was bouncing up and down, and he couldn't seem to make it stop. "I don't think it's a bad thing."

"Okay." Carl lay his newspaper in his lap and focused on his son. "Shoot."

Devante stared at him helplessly for a few seconds, and then said, "Could you…" He held his hands up in front of his face like he was holding a newspaper.

Carl blinked at him blankly. "Could I what?"

Devante winced. "Could you put your paper back up?" he asked, voice cracking. "It's just, I don't think I can look at your face when I tell you."

Carl looked even more surprised, and more than a little concerned, although his face didn't actually change much. It was all in the lines around his eyebrows and forehead, Devante thought to himself. Carl sighed, but he unfolded his paper again and held it in front of his face.

Devante immediately started breathing a little easier. "Okay. Thank you. So it's about where I've been spending my nights when I'm not at home." Carl didn't say anything. *Come on, Devante. You're in this far.* "I haven't been spending them at Charlie's."

"I know," Carl said implacably from behind his newsprint screen.

"Right. Okay. Of course you do. How do you know that?" Devante said, aware that he was babbling and unable to stop.

"You're a shitty liar, son."

"Right. Okay." Devante rubbed his hands together, then passed them over his face. "I've been seeing someone," he forced himself to say, "and I've been spending the nights there instead."

"Figured as much," Carl rumbled placidly.

His father's total lack of surprise, oddly, emboldened Devante; the thought that maybe Carl already knew was the only thing that let him say, "His name's Michael."

Snap.

The look on Carl's face when he cracked the paper down put paid to the idea that he'd known the gender of Devante's partner before he'd said it—pure, blank shock. His face was furrowed, like he was thinking very, very hard, and his gaze was piercing. Devante squirmed, trapped in it, heart racing, stomach churning, completely unable to hide from his father in that moment.

And then Carl blinked, and up went his paper again, hiding his face like Devante'd asked him to. "Ask him to dinner on Friday," he said, not the slightest hint in his voice that anything was wrong. "I'll make my spaghetti sauce."

Devante collapsed, face falling into his hands, elbows on his knees as he shook. Relief clubbed him over the head like a baseball bat, until he was dizzy and faint with it. "Thank you," he managed through his harsh breathing.

"Ain't gotta thank me, kid," Carl said from behind his paper, voice sharper than it had been. "You're my son."

Devante laughed, a little hysterical. "Lotta parents don't see it that way."

"Lotta parents are assholes," was Carl's reply, and, well, Devante couldn't argue with that.

Carl let Devante sit and shake for a few more minutes, silence that was almost comfortable stretching between them, before he said, "So tell me about him."

"Right," Devante said shakily. He wiped his hands over his face, not surprised to have them come away a little damp. "His name's Michael, Michael Lopez," he said, thinking of Michael, trying to find some calm in his memory. "He lives next door to Charlie. Charlie brought him to drinks last year and we hit it off."

"How long've you two been together?" Carl asked, and then, "Do I have to keep this paper in front of my face?"

"No," Devante said, laughing again, a little saner this time. "No, you can put it down." Carl did, folding it and dropping it onto the stack at his side. "We've been together since November," he said.

Carl nodded. "What's he do?"

Back came a few of Devante's nerves. "He's a competitive athlete," he said, and then, tentative, "Figure skating."

But Carl just nodded again. "He any good?"

"He's *very* good," Devante said, his anxiety becoming slightly taken over with the warm pride he associated with thinking about Michael's skating. "He just won silver at Nationals."

Carl looked impressed. "Alright then." He turned serious again. "And you like him? He's good to you?"

I love him. "Yeah, Dad, I like him," Devante said softly. "He's great to me, I promise." He cleared his throat. "It was like what you said with Mom," he said. Carl raised an eyebrow. "When I met him," Devante clarified. "It was like how you said it was with you and Mom. For him too."

Carl bobbed his head ever so slightly. "I'm glad for you, son," he said carefully. "Do you have a label?"

"A label?"

"Yeah, you know, a label," Carl repeated. "I saw it in the paper last year. Gay, bi, what was the other one…pot?"

Devante giggled; he couldn't help himself. "It's pan, Dad," he said. "And I'm gay."

"Right," Carl said. He rubbed his hands on his thighs. "I got a gay son." He didn't look put out by it, just like he was coming to terms with a neutral fact. Devante's heart ached.

"Yes, Dad, you've got a gay son," he said, a smile tugging at his lips.

"Well, that's alright then," Carl said. He nodded, once, and Devante nodded back, and that was that. "You gonna talk to him today?" Carl asked.

"Yeah," Devante said. "I should probably call him, let him know we talked and everything's okay. Everything's okay, right?" he added, suddenly sick with the need to be sure.

"Everything's fine, kid," Carl said, as close to reassuring as he ever got. "Go call him." He reached for his paper. "I meant it about Friday," he said, pointing at Devante before he disappeared behind it. "Spaghetti sauce."

"I'll let him know," Devante said, and stood up, feeling as though he could dance his way up the stairs.

He remembered halfway through his phone ringing out that Michael was at practice just then, and almost hung up and sent him a text instead, but to his surprise Michael answered, sounding out of breath. "Hey, sweetheart," he said, voice as bright and cheerful as ever. Devante thrilled to it. "What's up?"

"Am I interrupting practice?" Debate asked.

"Nah," Michael said, "Sara gave me fifteen minutes to breathe. I've got about ten left, and I'm more than happy to spend them with you." Devante heard an exhale as Michael sat down, presumably on the bleachers. Devante also sat down, on the edge of his bed. "Something on your mind? You don't usually call me while I'm at practice."

"I just came out to my dad," Devante said.

"Holy *shit*, Devante," Michael yelped immediately. "Are you okay? Do you need me to come get you?"

"No, no," Devante said quickly, "I'm fine, I promise. Everything's fine." More tears sprang into his eyes, and he rubbed his free hand over them and flopped backward onto the bed. "He was really great about it, actually."

Michael let out a long, pained breath. "Jesus, sweetheart," he said, laughing a little shakily. "You sure do know how to get my blood pumping. I didn't know you were planning on coming out to him today."

"I wasn't," Devante said. "It just sort of…came out. If you'll pardon the pun."

"Well, you know I love puns," Michael said. "I'm glad he was okay with it."

"There's more," Devante said. "Can you eat pasta on Friday?"

"I can move my cheat day, I haven't had it yet this week," Michael said slowly. "Why?"

"Dad wants to meet you." Devante pushed himself back up into a sitting position. "He's invited you over for spaghetti on Friday evening. He's gonna make his famous sauce."

"Jesus," Michael said faintly. "I'm gonna meet your dad this week? In three days?"

"If you can make it," Devante said. "I can always tell him you're busy."

"Of course I can *make* it, it's your father," Michael said. "I guess I was just expecting a little more lead time."

Devante smiled. "More lead time would just make you more nervous."

"Fair," Michael allowed. "Okay. Friday. Yes. I will be there." Devante laughed at how scared he sounded, which made *Michael* laugh. "You're okay though, seriously?" he said, sobering. "It's a big thing you just did."

"I'm okay," Devante said quietly. "I just…I couldn't take it anymore. Him not knowing, I mean."

"I get it," Michael said. "I'm proud of you, sweetheart."

I love you. "Thanks." Devante took a deep breath, and was pleased at how steady it was. "Your break must be almost over."

"Almost," Michael said. "I'm glad you called." They sat in silence for a moment, Devante listening to the sound of Michael's breathing through the phone. "I've got to go now," Michael finally said, regretful. "Sara's calling me."

"Have a good rest of practice," Devante said. "I'll talk to you later."

"Talk to you later," Michael echoed. "Bye, Devante."

"Bye, baby."

Devante washed his face in his tiny bathroom and went back downstairs, carrying his laptop. "Michael says he's in for Friday," he reported to Carl, who nodded from behind his paper, NPR still playing off his phone. Devante settled onto the couch and opened his computer, letting the soothing tones of Terry Gross serve as the soundtrack to his daily check in with figure skating Twitter.

Chapter 24

CG: HEY

CG: Just a heads-up that Michael's on his way to your place

CG: I know because I spent the last hour at *his* place watching him try on outfits

CG: Your boy's a little nervous

CG: I told him Carl is chill as hell but it didn't seem to help

CG: Good luck!

The house smelled *amazing.* Carl's famous spaghetti sauce, with mushrooms and ground beef, was bubbling on the stove. Carl himself, Devante was amused to note, had dressed up, his usual white t-shirt abandoned for a deep blue polo that he hadn't worn since Devante's library school graduation. Devante, getting in the spirit of things, had ironed his pineapple shirt for the occasion.

He was surprisingly *not* nervous, for all he was bringing his first boyfriend home to meet his father today; he loved Carl, and he loved Michael, and he knew, deep down in his core, that they would like each other too, once they got over their anxiety about each other.

Michael knocked on their door at exactly 6:30 P.M. Devante exchanged a look with Carl and went to answer the knock.

The sight of Michael standing on his porch took Devante's breath away for a second. He was wearing his best dark-wash jeans, and Devante's favorite of his shirts, the green short-sleeved button-down. His hair was freshly washed and pulled back into his skating ponytail, sharp and clean. He looked terrified, but softened when he saw Devante, as he always did. "Hi," he breathed, hands hanging out of his back pockets.

"Hey," Devante said, stepping aside to let him in. "Did you have any trouble finding the place?" he asked as he closed the door.

Michael looked around as he stepped inside Devante's house for the first time. "No," he said, finishing his sweep to look at Devante's face and smile. "Your directions were exact."

"Good." Carl was still in the kitchen, so Devante leaned in and stole a quick kiss. Michael hummed happily as their lips met, licking his own when Devante pulled back. "Come meet my dad."

Michael made a face, which Devante just laughed at, but he gamely followed him into the kitchen. Carl turned when they entered, from where he was stirring his sauce on the stove. "Michael?" he asked. Michael nodded. "Carl Miller," he said, holding out his hand.

"Michael Lopez," Michael said, shaking it firmly. "Pleasure to meet you, sir."

"You too." Carl turned back to the stove. "Just about to put the pasta on," he said. "Fifteen minutes until dinner."

"Sounds great," Devante said. "I'll set the table."

"Can I help?" Michael asked.

Devante shook his head. "I've got this down to an art form," he said, winking. Michael gave him a dazzling, breathless grin. "You just have a seat."

Their table was only just barely big enough for three, but Devante made it work, laying out placemats, plates, and silverware. He pulled two beers out of the fridge and showed one to Michael; Michael nodded, and Devante set them on the table and fetched a third for Michael's place. He let a hand trail over Michael's shoulder as he passed; Michael looked up at him gratefully, and not a little adoringly.

Carl drained the pasta and poured it back into the empty pot, and then announced, "Dinner's on." Michael stood, and they all gathered their plates and filed in front of the stove to load up on noodles and sauce. There was a small loaf of crusty bread Devante had bought the day before and sliced earlier for the middle of the table.

Michael made a soft, surprised noise in the back of his throat when he took his first bite, and then covered his mouth with his hand while he finished swallowing. "Sorry," he said, looking embarrassed. "That's amazing, sir."

With that, the nervous tension in the room broke a bit. Carl swelled a little with pride. "Glad you like it," he rumbled, loading up his own forkful.

There were a few minutes of devoted eating, and then Carl cleared his throat, took a pull of his beer, and said, "So, figure skating, huh?"

Michael wiped his mouth on his napkin. "Yes, sir."

"How long you been doing that?"

"Since I was a preteen," Michael said. "Seriously, as a career, for two years. Since I graduated college, more or less."

Carl nodded. "You're good," he said surprisingly. Devante and Michael both blinked at him. "Looked up some of your performances on the YouTube."

"You know what YouTube is?" Devante asked, at the same moment Michael said faintly, "You've seen my skates?" He shared a look with Devante; Devante knew they were both thinking of the moment in his short program where he ran his hands up his hips, presenting his ass to the audience.

Carl scowled at Devante and turned back to Michael. "I saw what I could find on the YouTube," he said. "Muted, after the first one. Couldn't take those narrators."

"Yeah," Michael said. "They're pretty terrible most of the time. But the judges are usually mostly decent."

Carl huffed. "That's something. Devante says you came in second recently?"

"Yes, at Nationals. And I got bronze at an international competition at the beginning of December."

Carl nodded. "'S good. It ain't easy."

Michael shook his head. "No, it's not."

"I got kids coming through the Center who can't wrap their heads around the fact that second place is *hard*, and something to be proud of," Carl went on. "It's first place or nothing, with some of them. Ain't healthy."

"I agree," Michael said, taking a sip of his beer. "Even back when I was much lower in the rankings, I still always tried to find something to be proud of myself for."

"Good," Carl declared, spinning pasta around his fork. "Healthier that way."

They ate for another few minutes, Devante getting up for seconds. Then Michael said, "Devante says you've been at the Reggie Lewis almost since it opened?"

"Mhm." Carl got up for his own second plate. "Started cleaning floors, then worked my way up to trainer. Been there ever since."

"He's the best they have," Devante put in. "The runners he trains consistently rank higher than any other students who train there."

"That's great," Michael said. "I've often thought about what I'll do after I'm done competing, and I keep coming back to being an assistant coach or a physical trainer, or something along those lines."

"Really?" Devante looked at him, and he nodded.

"Hopefully I've still got a good few years of competing left in me, but there's no denying that I'm getting older, and I'll age out eventually. But I want to stay involved in the competitive scene however I can, you know?"

"Makes sense," Devante said.

"'S good to have a plan," Carl rumbled, reaching for a piece of bread. "Gotta look to the future. I was just saying to Devante, that's one of the things I'm proudest of," he added, looking to Michael. "He's always had a plan."

"I agree," Michael said, voice going fond. They both looked

at Devante, who flushed and shoved his mouth full of spaghetti. He should have known they would team up on him like this.

"Devante says you just moved to Boston," Carl said to Michael next. "Where were you before?"

"Texas," Michael said promptly. "Just outside Houston."

Carl grinned. "Texas, huh? How're you liking your first Boston winter?"

Michael shuddered theatrically. "I wasn't prepared," he said dramatically.

"It's true," Devante put in, to get a little of his own back. "Half our texts are just him complaining about it."

Michael gave him a shocked, betrayed look. When Devante frowned, trying to figure out if he was serious, though, he flashed him a quick wink. "Whining is warming," Michael said. "That's what boyfriends are for."

"God knows that's true," Carl said, putting his fork down next to his empty plate and leaning back in his chair. "Devante's mother, now. Born and raised in Jamaica Plain, so you'd think she'd be used to it, but no. Our first winter together was nothing but her complaining about the cold and trying to stick her icy feet on me."

"Really?" Devante asked. "I didn't know that."

Carl nodded. "Woman was a reptile," he said. "Not in the bad way, just, cold-blooded."

"That's Michael all over," Devante said. Michael made a face at him. Under the table, his foot nuzzled Devante's.

Carl insisted on packing two containers' worth of spaghetti and sauce up for Michael, and wouldn't let him anywhere near the dishes. "You're a guest," he said gruffly, putting the food into a plastic bag. "Maybe one day you won't be anymore, but for now you are, and we don't let guests clean up in this house. I'll do the dishes."

"I can do them," Devante objected. "You did the cooking."

Carl waved this off. "Nah, 's alright. I'll take care of it. You walk Michael out." He held out his hand again to Michael, who shook it. "Pleasure meeting you, kid," he said.

"You too, sir," Michael said firmly.

Carl chivvied them out of the kitchen after that. Michael put his coat and shoes back on at the door, and together they stepped out onto the porch. "I think that went well," Devante said, when the door was safely shut behind them.

Michael let out a long, gusty breath. "I think so too," he admitted. "Your dad's lovely."

"He's great," Devante said fondly, and then put a hand on Michael's shoulder. "And so are you."

"Did he like me?" Michael asked plaintively.

Devante nodded. "You'd know if he didn't," he promised.

Michael bit his lip, then burst out, "I have something to say." Devante furrowed his brow at him, curious. "You haven't said it since that first morning," Michael said, words tripping over themselves in his nervous haste, "and I've been waiting for you to say it again, but I sort of can't, anymore, not after meeting your dad and seeing you with him, and it's okay if you don't actually feel it, I just have to—"

"Michael," Devante interrupted, squeezing his shoulder. Warmth was suffusing through him, starting from his heart and emanating out to his fingers and toes in waves, until he felt like he could melt in the cold January evening. "It's okay." He smiled. "I've been waiting for you to say it."

"I love you," Michael said helplessly. "I'm so in love with you, Devante Miller, it's, it's *crazy*, I feel like I'm going insane. I just, I want to be with you *all the time*, I think about you *all the time*, you make me feel so safe and happy, and I just…" He shrugged, eyes wide and begging for Devante to understand. "I *love* you."

Devante leaned forward and, in public, on the porch of the house that he shared with his father, kissed Michael. Michael whimpered against his lips. "I love you too," he murmured, pulling back just far enough to press their foreheads together. "So much, Michael."

"Promise?" Michael asked, a little desperately, and then

looked ashamed of himself for asking.

Devante laughed and kissed him again. "I promise. I love you."

"I love you too," Michael said.

Devante pulled him into a hug, and they clung to each other through Michael's bulky coat. Finally, Michael stepped away, and Devante pretended not to notice him sniffling a little. "This was a lovely way to spend an evening," he said, getting himself together. "Tell your father thank you for inviting me."

"I will," Devante said. "I'll see you tomorrow."

"See you tomorrow, sweetheart," Michael said, and then, "I love you," like he couldn't help himself; like the words tasted good in his mouth.

"I love you too," Devante said. With a smile, Michael left the porch and headed off for his bus stop.

Carl was just putting the big saucepan in the sink to soak overnight when Devante came back inside. "Well?" Devante asked, leaning against the kitchen doorway, not really worried about Carl's answer.

"I like him," Carl declared, as Devante had known he would. "Seems like a good match for you." He dried his hands, brow furrowed in concentration as he tried to settle on what words to use next. "He looks at you right," Carl settled on, with a decisive nod. "You look at each other right."

Devante smiled, swallowing hard. "Thanks, Dad." Carl nodded again. "He likes you too," Devante went on. "He says thanks for inviting him."

"We'll have him back," Carl said. "Give me an excuse to make my gumbo."

"Something wrong with *my* gumbo?" Devante demanded, a grin tugging at his lips. Carl winked at him and nudged him out of the way so he could go into the living room and drop with a sigh into his armchair.

Devante stretched out on the couch. He wiggled his phone out of his pocket to find a new text from Michael, a simple heart emoji. He sent one back, and then pulled up The Friend Group chat.

DM: Everybody give a round of applause to Michael

DM: He's been through the Boyfriend Gauntlet today

CG: How'd it go???????

DM: It went great

PC: What happened?

CG: Michael met Carl today

PC: Holy shit

PC: Dev, you brought Michael home?

DM: I did

NM: As a boyfriend or as a friend?

DM: As a boyfriend

DM: I came out to my dad earlier this week

PC: WELL DONE DEV

MC: Wait, what?

MC: Michael met Carl?

ML: I did! And I did not crap my pants before, during, or after

ML: Which I think is worthy of a medal

NM: Well done!

NM: What did Carl cook?

DM: Spaghetti sauce

NM: Oooooh, the big guns

ML: It was delicious

CG: Everything Carl cooks is

ML: He passed that gene onto Devante, based on his gumbo

PC: You've had Devante's gumbo?????

PC: He NEVER shares his gumbo

DM: Michael!

ML: Sorry!!!!!!

PC: Ugh

PC: Anyway, congrats you two, I'm glad it went well

NM: Congrats!

CG: Congrats!

NM: Mike?

MC: Yeah, congrats

ML: Thanks, everybody!!!!!

Chapter 25

DEVANTE FELT ITCHY in his skin, unsettled, all Friday night after Michael left, and all Saturday. His arms ached for Michael, his skin prickled to feel Michael's pressed against him, and it didn't stop until Saturday night, when he went to Mood to meet his friends and could pull Michael into his arms again.

Michael gave him a kiss and a dazzling smile, and they settled into the booth together, signaling Katie at the bar for their drinks. Devante slung an arm around Michael's shoulders and Michael reached up to take his hand, interlacing their fingers with a happy sigh.

"I missed you," Devante murmured into Michael's ear.

"I love you," Michael murmured back. Devante's heart thumped in his chest and he tugged Michael a little closer.

They were the first ones there, and had a good five minutes of cuddling before Natasha showed up with Mike in tow. "Evening, boys," Natasha trilled, waving at Katie before settling down opposite them. Mike slid in next to her. He flicked his eyes over to Devante and Michael once, Devante noticed, before turning himself to face Natasha.

"Evening," Michael said easily. "Good day?"

"Lovely day," Natasha said breezily. "Last semester of journalism school is off to a great start." She started talking about her capstone course, but Devante couldn't quite listen to her, attention drawn by the way Mike's body was totally perpendicular to them, and the way that, when Katie brought him his can of Pabst, he drained half of it in one go.

Preeda got there before Natasha finished her story, followed by Charlie in another five minutes. Preeda sat on Michael's other side, flashing them a sweet grin, leaving Charlie to sit next to Mike. Katie brought their drinks, and, when Natasha was done, Preeda said, "Guess who has a job interview."

"No way!" Charlie yelped. "Where?"

Preeda winced. "That's the thing. New York."

Devante's stomach dropped. "The NYPL job?" he asked. "The one that was posted three weeks ago?"

Preeda nodded. "I applied then, didn't think much of it, but they called me yesterday. I'm going down next weekend."

"Damn," Natasha said. "I don't know whether to congratulate you or sabotage you."

"Neither, hopefully," Preeda said. "No congratulations until I have a job offer or you'll jinx me."

Charlie raised his Corona. "To Preeda," he said. "Good luck, although we'd miss you greatly."

Everybody toasted her. Michael snuggled in closer to Devante's side, tucking his foot between Devante's below the table. Across from them, Mike drained his Pabst and caught Katie's eye, lifting the empty can. She nodded and brought him another.

"I have a question," Natasha announced, putting her elbows on the table and peering at Michael. "Michael, my good friend, what did you think of Carl?"

Michael laughed. "I saw a lot of Devante in him," he said. "Hard not to like him after that, although I would have anyway."

Natasha nodded. "Like father like son," she said. "And did he like you?"

Michael looked up at Devante, who nodded, then back at her. "Devante says he did."

"He did," Devante confirmed. "He wants to have you back over for dinner again sometime."

"If it's as tasty as his spaghetti sauce, I'll be there with bells on," Michael said. "That was *delicious*."

"I still can't believe Dev gave you some gumbo," Preeda said. "I've been trying to wheedle some of that shit off him for *years*."

"The secret is for me to have a crush on you," Devante said. Preeda cackled.

Across from them, Mike signaled for a third beer. Charlie gave him a look and caught Devante's eye. Devante shrugged; whatever was eating Mike, he'd either talk about it or he wouldn't. More likely he wouldn't, knowing Mike, but his hangover tomorrow was his own business.

"Sick jump in your Insta story on Thursday, bro," Charlie said to Mike. "Was it a Lutz?"

"No," Michael said regretfully, "Not yet. Sara says I can't start working on my quad Lutz until after the Four Continents. But soon."

"Not after Worlds?" Natasha asked, sipping her drink. "Don't you have to focus for that too?"

Michael laughed. "It was our compromise," he said. "I wanted to start after the Final, she wanted me to wait until after the season. So we split the difference."

"Where's Worlds this year?" Preeda asked. "Anywhere exotic?"

"Barcelona," Michael said. "Definitely gonna hit the beach while I'm there."

"Oh man," Natasha said enviously. "I'd love to go to a Barcelona beach in March."

"The men's singles group chat is planning an outing," Michael said. "Georg's been sending me pictures of all the sluttiest bathing suits he can find, trying to pick one."

Most of the table, including Devante, laughed, but not Mike, who grumbled something and took a pull of his third beer. "What was that?" Michael asked. His tone was pleasant enough, but Devante felt him go a little tense in his shoulders.

"Fucked up," Mike mumbled. His voice was a little slurred, and he was sweating.

"Dude, did you pregame or something?" Charlie asked him. "You're drunk."

"What's fucked up?" Michael asked, still pleasant, although now Devante could hear a bit of steel in it.

"You're fucked up," Mike snapped, suddenly going from "drunk and mildly irritated" to hostile. "Talking about your fuck buddy sending you slutty bathing suit pictures while Devante, your *boyfriend*, is right there with his arm around you."

"Don't bring me into this," Devante said sharply. "You have a problem, you own it, Mike. Don't push that shit on me."

"Yeah, I got a problem," Mike sneered. The atmosphere at the table had soured; Charlie and Natasha exchanged a panicked look over Mike's head; next to Michael, Preeda seemed to be trying to disappear into her wine glass. "I got a problem with this *slut* talking about how he's planning on cheating on you just as soon as he's out of the country."

"You're out of line," Natasha said. "Stop now, Mike."

"No, no, let him go," Michael said. He shifted forward, Devante's arm falling off his shoulders. Devante put a hand at the small of his back instead, finding it tense and hard through his shirt. "I want to hear what good old *Mike* has to say."

"*I'm* out of line?" Mike asked the table at large, outraged. "*I'm* out of line, for pointing out that *Michael* is probably fucking someone else behind our Dev's back? Probably a lot of people," he went on. His face was lobster-red, fists clenched on the table. "Probably everyone he can get his hands on, man or woman. Or otherwise," he added, like his adherence to the gender binary was the problem.

"I'm done," Devante said. "I'm not listening to this anymore. Michael, let's go." He stood up and started shouldering himself into his coat.

"Wait for me outside," Michael said, voice even and calm. He hadn't taken his eyes off Mike since Mike started talking.

"I'm not *leaving* you here—"

"It's alright," Michael snapped. Devante just looked at him; Michael flicked his gaze over to him for a moment. "It's alright," he said more quietly. "I just want to make sure I understand all of good old Mike's problems with me. Wait for me outside?"

Devante hesitated for a moment, but Michael looked stubborn enough not to move until he was good and ready, so Devante nodded and left the booth.

"Mike, shut *up*," he heard Charlie say as he left the bar, and then Mood's front door swung shut behind him and there was nothing but the sound of traffic and the wind in his ears.

Devante pulled his phone out of his pocket and ordered a Lyft, destination Michael's apartment. The app told him the car would be there in five minutes. He texted his father: *Minor crisis, staying at Michael's tonight.*

Hope everything's alright, came Carl's reply.

Michael came outside just as the car was rounding the corner. His expression was like nothing Devante had ever seen on his face before, stony and eerily calm, utterly unmoving. Devante put a hand on his back and he acknowledged it with a distant nod. "I got us a car," Devante said, pointing to the Toyota Camry that was just now pulling up to the curb.

"Good thinking," Michael said. Devante hated the way his voice sounded, and was guiltily grateful when he didn't say anything more, just climbed into the car's backseat and looked out the window. Devante put his hand over Michael's, and thankfully Michael took it, his grip tighter than his face would have indicated.

It was a ten-minute drive to Michael's apartment, and Michael spent it with a death grip on Devante's hand, his face turned away from him to look out the window. Devante watched his profile like he would a wounded bird, trying to figure out the best way to help without hurting it further.

Devante got Michael out of the Lyft and up the stairs of his building. "Keys," he said, holding out his hand. Michael fished them out of his pocket and passed them to him, and Devante unlocked the door and ushered Michael inside.

They both toed off their shoes. Michael got his coat off before Devante, and disappeared into the kitchen; when Devante followed him a moment later, he found Michael with both hands on the counter, head bowed, eyes screwed shut. "Oh, baby," Devante said helplessly. "What can I do?"

Michael's answer was a sob, sudden and broken and loud in the still silence of his apartment. He groped blindly for Devante, and Devante pulled him into his arms, Michael's face going into his neck. He sobbed again, his body shaking; Devante felt the tears on his neck as they started to fall from Michael's eyes.

Michael cried for five minutes, falling apart in Devante's grip, before he gasped and started getting his breathing back under control. Devante murmured whatever he could think of into his hair, *it's okay* and *I've got you* and *I'm so sorry* on a loop until Michael took a deep breath and stepped away, wiping his face with his hands. "Ugh," he said expressively, looking at the tears that were now on his palms and rubbing them on his jeans. "I hate crying."

"I've never seen you do it before," Devante said.

Michael stepped forward again, reaching for Devante's face to pull their foreheads together. "That sucked," he proclaimed.

"I'm sorry I left you," Devante said.

Michael shook his head as best he could without moving his forehead from Devante's. "I wanted you to," he said. "I didn't want you to hear any more."

"I didn't want *you* to hear any more," Devante pointed out. "What else did he say?"

Michael sighed. "Just some shit about how if I'm going to skate like a slut, I shouldn't be surprised when people know I'm a slut in real life too, and more shit about me fucking Georg behind your back."

"You know I trust you, right?" Devante said. He pulled his head back to get a better look at Michael's face. "I don't think that, at all——"

"I know," Michael said. He kept his hands on Devante's neck; Devante's hands were on his waist. "I know you don't, we talked about it and I know you would tell me if you had a problem."

"I would," Devante said firmly. Then, a bit more questioning, he went on, "If you knew that, though, I'm surprised he got you so upset."

Michael made a wry face. "He got me in a sore spot." Devante furrowed his brow curiously. "I hate the way I've been skating this season," Michael confessed. "The whole super-sexy playboy thing, it's not me at all, but it's the only thing I've ever done that has made the judges pay attention to me. It was fun at first, putting on a performance, a character like that, but it's getting more grating as time goes by, what with everything it makes the commentators say about me, and then to get it from someone I considered a friend tonight..." He shrugged. "It was just a bit too much."

"Has Sara been pushing you into it?" Devante asked. "Do you need a new coach?"

Michael shook his head. "The persona was my idea initially," he said. "She was on board, but if I told her I needed a change, she'd run with it, I think." He bit his lip. "I just don't know if I want to change now and risk losing what positive attention I've gotten."

Devante held him a little tighter. "That's a decision for another time," he said. "For now, what can I do that would make you feel better?"

Michael looked at him consideringly. "I don't know if you'll mind, but..." He trailed off, and then used his hands on Devante's jaw to tug him into a kiss, hungry and wanting right from the jump.

Devante kissed back, hands slipping from Michael's waist to his back. "Are you sure?" he murmured against Michael's mouth.

Michael nodded, catching his lips again for a swift moment. "I want to be close to you," he murmured back, and then grinned, the sight of it after his weeping more beautiful than Devante could have imagined. "Plus, you know, endorphins," he added.

"Can't argue with endorphins," Devante said breathlessly. He kissed him again, tongues slipping together in Michael's mouth. "I wish I thought I was strong enough to carry you to the bedroom," he said ruefully.

Michael's eyes went dark. "We'll work up to that," he said hoarsely. "For now, I'll drag you by the hand."

"No need to drag me," Devante said, laughing, but Michael was already off, hauling Devante after him toward the bedroom.

Once they were there, the mood sobered a bit again. Devante stripped Michael bare, and then himself, and laid them both on the bed. He fetched two condoms from the box on Michael's nightstand, ripped one open, and tossed the other to Michael. Once they were both covered, he laid his body over Michael's and slowly let his weight bear him down. The more of his body weight Devante put on Michael, the higher and hungrier Michael's whine went, so Devante kept going until most of himself was pinning Michael to the mattress, and then he started to move. They rocked together, Michael's legs hooked on Devante's hips, kisses becoming longer, sloppier, less formed kisses and more slack mouths panting against each other, until Michael shuddered and sighed under him. Devante took himself in hand and followed him bare moments later.

Michael had long kept his bedroom trash can to right next to his bed. They disposed of their condoms, and then Michael wedged himself into Devante's arms, head pillowed on his shoulder and one leg thrown over both of Devante's. "Love you," he mumbled sleepily into Devante's chest.

"I love you too," Devante told the top of his head. Michael hummed happily, wriggled somehow even closer, and they both were asleep in moments.

Chapter 26

DEVANTE WOKE TO a feather-light kiss to his jaw. "Mmm, morning," he rumbled, winching his eyes open to look at his sleep-mussed boyfriend.

Michael responded by kissing him full on the mouth, a deep, searching thing that seemingly held no regard for Devante's morning breath. "Still horny, then?" Devante mumbled.

Michael laughed. "Still horny," he said. He pressed a kiss to Devante's neck, then to his collarbone, then to his sternum.

"You're going the wrong direction for me to do anything about that," Devante observed, folding his arms behind his head and watching Michael kiss his way down his torso.

"On the contrary," Michael said, as casually as if they were discussing the weather. "I'm going," he licked under Devante's belly button, making him squirm, "exactly the *right* direction."

He had a condom in his hand, and ripped it open with his teeth. "One day," he said, tone still light, "I'm going to start a conversation with you that will end, I hope, in a round of testing for us both, and then us never having to use one of these things again."

"Oh fuck," Devante whined, his body thrilling at the thought. "I am—*shit*—very open to that conversation," he panted, as Michael rolled the condom onto him.

"Good to know," Michael purred, and then bent to his task.

Michael let Devante bring him off afterward, kissing him slow and sloppy as Devante's hand worked between their bodies. When it was over, he pulled Devante into the shower with him, even though there was demonstrably not enough room for them both in it.

"Goal for next apartment," Michael said as Devante soaped his back. "Bigger shower."

"Bigger shower, bigger couch," Devante added, kissing his shoulder.

Devante was, at his heart, his father's son, and he'd been battling the need to feed Michael ever since Mike had started spouting off the night before. After their shower, he sat Michael on the counter next to the stove and cooked a batch of pancakes of which his father would have been proud.

Devante's phone rang as they sat down at the table to eat. "It's Natasha," Devante told Michael, picking it up and accepting the call. "Hello?"

"Hey," Natasha said briskly. "Is Michael there? I have a status update."

Devante pressed the phone to his shoulder. "She wants to talk about last night," he said to Michael. "Status update."

Michael made a face but nodded. Devante put the call on speakerphone and placed the phone in between them on the table. "Go ahead," he said.

"First off, Michael, how are you?" she asked.

"I defy any man to be sad when Devante Miller has cooked him pancakes," Michael declared. "Such a treat could turn even the worst of situations into a decent morning." Devante smiled at him and he winked before shoving his mouth full of pancake.

"Fair enough," Natasha said. "On behalf of The Friend Group, I've been authorized to extend an apology to you for what happened last night."

Michael swallowed thickly. "I appreciate it, but I don't blame any of you," he said. "You tried to stop him talking."

"Not hard enough," she muttered, "but I'm glad to hear you're not angry with us."

"I am not," Michael confirmed. "Just with Mike."

"Mike's out," Natasha said brusquely. "Charlie put him into a cab last night not long after you left, and he's been forbidden from future drinks nights and booted from the group chat."

"Wow," Michael said, looking impressed despite himself. "You guys work fast."

"There's no room in The Friend Group for that kind of toxicity," she said. "He came for your throat, and we can't have that."

Michael looked genuinely touched. "Thanks, Natasha."

"Don't mention it," she said. "I told him not to contact you guys to give an apology for at least a few days, but I'm not sure how much he was processing at that point, so we'll see if he took it in."

"Why a few days?" Devante asked.

"You know Mike," Natasha said with a sigh. "When his head's that far up his own ass, it takes a good while for him to unstick himself."

"Fair," Devante allowed.

"I'm not sure I'm ready to accept an apology yet anyway," Michael said. Devante looked at his face, and Michael gave him a wry smile. "Soon, probably, but I'm sort of enjoying being angry, if that makes sense."

"Oh, I completely understand that," Natasha assured him. "Few things are as delicious as a well-earned grudge."

"Cheers," Michael said, taking a sip from his coffee mug.

"Anyway, I won't keep you," Natasha said. "I just wanted to check in and see if you were okay, and let you both know how things stood."

"You're a god among women," Michael proclaimed. "I couldn't have asked for a tidier status report."

"Call if you need anything," she said. "Or call Charlie, he's right next door and I had to fight him for the chance to have this conversation."

Michael chuckled. "We will. Thanks, Natasha."

"Talk to you later," she said, and hung up.

"She's frightening," Michael remarked, loading up another forkful of pancake and syrup. "I like her."

Devante gave him a tentative smile, then said, "Are you really okay, or were you just putting on a good front for Natasha?"

Michael sighed, trailing his fork through a puddle of syrup on his plate. "Mostly okay?" he said. "I have a strong enough sense of self that I don't really *believe* any of the shit Mike said about my character last night. If our relationship, yours and mine, weren't so strong, maybe that wouldn't be true? But it is, and so I'm aware that Mike was just talking shit." He paused for a moment, gathering his thoughts. "But I'm sad," he said slowly, "and my feelings are hurt, and I'm angry. It's bad enough I get judged like that professionally; I don't deserve it from my friends too."

"You don't," Devante said, putting a hand on his arm.

Michael flashed him a small smile. "I'm in for a shitty few days," he said. "But it'll pass, and I'll feel better."

"Do you want me to stay?" Devante asked. "My job starts on Thursday, so I can't stay longer than maybe Tuesday, but if you want me to—"

"I do," Michael said quickly, looking relieved. "I didn't want to ask, but I'd love it if you could stay a few days."

"I'll let Dad know," Devante said. "I told him you had a crisis last night, so he'll understand."

Michael winced. "Please tell me he doesn't, like, love Mike, and will hold it against me if you never see him again."

"He doesn't," Devante said. "He got along with him the few times they've met, but Mike's never been his favorite of my friends."

Michael relaxed. Devante squeezed his arm and let go, and they went back to their pancakes.

Michael washed up after breakfast, leaving Devante some time to text his father that he'd be staying in Brighton for a few days. He stuck to the bare minimum, just saying that Mike had gone off on Michael at drinks and Michael needed support for a while. *My best to Michael. Take your time,* Carl wrote back, so Devante sent him a heart emoji and went to dry the pancake pan when Michael was finished with it.

"I've got a workout this afternoon," Michael said, drying his hands when the dishes were done. "Shouldn't take more than two hours. I'm sorry to leave you alone at all, though."

"Don't worry about me," Devante said firmly. Michael dropped the dishrag on the counter and walked forward until Devante took the hint and pulled him into his arms. "If I get bored I'll go knock on Charlie's door. Or take a nap."

Michael hugged him around the waist. "I'm really glad you're here," he mumbled into Devante's shirt.

"Me too, baby," Devante said into his hair.

They spent the rest of the morning on the couch, Michael reading *The Silmarillion* and Devante paging through a copy of *The Hound of the Baskervilles* he'd stolen off Michael's shelf. "I really feel bad for Maglor," Michael said, a few hours into their reading and cuddle time. "He's clearly done with the whole oath thing and just wants to raise his two adopted sons in peace."

"I always wanted a TV show about them," Devante said.

"A family can be two brothers and their stolen, adopted sons whose parents they drove off the continent," Michael said. Devante laughed, and Michael twinkled in triumph at him.

Michael left for his workout at one P.M. Just before he left, he approached Devante with something in his hand. "I'd hoped to give these to you under better circumstances," he said, extending his hand to Devante. "But I swear I planned on giving them to you anyway, they'll just come in useful if you go to Charlie's." He opened his had to reveal a set of keys.

"Oh, Michael," Devante said, taking them. "Are you sure?"

Michael nodded. "I want you to be able to get in even if I'm not here. I trust you completely."

Devante kissed him. "Thank you," he murmured. "If I had an apartment of my own, I'd give you a set of keys too."

Michael smiled. "One day."

"One day," Devante echoed.

He did wind up going to Charlie's while Michael was out, locking the door to Michael's apartment with his new keys and knocking on Charlie's door. Charlie let him in with his trademark wide smile.

They each took a couch in Charlie's main room. "How's Michael?" Charlie asked, swinging his feet up onto the cushions.

Devante shrugged. "Soldiering on," he said. "He'll be alright."

"I think Mike must have pregamed pretty hard before showing up at Mood," Charlie said speculatively. "He was pretty out of it when I put him in the cab after you guys left, and he only had the three beers."

"I don't really care," Devante said honestly. "Three beers or six, he was out of line."

"Oh, totally," Charlie agreed. "Natasha made it very clear to him, although I think he knew it while he was talking."

"Thanks for handling it after we left," Devante said. "I just had to get Michael home."

"Totally," Charlie said. "Least we could do."

"Enough about Mike," Devante said, waving his hand. "How've you been lately?"

Charlie launched into a story about his accounting firm, where he was up for a promotion at the end of the fiscal year. Devante had always liked listening to Charlie's stories, even the boring ones—he was a good storyteller, and he had Devante laughing and light-hearted for the first time since Mike had opened his mouth the night before.

He stayed at Charlie's for almost two hours, before a text from Michael saying he was on his way home drew his attention. "I should get back next door," he said, standing with a grunt. "Thanks for keeping me company."

"Anytime," Charlie said. "You know I love you, man."

"Love you too," Devante said with a grin, clapping him on the shoulder.

He let himself back into Michael's apartment and set up a snack, cheese and crackers and some pepperoni from the back of Michael's fridge. Michael got there ten minutes later, greeting Devante with a warm, sweaty kiss. "Shower," he said into

Devante's cheek, "then food."

"I made a cheese plate," Devante said. "Go shower."

Michael moaned hungrily. "I love you." He winked at Devante and disappeared into the bathroom.

Precisely seven minutes later, Michael came out of his bathroom, hair damp, and insinuated himself into Devante's lap on the couch. "How was practice?" Devante asked, pressing a kiss to the back of his neck because it was right there.

"Tiring," Michael said, stacking a cheese cube onto a cracker and popping it into his mouth. "But cathartic."

"Oh yeah?"

"Yeah!" Michael said cheerily. "Doing eight triple axels in a row really helps sweat the feelings out."

"You'll never need therapy," Devante remarked drily.

"Not till I retire!" Michael chirped. He consumed three more cheese-and-cracker stacks and then leaned back into Devante with a happy sigh. "Did you go over to Charlie's?"

"Mhm." Devante hugged him. "We hung out for a bit."

"Good, so you didn't take a nap," Michael murmured sleepily. When Devante looked down at him, his eyes were closed. "Want to do that now?"

Devante chuckled. "I'm not tired, but you go ahead."

"Mmm sure?" Michael slurred.

"I could sing you a lullaby if you like," Devante said jokingly. Michael made a happy noise and snuggled closer.

Devante didn't sing, but he did hum, a planless melody that spilled out of him until Michael was heavy in his arms, breath gusting hot over his neck with each breath. Devante looked down at him, heart thudding with adoration and love, and pulled him closer.

Chapter 27

THE THREE DAYS Devante stayed at Michael's place flew by. Between cooking meals, going for long walks around Devante's public library shift and Michael's practices, and the number of times Charlie knocked on their door "just to say hi," Devante barely had time to be nervous about how close his first day at his new job was.

But then it was Tuesday night, the night they had agreed that Devante would go home, and the only thing keeping his nerves at bay was the way Michael was kissing him goodbye.

"You're sure you don't need me to stay another night?" Devante asked in between kisses.

Michael laughed. "I'd love you to, you know I would, but I'm sure your dad misses you, and you have to get ready for your big day." He belied his words with another kiss, searching and passionate. "I'll miss you, though," he murmured, his lips brushing Devante's with each word.

Devante groaned regretfully but forced himself to pull back. "I'll miss you too," he said. "If I'm going, I should go."

"Mhm." Michael made no move to release him, so with a chuckle Devante took hold of his wrists and pried his hands off his waist. Michael sighed. "I love you," he said wistfully, leaning against the doorframe.

"I love you too," Devante said. "I'll see you Thursday evening."

"Until then," Michael said. Devante made himself turn and head down the stairs to the exit.

On my way home, he texted Carl from the bus. *Call it in*, meaning their usual pizza order.

Called in. See you soon, was Carl's response.

Devante picked up the pizza and French fries on his walk home from the bus stop. Carl opened the front door just as he walked up to it, standing aside to let him in. "Hey, stranger," he rumbled.

"Hey," Devante said, smiling warmly at him. "Good to see you too. Hungry?"

"Starved."

Carl had already set the table, and they settled down and tucked into their food. "Your first day's on Thursday, right?" Carl asked as he pulled his third slice out of the box.

Devante nodded. "It's mainly going to be Human Resources stuff," he said. "Orientation, trainings, that sort of thing." His new principal, Joel, had walked him through it when Devante had called to accept his offer. "I'll have to track down my Social Security card."

"It's in the safe," Carl told him. "I'll get it out for you after dinner. Need anything else?"

"No, just that and my ID card, which is in my wallet," Devante said.

"Mmkay." Carl took a bite of pizza. "Nervous?" he asked.

"Yes," Devante said honestly.

Carl shook his head. "You'll be fine," he said. "Nervous is natural, but there's nothing scary about a job. You've been working since you were fourteen."

"Yeah, but this is a *job* job," Devante said. "A career job."

"Career job's the same as any other job," Carl said. "Only difference is how much weight you give it."

"Wise," Devante said drily. Carl scowled fondly at him.

Devante spent all of Wednesday preparing. He ironed the clothes he'd chosen for his first day: black jeans, a crisp and clean undershirt, and his blue button-down with the pattern of cats. He'd asked Joel about the dress code for librarians in the district, and was told that he could Miss Frizzle to his heart's content. His original choice had been the pineapples shirt, considering how much luck that had brought him in the past year, but he'd left it at Michael's.

He also cooked his lunch, roasting a chicken breast he'd had Carl marinate the day before and some yellow rice. Once that was done, he washed up and put more chicken into the crockpot for dinner, along with a can of cream of chicken soup and half an onion.

Just when he'd run out of prep work to do and was starting to feel the butterflies in his stomach, Michael texted him. *Wait*, it read, *I just got to Maedhros's death. Is the Arkenstone a Silmaril?????????*

Devante laughed out loud, his nervous tension leaving him in a rush. *No*, he texted back.

ML: Seriously?

ML: Shiny rock that emits light and makes everyone around it go crazy with jewel-lust?????

ML: How many of those could there be in Middle-Earth????

DM: Maedhros jumped into a fiery pit. Erebor is a mountain

ML: A mountain that could have been a volcano that grew from, oh, say, a fiery pit??????

They argued about it all afternoon and well into the evening, a light-hearted back and forth that Michael approached with the same single-minded intensity he brought to his triple axels and camel spins. Finally, as Devante got ready to brush his teeth and get an early night, he gave in.

DM: Look, I still don't think it is, but if you haven't read the Annotated Hobbit, you may want to get your hands on a copy

DM: The editor agrees with you

ML: HA!!!!!!!!!

ML: I will!!!!!

DM: I'm going to sleep

DM: Good night, baby. Love you

ML: Love you!!!!!!! You're wrong!!!!!!

Michael sent him another text in the morning, wishing him luck. Carl made him an omelet, heaped with spinach and sausage and cheese. Devante dressed carefully, double-checked he had his identity documents for the I9 form, and made it to his bus stop with ten minutes to spare.

He met Joel and the district superintendent, a terrifying-looking woman named Nancy, in the middle school administrative office. From there, the day was a whirlwind: paperwork with HR; orientation videos at a desk in the corner of the administrative office; a tour of the middle school library and a chance to meet the librarian; and then getting into Nancy's car to tour the other libraries in the district, and meet their librarians.

Every single person he met, all day, complimented his shirt. He was *definitely* adding this one to the pile of lucky shirts.

The high school librarian, a round, apple-cheeked nonbinary person named Andy, asked him what his favorite book was. "Definitely *The Lord of the Rings*," Devante said without a moment's hesitation. "The whole Middle-earth saga, really, from *The Silmarillion* on down."

"Oof, you're a braver person than I," Andy said with a wince. "*The Silmarillion*'s defeated me twice."

Devante took a chance. "That's what my boyfriend said, before we got together," he said. Andy gave him a wink and a nod; Devante's chest filled with warmth and relief. "And now we spent all of yesterday arguing whether the Arkenstone is a Silmaril."

He could tell Andy didn't know what that meant, but they laughed gamely anyway, which made Devante like them even more.

Devante finished the school day with his head spinning, new faces and names and a long, long list of book recommendations in his Notes app. Nancy met him again at the end of the day, mostly to shake his hand and welcome him on board. "We'll have you in for some more training next week," she said, "on how to present to classes and what the students will be working on for the rest of the year. It's a pleasure to have you on board, Devante."

"It's a pleasure to be here," he could say with absolute honesty.

It was Thursday, so he stumbled from the last school to Michael's apartment, letting himself in with a quiet little thrill that the new keys on his keychain still brought him.

To his surprise, Michael was there; he got up from the couch when Devante came in, summoning up a warm smile and a kiss for him. "How was it?" he asked, taking Devante's hand and leading him into the apartment.

"Great," Devante said. "My head is still kind of spinning, but I think it's going to work out. What are you doing here?" he added, as Michael drew him onto the couch. "I thought you'd be at practice."

"Sara woke up with a head cold this morning," he said. "She didn't make it to the rink. I did some drills and ran through my programs a few times, but she told me I could take it easy today."

That didn't look like everything that was on his mind, to judge from his face. "Is everything okay?" Devante prompted, taking his hand.

"Mike texted," Michael said. "He wants to come over in an hour and apologize."

Devante grew solemn. "Oh." He searched Michael's face. "Do you want to let him?"

Michael nodded. "I want it to be over," he said. "I don't want to have to think about it anymore."

"Sounds like Mike should come over, then," Devante said. "Do you want me here?"

"Yes," Michael said instantly, grabbing his arm. "Yes, I do, and he specifically said you should be there too."

Devante's stomach twisted. "Well then," he said. "Let's do this thing."

Michael let Devante up to shower while he answered Mike's text. Devante took a long time under the hot water, trying to reconcile the busy lightness of his day with the tense conversation that was sure to happen when Mike got there. Eventually, though, he sighed and shut the water off, toweling dry and padding out to join Michael on the couch and cuddle until there was a knock on the door.

Devante answered it, leaving Michael on the couch. Mike was dressed for the cold weather, in his North Face jacket and Timberland boots. His face was wretched, clearly nervous, his remorse written all over his face when he saw Devante. "Hey," he said, letting out a breath.

"Come on in," Devante told him, stepping aside to let him pass.

Michael's main room didn't have much space for furniture, just his too-small couch and the coffee table. Devante joined Michael on the former; Mike stood on the other side of the latter, shoulders squared, feet apart, like he was facing a firing squad. There was a moment of awkward silence, and then Michael said, "Go on, then."

"I'm so sorry," Mike said quickly, the words rushing out of him like squirrels tripping out of a tree. "Michael, what I said to you was inexcusable, and furthermore it was bullshit, and also it was none of my business."

"Good start," Michael said, his whole body a tense line pressed against Devante's side.

Mike acknowledged his words with a nod. "I was drunk, and I was angry, and I wanted to hurt somebody. You," he added. His hands were behind his back, but Devante could tell by the set of his arms that they were clenched into fists. "I wanted to hurt you."

Michael huffed a breath. "Why?" he asked, his voice as tense as his muscles. "What have I ever done to you?"

Mike sighed, looking down at his feet and breaking eye contact for the first time since he'd taken position. "I was hoping you wouldn't ask me that," he admitted.

"I'm asking," Michael said harshly. "What the hell is your problem with me?"

Mike sighed again, looked up at the ceiling for a moment,

and said, "I've been—I've *had feelings* for Devante for a long time," he said, as though the firing squad were taking aim.

Devante sucked in a shocked breath. Next to him, Michael relaxed, as though something he'd long suspected had been confirmed. "I see," he said.

Devante turned to blink at him, but Michael just looked at him quickly and then back to Mike. "It was fine while I thought Devante was straight," Mike went on, "but when you came around, and he wasn't…I just couldn't cope with it." He shut his eyes tight for a moment, then opened them and looked at Devante. "I guess I felt like, now that you had come out, if I could just separate you two, I might have a chance."

Devante's shock was fading, and it was being replaced by a low, bubbling rage, unlike anything he'd ever felt. Before Michael could say anything further, Devante opened his mouth and said, "I'll tell you one thing, Mike Cooper. I might have dated you, if you'd asked before Michael showed up. But if I had, I'd have left you for him when Charlie brought him around."

He could feel Michael wince. Mike, though, just took the blow like a trained fighter, shutting his eyes again and lowering his head. "I guess I deserved that," he murmured.

"You don't get to pine for me for however long, and then try and drive off the man I actually chose," Devante said, his anger bubbling over. "You don't get to call that *love.*"

Again, Mike withstood Devante's words stoically. "Very fair," he said. "I was totally and completely out of line, and Michael, and Devante, I apologize."

Michael coughed. "I accept," he said.

"I don't," Devante said. "If you want to come back to drinks, and be in the group chat again, then fine, but you need to take a huge step back where I'm concerned."

"I don't, actually," Mike said, surprising him. "Not…Not right away. I think I need some time away, to get my head on straight. To get over you."

"I think that's smart," Devante said. Michael put a hand on his knee, gentling and calming him. He let out a deep breath at the contact, trying to funnel his anger out with the carbon dioxide.

Mike nodded, a single sharp jerk of his head. "That's that, then," he said. "I'll see myself out." He cast a last look at Devante and left, the door to the apartment clicking shut behind him.

Michael and Devante sat in silence for a good minute, Devante turning the past few minutes over in his head. "How are you feeling?" Michael finally asked, squeezing the hand on his knee.

"How're *you* feeling?" Devante asked, turning to face him.

Michael shrugged. "Honestly, I wondered if it was something like that," he said. "It wasn't a great surprise to me. I can tell it was for you, though."

"'Surprise' is one word for it," Devante said. "How dare he?"

"I would like to remind you that I didn't make the first move with you either," Michael pointed out gently.

Devante leaned into his shoulder, suddenly exhausted in the wake of his fury departing. "You know what I think?" he said tiredly.

"What?"

"I think we should get married." Michael jolted against him in surprise. "Not right now," Devante clarified. "Not even soon. But I want that to be where this is going. Where *us* is going."

"I want that too," Michael said.

Devante leaned up and looked at him. "And I think when your lease is up in May, we should get a place together," he said. "Or put me on the lease here. I want to live with you, full-time."

Michael's smile was a beautiful, fragile thing. "I agree," he said.

"I'm sure of you," Devante said. It was urgent that Michael understand that. "I'm sure *about* you. I'm one hundred percent positive that the rest of my life is supposed to have you in it."

Michael kissed him, a soft, tender caress as fragile as his smile. "Me too," he whispered. "I'm so glad we found each other. I'm so glad I told my new next-door neighbor that I needed local friends, and he brought me to drinks with his friend group. I'm glad there was a man there, a super hot man in a shirt with pineapples on it, who caught my attention instantly. I'm glad that man turned out to be you."

Devante kissed him again, putting a hand to his jaw to draw him in at the right angle. "I love you," he said.

"I love you too, Devante Miller." Michael pulled him in again, and Devante tucked himself into the warm circle of his arms and chest, the scent of vanilla and pine filling his nose.

T.J. BLACKLEY IS a bisexual queerling with all the gender of your average river rock. During the day they live in the library, cataloging as many books as they can get their hands on, and in the evening they come home to their beloved cat and write as much queer romance as they can think of.

For more information, visit tjblackley.com.

Made in the USA
Middletown, DE
10 February 2022